Billy Christmas

Billy Christmas

by

Mark A. Pritchard

Billy Christmas is published by Alan Squire Publishing in association with Santa Fe Writers Project, Chris Andrews Publications Ltd, and Left Coast Writers.

ISBN: 978-0-98-262518-7

Cover art and jacket design by Randy Stanard, Dewitt Designs, www.dewittdesigns.com.

Front cover photo by Anthony Mattox.

Author photo by Matthew Pritchard.

Illustrations by Jack Brougham.

Copy editing and interior design by Nita Congress.

Printing consultation by Steven Waxman.

Printed by RR Donnelley.

First Edition
Ordo Vagorum

For Grace,
Sueñas siempre, amor mía.

Daddy

⋄December 13ᵗʰ⋄

Through the snow his footprints linked the ancient trees of Higginson Park. Pausing at each trunk, he pressed his palms against the cold bark, listening for clues, but heard nothing. He knew he would have to get closer to see what was happening.

Looking around, he made his way down to the landing platform at the edge of the river. Across the lawns beside the cricket pavilion, he could see the Christmas tree stall brightly lit against the dark park. The stall was more crowded than he had hoped for, though less busy than either night before, and he didn't want to return empty-handed again. Pulling his scarf high over his ill-fitting coat, he began to cross the park. An old memory surfaced and steered him towards the bronze statue of Sir Steven Redgrave. The knight looked out towards the river, blade in hand, ready for action. Hoping it would still work, Billy Christmas slapped Sir Steve across the backside, wishing grimly for luck before heading towards the stall.

At nearly six feet tall and all shins and elbows, he was recognised at once. The assembled families hurriedly fell into silence as he reached the deep rows of Christmas trees. Feeling the weight of their thoughts and stares, he hunched his shoulders and looked for the owner of the stall.

Mr. Shaw was a tree surgeon by trade and appeared to be built from oak himself, his body seasoned from a life-time of working wood. When he saw why his customers had become silent, he threw them a displeased glance before turning back to Billy with a smile that was full of warmth.

"Well hello, Master Christmas. Are you after a tree?"

"You know my name?" said Billy.

"'Course I do," said Mr. Shaw, and then a bit more quietly, "your mother not here then, son?"

"No, she's not. I can pay though. I've saved up."

"Your money's no good here, Master Christmas. You just take your pick."

Whilst hating any hint of charity, Billy sensed it would be pointless to argue. He also knew the money he could now save would feed his mother and him for another week. He nodded his thanks to Mr. Shaw and headed towards the labyrinthine rows of Christmas trees.

Walking into this impromptu forest, he drew in the scent of pine and began to relax. However hard it was to leave the house these days, he still delighted in the sights and smells of the outside world. Starlight danced off the dusting of snow on the tree branches. Billy thought that no decorations they had at home could exceed how nature had dressed these trees.

Abrupt voices sent him scuttling underneath the nearest pine.

"It was definitely him?"

"For sure, the little attention-seeking prat. He went down here."

"What you got planned for him then?"

"What do you think?"

Billy didn't need to look up to recognise the tones of Robert Lock, familiar from so many schoolyard taunts. While he couldn't be sure, he thought the other was probably Olly Thatcher. He lay quite still until they moved on.

A faint sound from somewhere behind him attracted his attention. He took a moment before moving, absorbing the new sound and allowing the unwelcome voices to fade away. It was music he heard now. The chords were faint but precise, reminding him of the miniature tuning forks Katherine carried in her canvas rucksack. Billy rose and spun into the path behind him, towards the music.

To his delight, the source appeared to be a small Christmas tree. A gentle breeze was making the snowflakes spin off its branches, splitting light into colours and casting sound that reverberated against the other trees. As if responding to Billy's thoughts, the tree turned and seemed, somehow, to look at him and blinked when their gazes met. They paused, stock still, regarding each other.

Without warning the refracted light snapped off, and Billy felt his jaw crack. The force knocked him flat, a flurry of long limbs in the snow.

"Got you, you stupid little sod."

The thumping pain from his jaw did not stop Billy wondering at Robert's poor choice of put down. Billy was over a foot taller than his adversary, not that height was an advantage in these circumstances. In fact, sometimes his height created these circumstances. Billy bounced back onto his feet, just in time to see Robert's accomplice, Olly Thatcher, appear, cutting Billy's odds of making it out of this unscathed.

There was a noise behind him. Billy didn't turn, but was relieved to see disappointment cloud his opponents' faces.

Robert looked straight at him, making sure his parting words hit home. "See you at school, Billy." Taking his time, he turned back and followed Olly into the darkness.

As they retreated, Billy wheeled around, coming face to face with himself, reflected in the blade of an enormous axe. The image was so clear he could see Robert and Olly slinking away behind him.

"What toe-rags." Mr. Shaw lowered the axe from Billy's face. "I'm so sorry, son, I should have been quicker."

"No, thanks. I'd have been in real trouble."

"Honestly…at this time of year too," said Mr. Shaw. "I've seen you coming down the last few nights, not wanting to come in. I'd put a tree aside and I was gonna bring it over tonight."

"That's OK," said Billy. "Mum isn't the best for visitors. Especially now. At Christmas I mean."

"Well, that's no surprise," said Mr. Shaw. Clearly hating himself for asking, he continued, "There's still no word then?"

Billy's eyes fell. "No word, no."

Mr. Shaw exhaled, his huge lungs creating a cloud in the night sky. "It was your dad who set me up with this stall in the first place. Before you were even born."

However well intentioned, Billy found these stories hard to bear. Everybody had a memory they wanted to express, unaware of what it did to him. What it had done to his mother.

Mr. Shaw seemed to sense Billy's unease and changed the subject. "So did you find a tree you liked then, young Master Christmas?"

He'd almost forgotten about it. "If you're sure it's OK, I'd really like this one please," he said, pointing at the small tree that was now just as still as the others.

Mr. Shaw looked at him in surprise. "I was wondering who would end up with that one. Why did you pick it?"

Billy couldn't explain, so he shrugged.

"Only reason I ask, other than boys normally wanting to get the biggest tree they can find, is that I didn't buy that tree in. It just arrived. Imported an' all. No idea where from." Mr. Shaw leant forward on his axe, his huge arms straining against his jacket sleeves. "And it came with its own set of twelve decorations in little velvet bags. People been trying to have them off me but I couldn't let them go without the tree. Mr. Lennon. Instant karma, you see?"

Billy didn't see.

Mr. Shaw rolled his eyes. "Look, you bring it up the front and I'll fish out the decorations for you. All right?"

Before he had a chance to reply, Mr. Shaw was off, swinging the axe over his shoulder. Billy turned back to the tree. It was still; the slight breeze had passed and there was no more music. It had seemed real at the time, but perhaps...? The clock started chiming the hours. Eight o'clock, and his mother wouldn't have eaten since he'd cycled home at lunch. Billy turned and grasped the tree low on the trunk. Even bending double he was still taller than it, and was able to carry it easily on one shoulder. He started off after Mr. Shaw.

Being so small, the tree was spared the usual plastic netting. "Much better for the tree, Billy, but don't be telling my other customers that."

Mr. Shaw brought over the sack of decorations. At this hour in the park, it was hard to tell whether the sack was purple or black, but it was made of the softest velvet. Billy opened it to reveal twelve smaller but otherwise identical velvet pouches, each containing a single decoration. Then he slung the sack over his other shoulder.

Thanking Mr. Shaw again, Billy headed back across the park and into Marlow. As he walked along the quiet High Street, he caught sight of himself in the plate glass window of a flower boutique. His height was new, but not unexpected; his father was closer to seven feet than six. It was the speed of his growth that had been so breathtaking. He had outgrown everyone in his own school year, and those in the year above, by putting on an entire foot since last Christmas.

As he reached the twenty-four-hour garage, he was forced to stop. The cord from the velvet bag was digging deeply into his shoulder and seemed to be getting heavier with each step. He caught sight of himself again, this time in the garage window. Bright shins glared beneath the bottoms of his trouser legs. His current pair were supposed to last until at least February. Katherine had joked when they met up for their daily cycle to school, "It's just as well your mum isn't cooking. Imagine how much more you'd grow with proper food inside you." As the only person who could get under Billy's armour as far as the subject of his mother was concerned, Katherine had received a rare Christmas smile. More and more he found her tucked into his thoughts, though he knew the cool gulf between them was too great for anything more than neatly tucked thoughts. Unable to think of a better way to carry everything, Billy swapped shoulders and grimaced as he climbed the slight incline to Marlow Bottom.

Several stops and shoulder swaps later he rounded the corner which led to his road, High Heavens Wood. In the dark it was difficult to see the ageing, red-bricked house, which had originally been built as a chapel, but then converted before consecration. It was the only home Billy had ever known.

Billy took his usual path around to the kitchen door at the back of the house. Light spilled out from the window into the back garden, and he could make out his mother moving around. He bent down, placing the tree and the sack of decorations on the rear step before tugging at his laces and kicking off his snowy hiking boots. Pushing open the door, he picked up the tree and sack and stepped into the kitchen. His mother's gaze didn't lift from the spout of the kettle, but he hadn't expected it to. She stood with one arm propping her frame against the counter, with her hair freshly greyed from all the wrong reasons. To one side he noticed a few crumbs on a plate and assumed she'd at least had some toast tonight. Billy took a breath and walked past her with the tree.

Behind Billy, a branch reached out and glanced against his mother's wrist. Her eyes lifted from the spout.

"Tree, Billy?"

Billy stopped and turned. "It's Christmas, Mum."

At this her eye hazed over and returned to the kettle. Billy ignored the pinch of disappointment this brought, and simply headed out of the kitchen and into the house.

The living room betrayed the earlier intentions of their home. Running from the front to the back of the house, it rose in a tall arch with dark wooden beams meeting at the crux from either side. To one side was a large fireplace, with a wooden mantelpiece above, which was charred underneath from the heat of the fire. With such a tall room, a fire was essential during the winter, though these days the room was barely used. These days the sheer space made the house feel emptier than ever.

Billy collected all the things he needed to plant the tree in the living room: a galvanised bucket with earth and large stones, a watering can and some sheets of newspaper to protect the carpet. He hadn't done this alone last year, but he thought he could remember how it was done, and this year the tree was not nearly so large. Once finished, he stood back and bumped into his mother. She was carrying a box of white lights, which she placed just inside the door.

"I thought you might be able to use these."

Astounded, he grinned, and darted down to his knees to examine the contents. "That's great, Mum, would you like to help?" But as he looked up, she was already leaving, heading for the stairs and the spare room.

He watched the door swing shut, drew a long breath, and turned his attention to fitting the lights. He couldn't remember whether his father had said they were the first or last things that you put on a tree, and at once stopped trying to recall the moment. Once those thoughts started, they were hard to stop. Instead he set to winding the lights around the tree. There were so many that they swamped the small pine. He sat back and wondered what to do next, before remembering the velvet bag still sitting on its side in the kitchen.

The bag had become light again, making the journey home seem somewhat unreal. Here in the kitchen he could see that the velvet was indeed purple. Taking the sack to the living room, he loosened the cord and laid out the twelve smaller pouches. He took the first pouch and undid the neck, which was strung with the same soft black cord as the larger sack. Inside was a miniature pair of ice skates, not made of silver or gold or even glass, but of all the materials that would have made them up had they been real. As he looked closer, they even appeared to have minute stitching holding the leather together, and small leather guards protecting the blades below the boots. Katherine, whom Billy had watched skating at numerous events, would love these. Though with his mother so withdrawn, he now discouraged his friend from visiting, and she was therefore unlikely ever to see the skates. He placed them back on top of their pouch and moved along to the next.

This time he brought out an axe. Close inspection showed that the handle had been varnished and the dark lines of grain were clearly visible. He bent down and nipped at the old carpet with the blade. A chunk of fluff came away in his fingers. Smiling but confused, Billy laid the axe on its pouch, rubbing the wiry threads away between his thumb and forefinger.

As he opened the next pouch he checked, then rechecked, what he'd seen. The pouch contained a perfect replica of his own bike, the one he'd outgrown this year. It even had the cracked rear reflector that was there the day he and his father had collected it at the bike shop behind Boots department store in the High Street. Both Billy and the shop owner were equally distraught about the state of the reflector. His father had told them both that, over time, it was the flaws and chinks which made special things, and people, unique. Billy hadn't believed this at the time, getting a bit cross when his father had refused the owner's offer of a new one. Now he was delighted to be able to recognise it.

He looked up at the tree. It was still, and remained so, only glistening now from the melted snowflakes. This tree, his tree, how could it possibly come with a replica of his bike? Pausing and calming his thoughts, he reasoned there were kids all over the country with drop-handled Trek racers, and the reflector could have simply been cracked during transit. But cracked in transit from where? Even Mr. Shaw hadn't known that. He set about opening the other pouches.

The next contained a pie which smelled like it had just been baked; he barely resisted the temptation to have a bite. Then five gold rings—or at least, they looked and weighed like real gold. A strange iron bar shaped like the letter *S* followed the rings, followed in turn by a sprig of mistletoe, thick with white berries and clearly not plastic, but tiny and perfect and real. Billy placed the decorations in a straight line before the tree.

The next pouch produced a piece of sheet music with writing which was too small for Billy to make out the title. Next came four gold rings, connected end to end, making a shallow curve like the arc of a late moon. Feeling baffled by the odd decorations, he went to the next pouch and thought he'd found an empty one. He delved further and found a tiny silver cylinder; peering closely, he saw a line about a third of the way down it. The edge of a lid? Yes: and as soon as he removed it, the familiar smell told him it was a tiny lipstick. Bizarre in itself, but also odd that it had such a strong aroma.

As he picked up the next pouch, he felt sure it had moved, and it felt warmer than the others. With great care he delved in to pick out what appeared to be a grey dog

wrapped in a thick sheet. It had a hook for the tree that picked the creature up in the way storks carried babies in cartoons. He realised it was getting late, and he was tired, but he thought he could make out gentle breathing from the dog. An old memory recognised the breed: an Irish wolfhound. Billy wondered if the tree and the dog might be robotic: that would explain the earlier movement of the tree and the size of the decorations. Companies always loved to make things smaller.

The last pouch held a tiny candle. He didn't hold it for long, fearing that the heat from his fingers might melt it. He got up, took a step back and looked at the tree, adorned in lights, with the twelve decorations below it, almost as though they were presents. Not the spread of last year, but of course everything had changed since then.

Torn between weariness and hunger, he switched off the lights to the living room, leaving just those on the tree alight. Giving up on the kitchen and into tiredness, he checked the locks on the front door before heading up to bed. Following his routine, he checked on his mother before going to his own room. The spare room, which she now used, was at the end of the landing near the front of the house. He didn't think the sofa bed helped her back, but without breaking their unspoken agreement on unnecessary speech, what could he do? Often she would be turning in her sleep, calling out his father's name. For this reason, he shut both her door and his own. He had enough trouble sleeping with his own thoughts, theories and questions.

As he brushed his teeth, the strewn packets of pills reminded him of the doctor's last visit. He suspected she had prescribed his mother with some pretty substantial sleeping pills. He'd ploughed through the medicine cabinet trying to learn what they were, but the labels were never that helpful. He wasn't sure what Nitrazepam did, but was all too aware of what Prozac was: an antidepressant. On bad nights, when sleep wouldn't come, he had thought about trying the nitro stuff, but concluded that it wasn't a good time to experiment with these things, when you're the only one who can get to the supermarket. Buying the food, the loo roll, things for his mother that a son isn't often seen buying; it had been a tough year.

In his own room, he lay back and thought about the tree sitting downstairs. Well lit, and with the ornaments spread like presents underneath, it could have been part of a scene from any house in his street tonight. Against all odds, he had managed to bring a piece of Christmas back home.

⁓ December 14th ⁓

A noise from downstairs woke Billy in the middle of the night. He sat up, at once awake and alert and, from the foot of his bed, reached for his father's cricket bat. He had moved the bat into his room after he answered the door one night to Robert's gang. He had narrowly dodged a small brick intended for the front door window. They had egged the entire house and Billy spent the whole weekend cleaning off the drying yolks before the smell started attracting rats—or worse, attention from the council. With his mother withdrawing to some place deep down, away from her pain, he suspected bad things might happen if officials found out the extent of his efforts at home.

Billy ran the bat along the banisters as he walked down the hallway. He'd read that making noise was the best way to make burglars panic and run. With his increasing height and the help of a few shadows, he hoped he could at least appear to make an imposing deterrent. The sounds didn't cease, and as he started down the stairs he swore he could hear a voice.

"Confound it…century…tied up!"

The voice wasn't quiet, but was twisted by sharp angles and baffled by soft carpets and furniture. Not for the first time, Billy wished that he'd worked out how to pay the telephone bill before it had been disconnected. His heart pounding, he hoped his mother was well dosed up and continued down the stairs. Perhaps someone had come for the tree? Mr. Shaw had said he hadn't ordered it. Perhaps the person who had imported it had now tracked it down and wanted it back? His stomach lurched as it always did when he felt he'd been foolish or slapdash.

Well, Mr. Shaw had given him the tree and the decorations, and his father had helped Mr. Shaw start his tree stand. So in a way, whoever this was was stealing from his father. This last thought arrived at the last stair and was all Billy needed to throw on the lights and burst into the living room wielding the bat above his head.

Yelling, he ran past the tree to the far side of the room, deciding that would give any potential burglar a path of escape and him a better angle to remind them why they should retreat.

"Where do you imagine you're going?" said a deep voice from thin air.

Billy whirled about the long room in terror, looking for the owner of the voice, bat extended but hitting nothing.

"And why on earth have you tied me to the wall?" said the voice, which was old and somehow familiar. It sounded like his late grandfather, who had died when he was eight years old.

Billy slowed and turned to face the tree. The Tree was glaring at him through eyes formed by branches curling both together and away. He could make out a mouth, and the mouth didn't look pleased. In the bustle and distraction, he had forgotten the quality of the Tree's movements earlier that evening. Right now, it appeared to be tugging at the electrical cord which ran from the fairy lights to the plug in the wall.

"In over three thousand years, not once has anyone tied me to a wall. Outrageous! Explain yourself," said the Tree, giving up tugging for glowering at Billy through furrowed branches.

"It's the lights," said Billy, astonished not to be screaming in fright. "If I take out the plug, the lights will go out."

"Pull the plug, Billy. Or mine won't be the only lights going out," said the Tree with impressive sincerity.

Billy reached down beside the bucket and pulled the plug. The lights went out, but before he could move, the Tree had whipped the plug from his hand with a grasp of branches and shoved it into the earth around its roots. The lights blinked back on.

"Well they do look rather good, don't they?" said the Tree.

The Tree leant forward and picked up the large velvet sack which had held the decorations, and hopped into it, leaving the bucket behind. The Tree tied the cord tightly before looking up and taking two further hops towards him. "We have things to discuss."

"Why do you sound like my grandad?" said Billy.

"You have a talking Tree in your family room and you wish to enquire why I sound like a grandad?"

"My grandad," said Billy, fighting the urge to back away.

"I sound like him because you find his voice inspiring."

"Does that mean that this is…"

"…a dream, Billy Christmas? Oh no, I wouldn't call it a dream," the Tree leant in closer. "Though in time you may wish it was."

"Oh."

"I am old in a way humans cannot understand and old, very old, even for my kind. I outdate your religions…"

"My family…we're not really religious," said Billy.

"Really? My goodness, yes, the world was starting to change quite rapidly on my last visit. Has religion disappeared altogether then?"

"Not so as you'd notice, no. Were you here last year?"

"Ha! Last year indeed. I last appeared one hundred years ago as I have each hundred years before," the Tree drew breath through its thick branches. "But there is time enough for us to talk, Billy, talk of many things. I'm sure you'll explain to me how the world has turned. I'm starting to forget things now; even for my kind I really am very old. I thought my last visit might *be* my last, but here we are. What is the date?"

"It's the thirteenth of December, no the fourteenth," said Billy checking the time in the long clock beside the Tree. It was past midnight.

"Plenty of time then. It is rare that I appear before the twelve days start, which is always either Christmas Day or Boxing Day. Though I'm forgetting the rules, of course, the rules. But you will forgive me I hope and put it down to my age."

Billy looked down at the Tree. "You look so young."

"That will change when we begin what we begin," said the Tree. "Now, to business. The usual way of things is that I find out what we need to do. Perhaps you can start by telling me what has gone so wrong that I have come to be here, talking to you?"

Billy faltered. Tears prickled at his eyelids, and he slammed them shut, as he always did, to avoid a bout of crying that he did not know how to stop. In the last twelve months, no one had asked him what was wrong, because no one had needed to. Everyone already knew what had happened. He began to explain, and as he did, he gave up trying to cover his tears.

He'd been sitting in front of last year's Christmas tree waiting impatiently for his parents to return from the kitchen. There was an indecent spread of presents and most of them were in a separate pile, awaiting his attention. A twelve-year-old Billy, still in his dressing gown, was doing a kind of breakdance jig to alleviate the tension, television being banned on Christmas Day in the Christmas household. His father had appeared at the door, towering over him.

"I'm in trouble, buster," said Tom Christmas. "Big trouble with the big boss."

"Aren't you done in the kitchen yet?"

"You're not hearing me, my boy. I've only gone and forgotten the milk! No milk, no tea. And it's Christmas Day."

"I'm bored, Dad!"

"Well why don't you sling on some clothes and come down with me to the twenty-four-hour garage? See if we can get back in your mum's good books."

"I'm not out of them."

"Come on Billy, by the time we're back your mum will be done in the kitchen, and we can crack on with the presents."

"I've already been waiting for hours, I don't want to go out."

"Not for me?"

"No."

"Suit yourself. Try finding me the next time you need a hand," his father threw him a sad and exasperated smile before grabbing his coat and hat and disappearing out the door.

Billy stood and watched his father depart through the branches of the Tree. Shortly afterwards a lorry had pulled up sharply. It could have been a dustbin lorry, but for it being Christmas Day. He had felt a stab of regret that he had not gone with his father. It was the same wretched lurch in his stomach he now knew all too well. He had decided to make sure the rest of the house looked neat and tidy, just perfect for his return.

"But he never came back," said Billy.

"I see," said the Tree. "He disappeared on Christmas Day, you say?"

"That's right."

"And your deepest wish?"

"Is to have him back."

"So that is why I am here."

The Tree began to stalk around the living room, branching up a hand to scratch its chin. Eventually, it turned back to him. "Yes, I think it can be done, there should still be time, but what you're asking me to do involves deep magic. In order for me to draw on the magic to grant this wish, you will have to achieve certain tasks. Each task is represented by the decorations you have opened. It is a matter of faith, Billy. I'm talking about acting out the required tasks with utter conviction, not questioning them once. Do you understand?"

"I think so," said Billy, regaining some composure and, for the first time in almost a year, a small spark of hope.

"I doubt you do, yet. But understand this: I have been thrown on fires by children who couldn't find enough faith in themselves. I mention this because the fate of another person—that of your father—is woven into your wish. Good or bad, you alone will bear the consequences of your actions."

"But you can bring my dad back home?" said Billy, finding his feet and trying to keep his hands from shaking.

"I can," replied the Tree, "but time is now against us. Traditionally I would be revealed on Christmas Day and the tasks completed by the fifth of January. The twelve days. However, if your father disappeared on Christmas Day, to stand any chance we must begin tonight."

"Tonight?"

"I have your commitment?"

"If I have your word," said Billy, speaking much more firmly than he had planned. He dropped his eyes.

"Never question the tasks, complete them on time, accept no fear, no tiredness, no obstacle which may come your way and try to prevent you succeeding."

"You have my word," said Billy, taking a step towards the Tree.

"And you mine," said the Tree. "Now tell me what decorations came in the sack. Tell me quickly, and hang the decorations on my branches as you do."

Billy described the twelve decorations and hung the items as the Tree turned slowly before him: the candle, the dog, the lipstick, the iron bar, the pie, the sheet of music, the five rings, the four rings (which made the Tree smile in not an entirely nice way), the axe, the sprig of mistletoe (which made the Tree hoot), the ice skates and the replica of his bike.

"Iron bar and ice skates you say?" said the Tree, sending a branch up to scratch its brow.

"Do you know what they mean?"

The Tree turned and looked at Billy at eye level. Billy hadn't noticed, but the Tree must have grown. "You're going to find that I'm not a great one for questions. Partly because I'm not allowed, and partly because I'm old and I get to choose not to."

The Tree started hopping up and down the length of the room, muttering back the list of decorations. Billy stood back. He wasn't sure that he and the Tree had established a relationship he could trust, but what choice did he have?

He looked at the Tree and found it staring at him.

"Not having doubts already, Billy?" said the Tree quietly.

Billy decided to bite his tongue.

"Take the candle and put it on my highest branch, where people think angels like to land."

Billy did as he was told, wrapping the hanging wire as tightly as he dared below the wax guard of the silver candleholder.

"Next take the dog, and hold him over your shoulder, as you did me this evening."

Billy slung the small dog over his shoulder with some vigour and faced the Tree. "Good lad," said the Tree. "Now take a match from the striking box, and make your wish whilst lighting the candle. You must call out the piece of your soul which misses him the most and bring it here, right into the room."

Billy scratched around in his mind, trying to find a link to the person he had to keep at the very back of his thoughts. Several painful seconds passed with the Tree bowed and waiting. Billy took a breath as he dug deeply for memories he had kept locked away. At last a recollection rose up, of being disappointed to find only a card at breakfast for his twelfth birthday. He'd opened it to find a magazine picture of his dream bike, his Trek drop-handled road bike, and had suddenly felt very foolish and very loved, and had looked up into his father's eyes.

Billy ignored the box of matches and took the lighting wand that had been left on the mantelpiece. He struck a bright blue flame with a click of his thumb, making the Tree jump slightly. Billy barely reacted; he wasn't seeing the Tree at all, he was seeing his father, and every fibre of his being longed for his return. In the room, light and sound imploded for the barest instant. Green light began to pulse deep within the branches of the Tree, and then faded gently away.

The Tree breathed out, and seemed a little stunned. "It is done."

"Are you OK?"

"You must miss him very much."

Billy's emotions threatened to overwhelm him again, but he was distracted by a significant gain in weight and size over his shoulders. The dog was growing.

"Get to bed, and take him with you. Otherwise he'll wake up confused, and a confused deerhound is a bad thing," said the Tree. "He might imagine I'm here for his relief."

"I thought he was a wolfhound?"

"Scottish deerhound, Billy. Bigger heart. Go on, to bed."

"But what about the other tasks?" said Billy, trying desperately to balance the dog.

"This is the first task, but this task will last for twelve days. Your faith must be as constant as this candle. We will speak again tomorrow night." With that the Tree spun into the air, terrifying Billy that the candle would blow out, and landed back in the bucket. It was then as silent and still as every other Christmas tree in Great Britain. Billy had his own problems; the dog was really getting heavy now. He turned and headed up the stairs.

Moments later, he stopped climbing. The dog had shuddered, sending a wave of goosebumps across him. He felt its heart beating rapidly through the sheet. This was no dream—the Tree, the dog, the opportunity to get his father back—this was all happening to him. Billy moved quickly, afraid that the dog might wake up whilst on the staircase and struggle, causing all sorts of problems. When he got to his room, he kicked his door shut, slamming it much harder than he had intended to. He froze as the huge dog flinched in the sheet. Then, just as he was beginning to lose his struggle with the dog's weight, he felt it return to sleep and he laid the animal gently at the foot of his bed.

The dog was now fully grown. At least Billy hoped it was. A deerhound like this would cost a lot to feed, and they were already getting by on minimal funds. And how was he going to explain this to his mother? Of course, these days it might just go unnoticed. Tired of addressing unanswerable questions, Billy flopped onto his bed, and waited for the chill of the mattress to pass before he could drift off to sleep. School tomorrow.

BILLY SLEPT BETTER THAN HE had all year and greeted the daylight without dismay. Then, remembering he wasn't alone in the room, he looked around. The door was open. Hadn't he slammed it last night almost waking the dog up? Grabbing his dressing gown, he tumbled down the stairs wondering where the huge animal had got to. He stopped at the Tree. The deerhound was sitting up staring straight into the eyes of his mother. She was transfixed and very much *there*. He watched for a moment before turning back up the stairs.

"Billy, where did he come from?"

The voice shook his heart. It was his mother's old voice.

He turned back to her, but she was still transfixed by the huge hound.

"He arrived last night," said Billy, as truthfully as he could.

"Last night," his mother echoed.

Billy watched for a few more moments before remembering the time. Now he was late. He dashed back upstairs to get ready for school. On his way out, he passed the living room, where his mother was still looking deeply into the wide eyes of the deerhound. He'd been worried about what would happen to the dog during the day, but perhaps everything would work out now after all.

At the door he tripped and found himself tumbling into the snow.

"Watch where you're going, will you?" Katherine had been sitting on her canvas rucksack, shivering as she waited. "The thanks I get for hanging around for you!"

Billy's own rucksack had landed over his head. "Sorry, sorry!"

He caught his step and ran to the shed to get his bike. As he came back the familiar wonder began to overwhelm him. Of all the people she could spend her time with, why on earth did she bother with him? Though he was taller than she was, he somehow always felt smaller. Her light brown hair was tied in a loose ponytail, and left strands that drew you in, to guess whether those eyes were blue or green. Her smile always started just a little to the right, and somehow made colours brighter and sounds sweeter.

Her smile made him dare to believe that the world was not, in fact, broken.

The deerhound barked, the sound rattling from behind the kitchen door.

Katherine looked up in surprise. "Have you got a dog now?"

"He arrived last night," said Billy, hoping that today he would sound at least halfway intelligible in her presence.

AS ALWAYS ON THEIR WAY to school, they cycled the back route alongside the river. The season was more apparent here, with ice edging into the river and black leafless branches cast against unspoiled snow lines. Billy always made the most of this part of the day, the only time he could easily speak to Katherine. Out of loyalty he kept away from her at school. He didn't want to make it difficult, knowing that even her rising star might be tarnished by association with the oddest boy in school. They reached the river path, and Billy automatically took the side nearest the water.

"You know it's the concert soon?" said Katherine.

Billy knew where this conversation was going. He'd been a keen singer, and good as well as keen. He would be wheeled out to visiting music teachers to show how many octaves he could cover. However, with his father's disappearance and the subsequent publicity, Billy had dropped out of anything that required him to be in the spotlight. He'd already used the excuse of his voice breaking to Katherine, claiming he ought to rest it until it settled.

"Just hear me out, OK?"

"Shoot," said Billy. He was still in a good mood from events at home, and the cycle with Katherine would, he knew, be the highlight of his day.

"John Wintergate has been taken out of school," said Katherine.

"Why's that?" asked Billy. John had been going to sing a solo in the concert.

"I think his parents have been posted. Army family: zero notice."

She should know; her dad was a general. This also meant she knew about being direct, and about saying things in a way that pushed you towards her objective before you'd had a chance to form an opinion of your own.

"You need to get back into doing the things you like doing. And you love singing."

"My voice is broken," said Billy, reminding her pointlessly.

"Has broken," said Katherine, correcting him with a glint in her eye, "and so had John's. That's why he was going to sing the male part in 'Good King Wenceslas.' Really easy notes, all you need is volume and tone. You could do it with your eyes shut."

He stayed quiet, all too aware this approach wouldn't wash with Katherine. She stopped her bike. Oh boy, thought Billy, and drew up beside her, not quite catching her eye.

"I think I have a better idea than most people just how awful this Christmas is going to be for you," said Katherine, dipping her head till she'd caught his eyes. "So that's fine. But next year, if you wimp out on things like this because of the attention or what people say, well, I'm going to kick you where it hurts."

Katherine paused, waiting for her grin to land on Billy.

"Last one to school buys the milkshakes on Friday," and with that she sped off.

Although Billy knew he could beat her on his road bike even if it was too small for him, he let her get a decent head start. He was happy enough hanging behind and tucking her kind words into his thoughts. At first he had been suspicious of Katherine's friendship. It was only later he'd learned that moving bases with the Army had given her a way of making friends, and later still, that Katherine had lost her mother at a very young age, in the first Gulf War. Though they'd never spoken about it, he was relieved that she never tiptoed around him, and would accept nothing less than his best foot forward in whatever they did. He started off down the river path, putting on significant speed, determined not to lose too much of his journey to school with her.

LATER THAT DAY AS HE cycled home, Billy allowed himself to think for the first time about the possibility of having his father back. As a child, he'd found it hard to understand his father, who whilst very tall, wasn't sporty, or stylish, or anything that helped Billy with any sort of bragging rights in the playground. Then one year, he was made to read *To Kill a Mockingbird*. With that book it became clear: his father was like the principled lawyer in the story, Atticus Finch. Tom Christmas was a lawyer, a barrister with a strong sense of justice, one who appreciated and often offered his talents in cases where colleagues might pass, dealing with clients who were in custody. Billy saw why he should be proud.

He learned more from the many stories offered in the wake of his father's disappearance. It was during this time that Billy came to appreciate his father's rare qualities. He was famous for undoing people, particularly pompous people, with a streak of humour that was tinder dry. The hole the man had left in the Christmas family was large and eccentric. The hole he had left was as difficult to ignore as his father had been.

At first it had seemed inevitable that he would be back, that he would turn up having lost his memory or having been called away for some awful reason. Soon it became clear that nothing was inevitable. The police were unable to offer any lasting help. Friends were unable to do anything other than attempt to reassure Billy and his mother. As time wore on, they returned to their own lives. It was then the constant nights of vigil took their toll and his mother had started to slip away.

As his mother did less and less, Billy found what he had assumed to be their sole bank account. With what appeared to be a vast amount of money, he thought he could comfortably maintain them for as long as they needed. As the bills mounted, he learned that the account contained all they would have going forward. There were no provisions to fall back on. The insurance policies they had would only work if his father were actually declared dead; this was far too difficult for his mother to face. He had discovered how much money it took to run their home, and realised that until now they had enjoyed a pretty comfortable existence. As with everything else that year, that situation had changed beyond recognition. Now, by some bizarre and magical twist, he had the chance to resolve their nightmare. He simply must not fail.

He cycled into the shed door, knocking it with his front wheel to make it open, then double locked his bike. Satisfied it was safe, he made his way back to the house. Approaching the kitchen, he realised the door had been left open. He sped into the house.

"Mum, hello?"

No one answered. He flew through his home, finding each room by turn as empty as the last. Suddenly he realised that the dog was gone too. Had she taken him out? It was still early. He then thought, for the first time, that he really had no clue what his mother got up to whilst he was at school. He looked about and found he'd come to rest by the still, silent Tree. No help to be found there now. He slumped in the chair where he could watch the front path and, despite his worry, soon dropped off to sleep.

"HELLO BILLY."

Billy stirred from the couch. It was now dark outside. His mum was back, and looked frozen stiff. In her left hand she had the dog on a blue lead and collar. Her hands shook and her bones were white and visible through bitterly frozen knuckles.

"He needed a walk, and I didn't have a lead," said his mother, "so I thought I'd better go into town and get one, only the pet shop has moved…"

"…to the superstore at the M40, I know!" Billy surveyed his mother's grey joggers and T-shirt with mild horror. "Don't tell me you went all the way into town and then out to the superstore in just that."

"Well, I couldn't walk him without a lead."

"You managed for about nine miles somehow!"

"Well, I…"

"And left the kitchen door open," said Billy, torn between being cross that it was in fact possible for his mother to get up to go to the shops, and delighted to see her up and about at all. His mother wavered, her new bubble threatening to burst. At that, he stepped forward and gave her a quick hug, ending the discussion. After making some admiring noises about the dog's collar, he took himself out and directly up to his room.

As he shut his bedroom door, he felt a little loneliness hit him. The dog would stay with his mother now. If she had the deerhound for companionship, and perhaps got out and about, what did that mean for him? Billy forced himself into bed, hoping sleep wouldn't evade him. He eventually drifted away, completely forgetting that he had no idea what time he was supposed to meet the Tree.

≈ December 15th ≈

Billy Christmas!"

Billy jumped from his bed and ran straight into the branches of the Tree, knocking them both flying.

"What are you doing up here!" said Billy as he disentangled himself from the scratchy, sappy Tree.

"Oh I see, it is fine for the dog to sleep up here, but I can't even visit?" said the Tree, righting itself.

"I think you might prove a bit more difficult to explain."

"Fine, well I won't risk being around you more than I have to," said the Tree.

Billy noticed that the Tree had filled out, and was now at least a couple of inches taller than him.

"Look, I have a few questions…"

The Tree held up a branch to silence him. Billy looked closely at its ancient face. The half-light of his room cast shadows across the branched face of the Tree. The deep lines brought back more memories of his grandfather: laughter and tears were what he'd told Billy had caused them. But what had the Tree known of life? How many years had the Tree survived? Even if it only came once every hundred years, how long had humans had trees at Christmas? He wondered what had been there before Christmas.

The Tree shook itself out, and began to pulse. Like a green heart, it pumped luminescent sap out from the trunk along the branches till its needles shone. Shards of green light leapt over the walls of his room, making Billy gasp.

"The next task has been chosen."

It held out the branch with the pie on it. As the decoration met his hands, it gained in size and weight. For the first time Billy realised there was a plate beneath the pie, and he was soon very glad of this fact. The pie started sizzling and steaming, with terrific heat emanating from it. It smelled delicious, and Billy realised he had stomped off to bed without supper and was starving.

"You must not eat any of it," said the Tree in stern tones. "This pie is for the old lady in Marlow Park who feeds the ducks every day. See that she has it in her possession by half past eleven tomorrow morning. That is your task."

With that, the Tree turned and hopped out of the room, heading for the stairs.

"Wait," said Billy, as loudly as he dared. The Tree paused and spun on its trunk.

"Just one question tonight, I think. Make it a good one."

Billy thought fast, but found little. "What time shall I come down tomorrow night?"

"Twelve minutes past midnight, Billy, always twelve past twelve."

With one large hop over the banisters and several smaller ones as it descended the staircase, the Tree left him. Billy watched the bobbing candle until it was gone, then turned back into his room. The sweet-smelling pie was making his stomach ache. He put it where the dog had slept the night before, then shut the door and pushed a chair against it, thinking that the deerhound might be even hungrier than he was. He flopped back into bed. Pie, Duck Lady, eleven thirty. Sleep overtook him.

BILLY WOKE IN TIME TO get out of the house before his mother was up; the first time he had needed to contemplate that for many months. He left via the kitchen, forcing a loaded jam sandwich into his mouth on his way and spilling a good dollop on his jumper. Overnight the pie had continued to sizzle and pop at the end of his bed, growing to the point where it was now as deep as two of Billy's closed fists and as wide as the largest pizza from Giuseppe's near school. He wrote a note for Katherine apologising for not being there and saying he would see her at school, before heading off to the park, balancing the precious pie on his handlebars. He had a plan: the Tree had said nothing about *not* delivering before eleven thirty. If he worked fast, he might still be in time for registration.

Unfortunately for Billy, the Duck Lady hadn't heard of his plan and wasn't there. Eight o'clock passed. He walked onto the landing stage where he'd scouted the tree stalls only two nights ago. The stalls were now silent and mostly empty. Perhaps Mr. Shaw had wound it up for the year? He strolled over to the statue of Sir Steve, and got caught slapping his backside for luck by a couple walking their dogs. They gave him a disapproving glare, but he had other things to worry about, and figured he needed all the luck he could get.

Nine o'clock passed, and Billy was getting worried. Half an hour late for school. He hated being late because it drew attention to him, and might raise questions about how he was being brought up in his freshly broken home. Now he would have to invent a cover story. He disliked making up stories—or, more accurately, telling lies. His father had always seen straight through them, and then seemed just a mite hurt that Billy hadn't felt he could be straight with him. Besides, once a lie was out, you had to tend and feed it, refer back to it as some other truth to be stashed alongside an already complex real life. He unwound the top of the tea towel that he had wrapped the pie in. It smelt even more attractive than before, but no, the Tree had forbidden it.

Ten o'clock. This was not good. He was now going to have to fake an appointment, which would need confirmation from his mother. He had forged her signature on numerous occasions but hated doing so, always believing that he would be found out. Marlow was a small town, and because of the publicity Billy felt that everyone who caught his eye had also recognised him. And people in Marlow talked. They were happy enough to talk about nothing, but give them something and they were unstoppable. He could imagine the thoughts of those who might have seen him this morning. *There's the boy who lost his father, Mr. Christmas; a Father Christmas on Christmas Day.* Tonight, they would check with their own children. Dentist, my foot, he was down the park this morning. But he couldn't give in, it was too important. He marched back to the bronze statue, avoiding a crocodile of infants and their teachers.

Eleven o'clock came and went and now hunger joined the doubt in his stomach. A further dreadful possibility dawned on him. What if she didn't come at all today? How long should he wait? What if it took till midnight?

Would that leave him enough time to get back to the Tree for twelve past midnight? If he hadn't completed the task, was there any point in returning at all?

At that moment, two female police officers entered the park. Billy turned around and headed off towards the cricket pavilion until the coast was clear.

Twenty minutes later, Billy was leaning on the statue keeping a good eye on either end of the park, both for the Duck Lady and the police. Just then, she crept into the corner of the park from the entrance near the white iron bridge. He recognised her immediately. Shorter than he, she walked bolt upright as if she wore a wooden corset. It would be difficult to tell if she did, as she had perhaps a dozen layers on. Petticoats, pre-petticoats, skirts and a green tweed jacket which had a matching green hat with a duck's feather in it.

Billy watched her move to the bench by the landing stage where he knew she would sit. Keeping a sharp lookout, he headed towards the Duck Lady, who had opened her bags of bread and was infuriating the swans by only throwing chunks to where one duck or another would manage to catch them.

"You big bullies," said the Duck Lady. "It's not for you, you hear!"

Billy approached her bench and sat at the far end. He watched as she continued to favour the ducks over not just swans but also the geese, moor hens and small garden birds trying to get in on the free feed. After a while, she turned to Billy, giving him a good stare through one eye, whilst half closing the other.

"Going to be up to me then, is it?" she said. "So be it. How do you do, Billy? My name is Agnes. Agnes Moorland."

"How did you know my name?" said Billy.

"Come on now, Billy Christmas, be serious," said Agnes.

Billy had forgotten the obvious. The Duck Lady, or Agnes, lived in and around the streets of Marlow, and probably spent most of her days listening to local gossip, which would include talk of his father's absence.

"Well, nice to meet you anyhow," said Billy.

"Seen you a lot about the place of course. Never talked to me before, have you?"

Billy didn't have an answer.

"But you never crossed the street to avoid me neither," said Agnes, "and as I never said hello to you, I guess that makes us even."

She cackled loudly, spooking all the birds including the ducks. "Ooh, sorry dears," she said, throwing out more bread to calm them. "'Scuse me Billy, but I guess you're having a bit of a week, aren't you?"

"I'm not sure I know what you mean," said Billy.

"Oh you know, with it being Christmas and all. Your dad still not found."

Billy felt his shoulders relax at the comment, surprised at how little it had got to him.

"Sometimes when people get lost, they stay lost. Sometimes it's hard trying to see the path home. Like me," Agnes said. "Though that needn't worry you too much, seeing as you've got that magic tree an' all."

Billy turned slowly towards her, his relief replaced by flashes of fear. What could she know?

"I'm sorry, I missed that."

"Fibber!" Agnes cackled, frightening the birds once again. "You just weren't expecting the old Duck Lady to have that much wits about her, were you? What did he bring for me?"

"He?"

"It's usually a man for a boy and a lady for a girl, depending on the person and who they pick. Not that many teenage boys are inspired by women, more's the pity."

"I am," replied Billy, looking away.

Agnes cackled twice as loudly as before, sending the swans to the far bank of the river. "Now I think you know that's not the same thing, Master Christmas, but good on you! World needs love aplenty at the moment, so you hang on in there no matter what you think she thinks. It's not always the same thing, you know."

Billy blushed and tried to ignore the rising hairs on his neck. How much hope could he take?

"So, what did he bring me then?" said Agnes, flashing her grey and white teeth at him.

Billy pulled back the tea towel to reveal the pie.

"Look at that." Agnes ran her fingers over the warm crust. "I ain't seen a Christmas pie like that in nigh on fifty years! In fact the last one I saw I might have made m'self."

He saw small tears form at the edges of her eyes, the low winter light making them sparkle.

"Thank you, Billy," said Agnes. "That's really very kind. You'd best be off to school now though. Better not be any later, eh?"

"But you have to tell me more about the Tree! How did you know about it?"

"Him, this time, Billy," said Agnes. She leant over and whispered, "and I think we're out of time, but I'm sure we'll meet again before the candle's out."

A hand clamped down on Billy's shoulder. He looked up blinking in the bright winter sun. The two policewomen, one who now had a hand on him, looked down. Billy's dreadful tightrope existence drew in piano wire tight. How could he have been so stupid? Apart from trying to get his father back, he also had to protect his mother, who until yesterday had effectively not been there.

"Unless I'm mistaken, school breaks up next week," said the police officer with her hand on his shoulder.

Billy had to think fast. "I was here getting a prescription for my gran," said Billy quickly. "They know at school, and I'm only a little late." He turned to catch Agnes, who winked back at him; she knew exactly what he needed her to say.

"Is that right, Agnes?" said the police officer. Billy looked back at her, confident she would come through for him.

"Never spoken to him before five minutes ago," said Agnes, without missing a beat.

Billy turned to her, open mouthed.

"Shame he isn't my grandson. Lovely boy. I'm sure he ain't been up to no mischief," said Agnes.

"Back to school for you then, son. Let's go."

He was so gob-smacked that he shook with the shock of it, unable to look at Agnes as the police officers led him away. He even forgot to worry about the consequences of crossing paths with the powers that be. The worry soon returned when he arrived back at school, on the playground, in a police car with blue flashing lights, and almost every kid in school pushed up against the windows trying to see if he had been handcuffed.

"OBVIOUSLY EVERYONE AT THE SCHOOL has nothing but the deepest sympathy for you, Billy," said Mrs. Herringate, the deputy head teacher, "but truancy at any time is totally unacceptable. If it were any other time of the year but this, I'd be calling your, well, your mother to let her know. However, you must realise that this is a dreadful time for her too. Surely you see that by acting up, you're being a bit, well, selfish?"

Billy hadn't had the energy to muster an explanation. He simply rode out the conversation to a point where he could be ejected onto the playground. This, of course, was no more comfortable. Robert Lock had been waiting for him, and led the throng which met his departure from the main office.

"Been out looking for your dad then, Billy?" said Robert.

There was a gasp of mock horror from Robert's gang, who waited for a reply from Billy, which never came. He simply turned and kept walking until they gave up following.

At least Agnes had accepted the pie, meaning that he could claim the task complete later tonight. What had Agnes been thinking? It would have been so easy for her to help him out. Instead she'd stitched him up like a kipper; a phrase that Billy knew fitted but hadn't a clue what it meant. And what had she meant about speaking with him again before the candle was out? If he met her right now, he'd steal her bread and throw it on the roof of the cricket pavilion where the ducks couldn't get it.

KATHERINE CYCLED HOME WITH BILLY. This was unusual, as she normally had something on each night after school. Today she was waiting patiently by the bike shed for him. Ignoring the stares and backhanded taunts of those around them, she greeted Billy with a quiet glance and they set off towards the river path. This would normally had Billy's heart in double-back somersaults; today he was simply grateful for the distraction.

They cycled in silence all the way along the river; with Billy not knowing how to start a conversation when he couldn't explain what had happened, and Katherine, he suspected, not wanting to rattle the cage of her friend who was clearly losing the plot. On the rare occasions that they did cycle back to Marlow Bottom together, Katherine would begin building up speed from a few hundred yards before his house, in order to tackle the hill up to her house at the end of the road. Today she coasted to a halt beside Billy at his gate.

"Thanks for waiting for me," said Billy. "It was going to be horrible with everyone otherwise."

On days when Robert's gang felt they had a good excuse, they would hound Billy on his way home; hence his love of road bikes with a good turn of speed.

"I know you'd have done the same for me," said Katherine.

"I thought the choir were rehearsing tonight?"

"They are. We didn't find a replacement for 'Good King Wenceslas,' so I had the evening off," said Katherine, without the hint of an edge.

Billy's face fell. He knew how proud Kathcrine had been to be allowed to sing a solo part, but hadn't realised that this was why she had wanted him to sing. With the day he'd just had, he had made up his mind that if he were going to complete these tasks, he must now keep his head down at school.

"Katherine, I'm so sorry."

"It's OK."

But it wasn't OK. His friend was looking away to hide her surfacing tears.

She broke the silence. "It's just, I'd worked pretty hard at this. I don't find it easy like, well, like you did."

"Katherine."

"I'm sorry, I know you've had a horrible day, and this is a horrible time for you." Katherine turned back to him with a sympathetic smile. "Next year, Billy. We're going to have such a good year. I'll see you in the morning."

She cycled twenty yards back the way they had come before turning and passing him at speed, looking straight ahead. Billy watched her with his heart in pieces. He'd thought this task was going to be easy, but here he was with his balanced world teetering. Katherine turned the corner to the hill and disappeared. After a minute, he turned and headed inside to make supper for himself, his mother and the dog.

⚜ December 16ᵗʰ ⚜

Billy's mobile began whistling like an express train. The only ring tone that would stir him at just after midnight, he'd decided. Despite the fact that he had only a few minutes of airtime left on it and no money to buy more, he kept it because he didn't have a watch, at least not one he could wear to school. Mickey Mouse was no longer acceptable. Still fighting sleep, he slung on his dressing gown and padded downstairs to the Tree. For some reason he had expected it, or him, to be dormant or asleep until the stroke of twelve past twelve. But the Tree was out of the bucket once more and had one of his dad's books out, thumblessly thumbing through the pages. It must have only just picked it up, as a cloud of dust from the neglected bookcase still twinkled around the Tree.

"Lot of adventure to be found on these shelves, Billy."

Tired and still smarting from his day, Billy was not in the mood for small talk. "How do you know Agnes Moorland?"

"Ah Agnes," said the Tree. "So you two had a chat?"

"We had a chat," said Billy, just holding his temper, "before she shopped me, for truancy, to the police."

"Now, Billy, do you imagine that someone like Agnes," said the Tree spinning to face him, "who is homeless, in a smart town like Marlow," the Tree took another hop towards him, "has the luxury of being able to lie casually to the police?"

Wrong-footed, Billy swallowed. "But how could she know about you?"

"Agnes was a young lady on my last visit."

"But that's impossible," said Billy. "That would make her at least a hundred years old, plus however old she was when you appeared."

"Yes it would."

"But she looked…"

"I wonder. How old does she look now?"

"At least sixty."

"Sixty! Oh my poor Agnes."

"Probably more in fact, but I still don't see how…"

"Put simply, she wished to live forever. It's the only time in thousands of years I asked a child to reconsider."

"Why did you?"

"When I met Agnes, she was fifteen years old. Great intelligence, but humble beginnings and few prospects for a girl with wit and ambition. I have been having a quiet look around, Billy, and technological marvels aside, I have to tell you that I had never anticipated that what they call 'gender roles' would have broadened out as they have.

Agnes saw beyond me on that count." The Tree popped the book back on the shelf and turned to Billy. "I gave her a vial. A token by way of compromise. I implored that she first taste life and love and try to understand its nature before becoming beyond nature. I wonder what she has seen in all those years? And why she took the vial so late?"

"She said that she'd got lost," said Billy.

"And that is why this task was so vital. She is truly lost, and would continue that way in static decay for a great many lifetimes."

A chill passed over Billy. Why had the Tree been so insistent that he should not try the pie?

"Is it poison?" Was he to be a murderer?

"Now that is a foul way to describe relief at a time of her own choosing."

"But what if she shares it with other homeless people?" What if she shared it with the ducks, he thought, horrifying himself by breaking into a grin.

"She understands the nature of the gift."

With the subject of death, his thoughts had drifted back to his father.

"What is on your mind, Billy?"

He was more prepared this time. "If my dad is dead, will it hurt him to, well you know, be brought back?"

"Ripped from the ground and shaken to life?" said the Tree.

Billy hadn't thought about this in such detail and shut his eyes against the image.

"In two nights, I will have located your father; if he requires such treatment, I will let you know."

He had frozen, suddenly caught with an image that he'd tried to ignore for almost a year.

"If he requires such treatment and you'd prefer to let life continue as it is, you can always fail at the tasks. The world is full of such choices, Billy."

"I believe you," was all he could manage whilst wrestling his tired mind away from the awful possibility.

"Did you find the task as easy as you'd thought?"

"Not really, no."

"I think that is a good thing."

"Meaning I'll be better prepared?"

"Meaning the next task awaits you."

The Tree backed away gently and started what Billy was beginning to recognise as a ritual of sorts. There was a moment of silence, and then it was as if a gentle electric current had passed through the Tree. The artificial lights went out and the needles seemed to stretch and then pulse a vivid green light of their own. By turn each decoration twitched, as if being prodded by an invisible hand, before the next task was chosen. The Tree bowed and passed Billy the tiny sheet of music. They both paused for a moment.

"Do you have any idea what it means?"

Billy looked up in surprise. "You don't know what the task is?"

"Not always. Sometimes they are quite personal. What is the title of the music?"

Billy had a double-edged, sinking feeling. He thought he might know what the music was, and knew he was going to have to go into his father's study to find out. Without a word, he put the sheet of music on the mantelpiece and left the room. He passed the staircase and opened the door to his father's study.

Moonlight cut the room in half, silhouetting the back of the old leather chair, the rug by the fireplace and the mantel. Memories were unavoidable here, and it was because the room had always welcomed him so warmly that Billy felt so much more the trespasser now. Often his father would shrug off his own work to help Billy with some indecipherable mathematics problem. Even now Billy smiled at the thought of his father attaching a Post-it note to the teacher when the problem had proved impossible. The note would read "*see me*" with a sum that was achievable, and his phone number for discussion.

Billy crossed the room to the only piece of inherited furniture in the Christmas house. His father's desk had been passed on to him by Billy's grandfather. Billy hoped that the desk was not now his, though it was impossible not to admire the regal, arched talon feet, embossed leather top and best of all, secret drawers. The magnifying glass was not in one of those, but the top right drawer. Billy reached for the strange green glass lamp that his grandfather had used to pore over stamps and turned it on. The small light cast fresh shadows across the dark room. Billy opened the drawer, recovered the glass and, turning off the light, retreated to the living room.

The Tree was by the fireplace when Billy recovered the sheet music. He had hoped it might have started growing by now, but it still seemed tiny. Billy brought the magnifying glass to his right eye, and lifted the tiny paper until it came into focus. The letters rolled into the centre of the glass, blobbing up just big enough for Billy to make out. "Good King Wenceslas," as he'd suspected.

"You know what the task requires?"

Billy knew where the task was going, but after today with the police it was impossible. He must keep his head down. "Yes, but I can't."

The Tree shuddered so violently that Billy thought he was about to be attacked and threw his forearm over his face. Through half an eye, he saw the Tree subside and draw up arms formed from branches rising slowly. As it did, every piece of glass in the room, from picture to pane, began to rattle and then sound. The Tree climbed methodically through a full octave. On the third note, the mirror over the mantelpiece bowed, terrifying Billy that they'd both be showered with lethal shards of glass.

By the fifth note, Billy had noticed a gnawing itch in his throat. At the sixth, he realised it was actually his vocal chords matching the frequency of the glass about the room. If it continued, he thought he'd throw up, but he didn't think he could speak to complain. By the eighth note, he was singing, because he had to breathe, and as he exhaled the notes sounded. The sound coming from him was both unfamiliar and unmistakably adult. The Tree had not finished with him. With the octave complete, it now flung the glass orchestra into a verse of "Good King Wenceslas," and Billy gave in and sang.

> Mark my footsteps, good my page;
> Tread thou in them boldly:
> Thou shalt find the winter's rage
> Freeze thy blood less coldly.

The Tree's loose arms fell back into branches and the glass orchestra rattled to a halt. "There is no doubt that you can do it, Billy. The only question is whether or not you *will*."

With that the Tree hopped back into the bucket. As the velvet whispered in against the metal, it was clear it had already returned to its dormant state and Billy was alone. Still flushed from his first singing in just over a year, he tucked the sheet music into his dressing gown pocket and went back to bed. Good King Wenceslas. Well, at least it would make Katherine happy.

THE NEXT MORNING, BILLY HEADED directly to speak to Miss Emerson, the music teacher. She was sitting at the baby grand piano in the school's theatre going over the running order for that evening's performance. She looked up as he walked into the room and a smile broke over her face.

"Billy Christmas."

He smiled back at her. "I wondered if you'd remember me."

"Remember you? I've been trying to get you back in this room for nearly a year!"

"Katherine might have mentioned it."

"How's Mum doing, Billy?"

Billy felt the flinch but showed only a small smile. "She's been getting a little better, thanks. Thanks for asking, I do actually have a favour I need to ask you…"

BILLY'S HEART POUNDED AS HE thought about the prospect of having to sing in front of a crowd again. He left the theatre to find Katherine pacing by the door to the playground. She rounded on him immediately.

"You were ages! What did she say?"

Billy found Katherine a few inches from him with her hands gripping his bony elbows. He paused, lost in her eyes.

"Well?" said Katherine, looking up at him.

"Well basically, she says we can sing tonight."

Katherine gasped and kissed a flabbergasted Billy on the cheek. At least he thought it was a kiss, his brain was so busy flipping and trying to remember the moment that he was lost to the world. When he came to, Katherine was dragging him back to the music room to practice.

THE CHOIR HAD ASSEMBLED BEHIND the curtain on the stage and were preparing to sing "Good King Wenceslas" as an encore. Billy and Katherine were standing slightly apart from the group ready to sing the bass and soprano solo sections of the carol.

"Oh god, I'm not sure I can do this," said Katherine, turning a little pale.

"We sang it forty times this afternoon. Once the music starts, you'll be fine." Billy hoped he was right. He was all too aware that this was the first time Katherine had attempted a solo part. It was entirely possible to go dry and mumble through a whole verse with a few hundred pairs of eyes on you. He lent Katherine his most confident smile and looked up at the curtain. The applause had started to wane, the song had to happen soon or they wouldn't be needed. Billy looked down at his sheet music, now fully grown, and wondered if there was anything else it was supposed to do. Katherine reached over and put a hand on his wrist.

"Oh god. I really don't…"

"No time now."

The curtain had flinched, the cue to the choir to stop picking their noses. Then it swept back to reveal a large collection of families, waiting for their set-piece encore of "Good King Wenceslas." The vicar, Mike Hayter, was beaming up at them from the front row, clapping for all he was worth. As his eyes had adjusted to the stage lights, Billy could make out Katherine's father, in uniform, standing by the theatre door. He glanced to his left. It was clear that she hadn't spotted the General, or even taken the time to look up. She was poring over the music, fingers looking for the points where she came in; not a good sign. He moved towards her and gave her a gentle elbow. Katherine yelped and looked up, eyes widening.

"Just follow me," said Billy through his teeth.

There was no reply.

The orchestra, consisting of two pianos and a drum kit, struck the first chord and then they were off. Katherine's head snapped up and she came in perfectly for the first verse. Billy let himself relax. Time to sing. He hadn't always hated attention, and the curious calm he'd experienced on stage before found him again. Striking the notes clearly and calmly, Billy poured his new older voice into the audience.

> Hither, page, and stand by me,
> If thou know'st it, telling,

Billy turned to Katherine, hoping that the story in the song, and his approach, would carry her on through the rest of the verse. Katherine appeared to be listening to him.

> Yonder peasant, who is he?

To his horror, he realised she was really listening to him. Just as the audience were.

> Where and what his dwelling?

Katherine opened her eyes. She caught sight of her father by the door, and the band played on without her. Billy thought fast and threw her a lifeline.

"Does he live a good league hence?" sang Billy, as Katherine's face fell.

"Underneath the mountain?" Billy snatched the score that she had been singing from, motioning to the audience that he had accidentally taken Katherine's sheet, and rolling his eyes by way of apology. He passed her the sheet music which had come from the Tree, praying something would happen.

It was blank. Katherine shot him an anguished glance. At precisely the same moment, large blue words floated up out of nowhere onto the page, scrolling and indicating time. She saw them clearly and sang out.

Right against the forest fence,
By Saint Agnes's fountain.

Billy was so proud of her that he almost missed his own cue.

Bring me flesh, and bring me wine,
Bring me pine logs hither:
Thou and I will see him dine,
When we bear them thither.

The choir, who had been watching the drama unfold, dived in and allowed the leads a moment of rest. Katherine, still amazed that the music was apparently moving over the paper, looked at Billy through grateful, if incredulous, eyes. Billy shot back his best impression of her own no-nonsense stare. They still had to bring this carol home. To his relief, they did it with something approaching panache.

Backstage, Billy took a moment to compose himself. It was the first time he'd put himself on display in over a year. He was surprised that it didn't feel more awful. A blank sheet of music appeared in front of his face and tapped him gently on the nose. Katherine's eyes were sparkling. Billy hoped she didn't have any awkward questions.

"Thank you," said Katherine. "Now please explain how this works."

"Special effects?" said Billy, grinning.

"Half the choir just saw me singing from a blank page. They think I'm crackers."

He giggled, the adrenaline from performing leaving him all at once.

"Don't you dare laugh at me."

But he continued, and soon they were both laughing. It felt good to be on the other side of this.

"My dad would like to meet you. Have a lift home?" said Katherine.

Billy smiled, torn. "I have my bike."

"Oh come on. We can walk in tomorrow."

"I can't risk it. My dad gave me the bike. But thanks."

Katherine gave him a look, then a hug and then went to join the throng of parents and friends. Billy had been tempted. The bike was well locked, but in truth he hadn't felt like any more attention from assembled families that evening. He had ventured out enough.

He headed out into the cold night, and over to the bike shed where he began unlocking his favourite present. Throwing the locks into his black rucksack, he put both lights on his bike and rolled it out of the shed. There was a bump above him, and he heard the sound of spitting just before the wet saliva hit his face. It rolled down his cheek and under the collar of his shirt. He threw his shoulder up trying to wipe it away. He could still feel the gob against his chest as he looked up in fury.

Robert Lock was grinning from the roof of the shed. "Nice singing, Billy."

Rubbing his shirt into his chest, Billy felt a cold rage rise within him. Could nothing ever just go right? He stared up at Robert. Unless he came down, Billy would be at a severe disadvantage. If he tried to climb up, he was certain Robert would stamp on his hands. He decided he would not let this idiot ruin his night.

"Don't you have a home to go to?" said Billy, and wheeled his bike away into the darkness.

"See you at school, Billy," said Robert, but this time his voice was faltering.

Billy cycled home as fast as he could, letting the night air flush the rage out through his lungs. As he slowed for his house, he looked along the road to the corner that went up the hill. He often wondered what Katherine was thinking about when she was up there. Tonight, he hoped with a touch more confidence, he might just be tucked in *her* thoughts.

After going through the routine of locking his bike, Billy headed back to the kitchen. The windows were steamed up, which only happened when someone was cooking. He opened the door, hoping he hadn't left the oven on. His mother was at the hob with a pan, something Billy had not seen in over six months. He realised he hadn't told her he was going to be late; she must have been starving. His mother looked up and spoke first.

"I fed Saul, because he was hungry. Then I felt hungry too."

Billy took a moment adjusting to the deerhound's new name. "I'm sorry I'm late. I can take over if you like?"

"It's OK," said his mother, turning back to the pan. "I think I'll finish it. Would you like an omelette?"

Billy walked through the kitchen in a pleasant daze. "Yes Mum, that'd be great. I just need a quick shower."

"Where did you say you got Saul?"

He turned back to her. "I didn't say. He just arrived."

"That's what I thought," said his mother, her eyes drifting in a much happier way than usual.

After a moment Billy left the kitchen, shaking his head. If he had known a dog would bring his mother back this quickly, he'd have found her one ages ago.

⇩ December 17ᵗʰ ⇦

A weary Billy walked into the living room at a minute past twelve and flopped into the large red chair next to the Tree. Letting out a sigh, he let his chin roll forward onto his chest. The broken nights were beginning to tell. He flinched, not sure whether he'd drifted off or not. The Tree was still inert, so he couldn't have been out for long. He fished his mobile out of his pocket. It was seven past twelve. He looked up at the branches above him and wondered what the Tree would want of him next. The axe glinted, turning slowly in the moonlight, throwing a tiny but bright reflection on the wall. What purpose would it serve? What were the four joined gold rings intended for? The black iron bar was barely visible, but he was still struck by its strange S shape. The Tree shuddered, snapping Billy away from his thoughts. All the Tree's branches lifted up as if it were stretching or yawning, before it hopped neatly onto the carpet and turned to Billy.

"So how did you get on?"

"You knew I'd do it?"

"You're still smiling. I take it things worked out?" said the Tree.

"Thank you."

"Don't thank me, Billy, you may find yourself taking it back before much longer."

He shifted his weight a little. "Any news for me?"

"Tomorrow Billy," said the Tree. "To that end I have to go out tonight, so we must get on."

Billy saw that the Tree was a good foot taller than he was now, and the needles looked fatter than last night. It was almost muscular in posture. What he wouldn't give for a few muscles on his own long bones. The Tree appeared to breathe in before the familiar green light pulsed out as before. It shuddered and started to bow towards Billy, who peered in eagerly to see which decoration had been chosen. As he did, the Tree lurched back and the pulsing light flickered, trapped as though it were one of his father's records which had got stuck. After a moment, the Tree bowed once again, but this time Billy was faced with not one decoration but two: the lipstick and the axe.

"Well, which am I supposed to take?" said Billy in confusion.

"The tasks are yours, Billy."

"Am I supposed to take both?"

The Tree's voice was so quiet it was hard to make out. "Just one."

He felt it was as though the Tree had used its remaining breath to whisper to him and now couldn't breathe until the choice was made; the pressure was incredible. He looked at the lipstick, a tiny perfect cylinder, and then the axe, remembering its sharp edge. Clenching his teeth at what it might mean, he leant forwards and took the lipstick. The Tree did indeed seem to heave a sigh of relief. After a couple of breaths, it spoke.

"I was sure you'd pick the axe…"

"Was I supposed to pick the axe?" said Billy, groaning at his choice.

"There is less 'supposed to' in all this than you might imagine."

He examined the lipstick again. It appeared to be another slow grower, showing no sign of movement. "I'm afraid I don't know what to do with this one."

"You are, of course, required to get a kiss from the girl you love," said the Tree. "Clearly, there is a girl you love. You can think yourself lucky I found you in the twenty-first century."

"And why is that?"

"You wouldn't believe how hard it would be to get a kiss from an eighteenth-century girl," said the Tree with the hint of a smirk. "It cost one young man the keys to a castle he'd wished for."

"This is not easy at all," said Billy, getting cross. "She's my friend, and this will ruin it. In fact, if I try to kiss her she'll probably punch me. She grew up in the Army."

"The tasks are no trifling matter," said the Tree suddenly, catching Billy off guard. "Perhaps the lipstick will have an effect. Perhaps it draws kisses by being worn. Perhaps it draws the person wearing the lipstick to the one who gave it. Do try to think laterally, Billy. You're in the midst of a magical quest, and you're concerning yourself with minutiae. Remember the goal, always."

Billy sank back into the chair, torn between wanting to fill his empty house and wanting to keep on good terms with Katherine, his only real friend. The Tree shook itself down and hopped out of the room. Billy remembered it had said it needed to go out tonight; he would have to unlock the front door. As he got up, he could feel the cold draft of night air. The Tree had somehow managed to open the mortise lock. He went out to the hall.

The Tree turned back on the doorstep. "My kind are not blessed with many friends, Billy, but it occurs to me that if you were a true friend you wouldn't keep such a secret as love from her."

With that, the Tree turned and sprang into the sky. Billy ran out and looked up into the darkness. It had vanished. After a moment, he turned back into the house, shivering slightly, hoping it would return, and knowing all the advice in the world would not make tomorrow anything other than appallingly awkward.

AS SOON AS HE WOKE up, Billy started to plan. It was Wednesday; Katherine would be back on after-school activities. Whatever it was, he would have to wait until she was finished. He had no experience of persuading girls to kiss him, but there was no way he was going to attempt this at school. He had been waiting at least half an hour that morning by his own gate. Normally it was Katherine waiting for him on his back step. His mother walked past him, this time, thankfully, wrapped up.

"Just nipping out to walk Saul," she said quietly.

He still wasn't used to his mother just nipping out anywhere. Despite being fond of most animals, he had to admit a certain amount of resentment towards Saul, who had simply ignored him from the outset.

Billy gave up waiting, and with a last glance to the corner of the hill, he sped off to make homeroom registration. Perhaps she had got a lift in with her father?

KATHERINE DIDN'T APPEAR AT REGISTRATION. Not wanting to ask the teacher out loud, for fear of the reaction of the class, Billy hung back until everyone had left. Once they had, he approached his form tutor, Mr. Rowe.

"I hear you had a good night at the concert, Billy." Mr. Rowe was a decent teacher who had allowed Billy the latitude to survive school over the last year.

"Yes sir, I just wondered what had happened to…"

"Miss Jennings? Her dad called to say that she'd be in at lunch."

"Did he say why?"

"She'll be in at lunch, Billy. Off to class now."

Billy struggled through the morning, wondering what had kept Katherine from coming to school. He hated the prospect of this task. Before today, he had simply ignored the thoughts he'd had of kissing Katherine because they seemed so ludicrous. Now the Tree had forced him into attempting this impossibility, with the cruel twist that if she turned him down he'd never see his father again. He was all too aware that this could ruin the only friendship that had stood up to his dire year. However, the Tree's parting words had struck a chord with Billy. What kind of friend was he that he'd pretend not to feel so much for her? With that, he broke off the train of thought and tried to return to his geography lesson and the machinations of meandering mountain rivers.

Katherine arrived at lunch break, and immediately Billy knew there was trouble. Despite her best effort to paint the evidence away, she had clearly shed many tears that morning. What could possibly have happened? He wanted to go up and find out, but the ever-popular Katherine was swallowed by a throng of girls fussed around her, questioning and then gasping. He was fighting the urge to go and throw these foolish girls off her and set about righting whatever had upset her. Beyond the gaggle of girls, Robert Lock stood grinning at him, almost daring him to risk communicating with the smarter set; ample excuse for a session of "Christmas time," as he had coined the attacks on Billy. Deciding not to add to whatever burden she already had, he leant back against the brick wall and waited.

The bell sounded and the reluctant return to classes began. Billy held his ground as the girls around Katherine faded away. After agonising moments, she looked up towards him. She raised her eyebrows, forced a small smile and nodded towards the bike shed. He got the message. The usual place, later. Though worried about what had happened, Billy couldn't stop his heart from soaring. She had turned to him.

Games provided a welcome distraction for a large part of the afternoon. He threw himself into the rugby, and managed to tackle Robert on two occasions. On the second, Robert had kicked up his boots, but Billy was all determination and fury; remembering Mr. Rodway's training, he dived and bound his long arms about Robert's legs, just above the knees, collapsing them totally. Not turning to allow a reaction, he was up like lightning, supporting his team to the try line and gaining victory from Robert's fumble. Enjoying the claps on his back on the way to the changing rooms, Billy barely noticed Robert, kneeling where he'd fallen, pounding clenched fists into the mud.

Back in the classroom, with his adrenaline sated, Billy was absorbing a grim reality check. If he failed to kiss Katherine, he would forfeit his father, as well as lose his only friend. He ran his thumb over the lipstick in his pocket. How was it supposed to help him? He had toyed with the idea of putting it on, in case it was supposed to be magnetic or something. He was at a complete loss as to how to approach this, so far was it from his experience. He thought of the Tree, and then of Katherine, and tried to put his own needs and desires aside. Katherine needed a friend. The bell sounded.

To his surprise, Katherine was already waiting for him with her bike.

"I left it here after the concert. Dad hadn't been expecting to make it last night."

Billy unlocked his racer, and they hurried away from the emptying school before anyone would spot them. Once they were along the river path, Katherine hopped off her bike and began to walk with it, her feet swishing in the weak, wet snow. Billy followed suit. This time, he chose to break the silence first.

"Can you tell me what is going on now, please?"

"He's been called up," said Katherine simply.

"Your dad?"

"Yes," said Katherine. "We're being relocated. Closer to the Gulf."

"The Gulf? But that is…"

"The other side of the world," said Katherine. "Obviously, they wouldn't put him there unless they had to. It must be serious."

Billy took a breath. "Isn't that where…"

"My mum died. Yes. It's not that so much. Dad is a lot more senior now. Looks very bad if your general gets shot," Katherine said, with a deal of venom. "But Dad will have to send people. People he likes, with families he knows. And it kills him. I can see it killing him. As if we haven't given them enough already."

His heart sank. All year, Katherine had been there, quietly backing him up, not speaking of her own troubles.

"But they keep sending us. With no real explanation. It's horrible, Billy. One of the reasons we moved off the base and into Marlow was that without meaning to I was scaring other kids. Scaring them that maybe they would lose a parent too."

Billy began to realise he would be losing his only friend. "When will you have to go?"

"They're not saying, which is not a good thing," said Katherine. "It usually means with little or no notice."

"There's nothing he can do to stop it?"

"It doesn't matter. He won't pass on what he's asked to do. It's not that kind of job."

They'd stopped pushing the bikes during the conversation. At this point in the river, there was a wooden fence by the bank. Billy moved over to it, brushing the snow off the bar, where it pattered onto the ice at the edge of the river. Katherine joined him and they were still for a while, pouring their frustration out into the water. Billy drew in several quiet deep breaths and reached into his pocket for the lipstick.

"I've got a present for you."

Katherine looked at him in surprise. "For me? Why?"

Billy didn't know why, and then remembered that presents are usually wrapped. Why hadn't he thought of this earlier? Not having an answer ready and feeling like it was his turn to forget his lines, Billy simply opened his left palm. The low light fading over the river bounced off the lipstick case, making it gleam.

"Is that lipstick?" said Katherine in amazement. "That's bizarre. Uh, is there some story with this?"

He'd had all day, why hadn't he worked this out? "It arrived for you," he said trying to make his voice sound mysterious, and succeeding only in sounding faintly odd. "I want you to have it."

"It has my initials on it," said Katherine, flashing Billy a look that he took to mean bemused, possibly verging on un-amused.

He looked closely at it, not remembering any such markings. He hadn't examined this decoration in the magnifying glass, and this morning he had simply switched it from one pocket to another as it slowly grew to the standard size.

"Of course it does," Billy took a deep breath. In his judgement, it was now or never. He closed his eyes, so he couldn't be put off by Katherine's reaction, which would doubtless finish him. He'd wanted to hug her earlier that day, to make her feel protected, but knew he'd still have to try to kiss her, and didn't want her to confuse his support with what he was doing now. He leant in to where he thought Katherine was facing him and kissed her—on the nose.

His eyes flew up. She had still been looking at the lipstick! He felt his cheeks flush red, but as Katherine recovered, she appear to bob back towards him. Billy also bobbed back in and this time they both bumped noses, quite hard. They laughed uncertainly. Then Katherine took a short look at him and reached up, putting her hands behind Billy's neck, and kissed him slowly on either cheek, letting him feel the full shape of her lips roll along each side of his face. Then, looking just a shade sadder, she retreated and put her hands back on the wooden bar.

Billy was lost in the kisses. He saw her there in front of him, hands back on the fence, but he also saw her, as clear as the dwindling day, there in front of him with her arms on his neck. The Billy that was left by the riverbank shook him out of it. Did kisses on the cheek count? He would never get another chance like this, away from school and prying eyes. He took her hand and tried to draw her back. The hand came, but Katherine did not. With no real perceptible force, she took her hand back and put it on her bike. Billy sank, had he taken it too far? Katherine got back on her bike and started cycling slowly down the path, and there was nothing to be done but follow her.

They cycled back to Marlow Bottom without a word or a glance. More accurately, Billy had shot worried glances at Katherine all the way home, but none were reciprocated. He hoped it was just the night that had grown chilly. Katherine finally broke the silence a short way from his house. "Thanks for the lipstick."

He didn't have a chance to reply before she started accelerating for the hill on the corner. At least she'd spoken to him before going. Why hadn't she said anything at the river? No one was there, she could have shouted at him, thumped him, called him a bad friend for taking advantage of her after all the support she had given him. It was confusing, and now he had to face the Tree. Did this even count as a kiss?

THAT EVENING BILLY DIDN'T GO to bed. His mother had seemed restless and hadn't been inclined to eat, let alone attempt cooking again. She moved listlessly about the house, approaching the forgotten rooms, appearing to consider entering them and then shaking her head and retreating to the safety of the kitchen and proximity of Saul. Billy asked her a couple of times if he could fetch her anything, but had received almost no recognition that he was even there. He tried not to feel hard done by, to take himself off the top of the agenda again. To remember the troubles Katherine was facing. Then he remembered that tonight was the night the Tree was supposed to tell him what had happened to his father, and whether he was still alive. This forced him into a ball on the chair by the Tree, and there he remained until midnight, drifting in dreadful possibility.

B illy."

To his frustration, he'd fallen asleep. He had wanted to stay awake; having some sort of control in this bizarre situation was essential. Cross with himself, he shook off the unwanted sleep.

"No bed to go to?" The Tree's voice was rasping and somewhat laboured.

"I thought I'd wait up."

"You should save your energy. You're probably going to need it."

He thought the Tree must have grown again, though this time it didn't seem to have gained any more height, just girth. Its voice worried him.

"Are you OK?" said Billy. "You seem a bit exhausted."

"I'm the last of my kind, Billy," said the Tree, "and probably at the very end of my days. This search has proved quite a strain."

Billy's heart sank. Did this mean that his father was dead after all? It must take more effort to find a dead person. Once again, the Tree appeared to read his thoughts.

"I can't tell you much, so please don't ask. I can tell you that your father is certainly still alive, if lost from you, and Marlow, and almost completely from himself."

Billy fell back into his chair. Alive. The relief, so unaccustomed, actually shook his body. The Tree's caveats about him being lost worried him, but this now stood as the first fact he'd had about his father since last winter.

The Tree hopped towards Billy. "I need you to tell me whether you kissed Katherine Jennings today."

With the news of his father he locked onto a decision and stood up again in front of the Tree.

"We kissed."

The Tree flinched slightly and peered down at Billy. Branches reached out and sniffed at the air about him. They had kissed, his mind insisted, supporting him with the basic facts; he wasn't lying. There was a long silence while the Tree continued to prod and smell the air near Billy.

"You understand that by lying you fool only yourself?" said the Tree.

"I'm not lying to you, we kissed."

The Tree took another good look at Billy before withdrawing its branches. The decoration ritual began before another word could pass between them. As the Tree began to pulse and shudder, Billy wondered whether he had passed this test, or whether he would even know until the end of the twelfth day. Knowing he would now carry this uncertainty, this half-truth, with him for over a week made him feel a little sick. The Tree bowed low before

Billy. This time there was no choice to be made. The axe had arrived.

He took the axe from the Tree and held it in his open palm, and realised at once this was different. This time he had the curious sensation of the weight arriving before the growth took place. He was forced to take a good grip on the handle, first with one hand, then with both.

"I shouldn't drop it," said the Tree.

Billy adjusted his grip to compensate for the weight. The blade sent flecks of shattered light across the room. Where the edge had seemed perfect when tiny, fissures and alloyed lines now appeared along its leading edge. If he held the blade at a certain angle, that edge looked like a row of teeth. The Tree took a couple of steps back; Billy suspected all trees would like to retreat if they were in close proximity to an axe such as this. Finally, it appeared to settle on a size that was too heavy for Billy to wave about.

The Tree remained at a good distance over by the unused fireplace. "How does it feel?"

"As if it's hungry," said Billy. The truth was it felt lethal, as though it could dispatch limbs given the faintest encouragement.

"The fence at the front of your house."

He looked over his shoulder. The garden was dark with thick clouds snuffing the moonlight. Beyond the path from the front door, he could picture the fence. It was only a few years old, made of tongue and grooved softwood, but nasturtiums and other creepers had quickly taken hold of it. Billy's father had been planning to cut back and poison the unwelcome visitors, and Billy had felt rotten about not taking care of it himself after his father had disappeared. Now he was faced with destroying the fence he had helped his father build. He felt anger build up inside him; what possible reason could the Tree have for this?

"I don't think so," said Billy, without turning back to the Tree.

At the mantelpiece, the Tree picked itself up to its full height, casting a long shadow across the room. It hopped slowly towards him until it was within an arm's length.

"The fence must come down," said the Tree, "by your willing hand."

"Set me something else to do. Anything except that."

"Do not question the tasks," said the Tree. "You risk our agreement."

Billy spun the axe in his hands. It wasn't a threat, just an expression of frustration, but he hoped it might help make his case. He was mistaken; the Tree didn't bat a branch. Inside, Billy's anger grew. Why cut down the fence? It had cost well over a thousand pounds, which was more money than his mother and he had lived on in the last three months.

"Pick something else."

"You imagine that it is me picking the tasks?" said the Tree, with sinister humour in its voice. "That it is me who placed the letters *K* and *J* on the lipstick case before I was shipped to Marlow?"

He couldn't imagine what the Tree meant, and was too cross to care. This was stupid.

"You were told on the first night. This is about faith. Faith requires your action regardless of convenience. What are you worrying about? That you'll wake up the neighbours? That you'll wake up your mother? At least she might have something to say to you!"

Billy cried out, the anger rising in him faster than ever before. He swung the axe back over his shoulder. Again the

Tree hadn't moved a millimetre. The rage flashed within
him again. Just as he might have been about to make a
move, something else caught his eye. There, twinkling on
the Tree at Billy's eye level, were his father's gold reading
glasses. Definitely there, definitely his; half-glasses with a

small kink on the bridge. It is the flaws and chinks which make special things, and people, unique. As this thought passed through his brain, the Tree turned, Billy dropped the axe and shot his left arm forward to recover the glasses, but as he did, the Tree rocked backwards, turned, and the glasses disappeared from view. The Tree turned back, and Billy righted himself. He knew the glasses were gone.

"What is it going to take to get you to remember how to believe?" said the Tree.

Billy took a step back and almost tripped over the fallen axe. It wasn't lying on the floor, but *in* the floor, the handle about two feet in the air and the blade buried through the carpet and deep into the wooden floorboards below. He picked it up. It still felt hungry.

NOW THANKFUL THAT THE MOON was covered, Billy headed down the path, trying not to ask questions, not to think about the noise, not to think about what his mother might or might not say about the fence coming down. He had seen his father's glasses, and he knew he must not fail. But he had another thought: the fence might have to come down, but the Tree had said nothing about the gate. Raising the axe above his shoulders, he slung it deep into the fence post. It bit in with a pleasing thump. He then unlatched the gate, which his father had hung with such care, and lifted it off its hinges. Placing it carefully by the pear tree on the front lawn, he could return to the task feeling he wasn't about to waste all their work.

The axe came out of the fence post with greater ease than he had imagined. He thought briefly about attacking the fence from the roadside, but it was clear that the garden provided a higher platform, albeit with a softer footing on the snow-laden lawn. With the axe raised over his shoulder, Billy swung hard into the fence post. The axe gave a low hum as it arced into the post, cleaving it three quarters through. Looking at his first swipe with some amazement, Billy tugged the axe back out of the post. The weight appeared to have evened out—perhaps just the effect of the blood getting warmed up in his arms? He swung again, and the top of the fence post spun off following the arc of the axe, twisting the adjoining tongue and groove slats. He was grinning despite himself, despite the waste of money and effort of loved ones; he had a task to accomplish and the tools in his hands.

Turning to the fence to the right of the path, Billy moved along, pacing himself as he took diagonal strikes at the slatted wood. Where there was a ragged triangle left standing, he kicked at it before perfecting a low swipe that would also clear each creeper that had poked and split the slats over the last year. Billy stopped for breath and to check if any lights were coming on around the street. The bungalow over the road had a light on, but he couldn't remember whether it had been there when he came out. He turned his attention to the fence on the other side of the main path.

So far the axe had bitten through the fence with ease. Billy wondered what else it was capable of. Taking several paces, he ran at the fence with the handle held across him, the blade hanging horizontally and out to his right. As he connected and passed through the fence post, Billy knew it was going to work. He continued to sprint, enjoying the sensation running through the handle each time the blade went through a fresh slat. Flipping the axe over, he gave the fence's top half a nudge with the flat side of the blade. It fell into the ditch before the roadside with a swish as the air escaped underneath it. Billy hacked swiftly through the remaining fence.

Looking back at the house, he could see the Tree, sitting back in its bucket by the living room window. At least it couldn't question his actions this time. Billy was smarting from the knowledge that the kiss might not count.

The shards of timber looked dangerous and ugly, still forming a barrier between the property and the road. The task felt unfinished, and this was the last way he wanted to be feeling after the earlier scrutiny from the Tree. Billy headed to the back of the house, returning with matches and a bottle of barbecue lighting fluid. He began spraying the splintered slats, soaking them as fully as he could.

Standing back, he took a match and upended the dark blob against the striking edge of the box. Pulling back his index finger, he flicked the match and it flew out, sparking loudly into the cold night air. There was a sound like a gas stove igniting, and flames rolled over the tangled wood, which crackled with surprise. After a few moments, the entwined evergreen creepers began to release a dense smoke, visible even in the dark. Billy put a hand on the axe and watched until the flames grew quite low. Believing the job now incontrovertibly complete, he shouldered the axe and returned to the house.

As he started up the stairs, the Tree spoke from the living room.

"Very impressive, Billy."

He continued up the stairs without replying.

STANDING WITH HIS BIKE IN the crisp morning air, Billy surveyed the charred remnants of the fence. Small wisps of smoke rose from the dark ashes. Billy was aware that traffic was slowing on the way past, with faces pressed against the glass to see what had happened. Some faces he recognised from school. Unsure whether his mother would notice the fence and not wanting to get into a discussion about it, he got up early enough to be outside the front of his house to meet Katherine.

He looked down towards the corner before the hill; still no sign of her. Would she have left early in order to avoid him after the fumbled kiss? He heard the back door close; his mother going to walk Saul. Billy thought about cycling down to the foot of Ragman's Lane, hoping that Katherine would appear in time. He saw Saul pulling against his lead before his mother followed. A look of confusion came over her as she saw the gate against the pear tree, and then deeper concern at the ashen lines where the fence had been. It was the first time in many months that Billy felt childlike, caught in the act of a plain wrongdoing. It sat uncomfortably in his stomach, and he felt sure that only a week ago she would not have noticed it at all, so lost had she been within herself. Billy clenched his jaw and shot another look over his shoulder for Katherine.

"What happened, Billy?" said his mother. "Who burned the fence down?"

"It was rotten, Mum," said Billy, not quite meeting her eyes. "It had to come down."

"Rotten?"

Katherine turned the corner at pace.

"I don't think it was rotten. It was quite new," said his mother, struggling to find a parental tone.

"It had to come down," said Billy, getting cross at being questioned, and even more aware of people in cars staring at them both. Neighbours from across the street were showing worrying signs of popping over to check that everything was all right. Katherine had started to slow down, her eyes widening at the scene that greeted her. Billy shot her a pleading look as he wheeled his bike away from the house.

"I'll explain later, Mum."

He hopped onto his saddle and started pumping the pedals, hoping his mother would cope with the neighbours on her own. He had no idea how he was going to explain this later, but without a task to concern himself with, he had all day to ponder the question.

KATHERINE CYCLED WITH BILLY ALONG the river path.

"Is everything all right?"

Billy had fallen into a sombre mood. It was unfair that he should be made to feel like some naughty child after all the effort he had put in this year. He knew that legally he was the minor, but hadn't he earned any credit for keeping himself and his mother afloat?

"Things are a bit tense at home."

"What happened to the fence?"

"Do you mind if I tell you after Christmas?"

Katherine looked over the river. "You'll have to be quick. We're leaving between Christmas and New Year."

Billy felt as though he had been kicked in the guts. He couldn't find the words to respond. Between Christmas and New Year?

"About yesterday?" said Katherine. "I think this is probably going to be hard enough for both of us. Let's just try and be friends, OK?"

Billy nodded in silent agreement, the whitening knuckles on his handlebars telling a different story. He longed for a task to distract him from this dismal day.

SCHOOL REVERTED TO THE TYPICAL. Typical identikit classes, with typical unpleasant breaks skirting typical abuse from the usual suspects, typical concern at his mood from teachers who aimed for him only to bumble quietly through classes as his fellow pupils did. There was not even the prospect of cycling home with Katherine, who was staying after school for hockey practice. Why practice now? Wasn't she about to leave all her teams? He stopped himself here. She was at practice for the same reason that he needed a task: to be distracted. At least he had the hope of his distractions, his tasks, taking him somewhere better. Between them both, it was Katherine, constant and stable, who was at the mercy of larger forces. With that thought, he burst the bubble of his bad mood and got on with his day.

Arriving back at home, he could see why his mother had been shocked. Piles of ash lay where the fence had been, and light wisps of smoke continued to rise up. A gentle breeze had carried away the upper layer of light greys, leaving the deeper charcoal colours to contrast with the thinning snow on the lawn. The other houses on his street looked picturesque and seasonal whilst his home looked broken and a little sad. Thinking back to the morning, he realised that his mother hadn't even raised her voice. What would he tell her now?

He walked into the kitchen to be greeted by the smell of cooking. Real cooking. His mother was hovering over the stove, all elbows and pans. Billy grinned; he liked to think he got his height from his father, but his elbows were undeniably from her. His mother looked up and returned the smile.

"I thought I'd give Jamie Oliver a run for his money."

"That could mean quite a lot of running, Mum, he's loaded."

As pleased as he was to see her in good form, could he enjoy this meal knowing she might sink back to her grieving self at any moment?

The smell of the food allowed his stomach to get in on the debate, and he surrendered. They sat at the table, enjoyed the meal and spoke without mentioning the fence.

❦ December 19ᵗʰ ❧

ot wanting to repeat the mistake of the previous night, Billy made sure he was awake and in the living room for midnight. He waited, looking through the front window onto the lawn, with his dressing gown arms ending at his elbows. It was a brighter night, and he could see the patches on the lawn where the snow had seeped away into the grass—just odd patches, as if a mole had been raising hills. Beyond the garden, he could see that the lights were on in the bungalow opposite, and more, that figures seemed to be peering through its window. He spun around and switched off the small side-light he'd been using each night. Had they seen him burn the fence down? Surely they weren't tuning in to see what happened next? Perhaps the house on fire this time?

Well, if they wanted to look out they would need to turn their own light off, he thought, scraping around for reassurance. A burning fence was one thing to explain, a walking talking tree quite another.

"Good evening."

The Tree made Billy jump, his attention snapped back to the room and he clenched his fists to calm himself.

"My apologies, I thought you were waiting for me," said the Tree.

"No problem. Just excuse me while I restart my heart."

"Aha, a joke. We've had precious few of those between us."

"It's been that kind of year."

The Tree was looking magnificent. Where the lights had once swamped its branches, it was hard now to see any of the wire between the lights; where before the needles were short and thin, they were now long and thick; and where once Billy had looked down on the Tree, it now topped him by over three feet.

"I understand. Agnes would tell me jokes. I should like to hear another before I'm gone."

"I can never remember them."

"I'm told the ruder the joke, the easier it is to remember," said the Tree.

Billy looked up at the Tree thoughtfully. Its eyes were now just above his own, a pair of blinking branches looking back at him.

"Do you think this is your last visit?"

"I don't know that for certain, any more than you would know whether tomorrow is your last day," said the Tree. "I feel old though, Billy, old age is creeping into my core. I used to have a good memory for the centuries I'd seen. But as the world has sped up, as it has over the last four centuries, I feel less sure of the things I have seen.

They are slipping away from me like the memory of a dream when you wake in the morning."

"But you look in such great shape," said Billy. "You look amazing."

"Smoke and mirrors, Billy," said the Tree. "With perhaps a little more in reserve. There is still much to do."

The Tree hopped out of the bucket, and Billy shot a look over the road. The lights had gone out. Had they gone to bed or made it easier to see across the street?

"You must focus, Billy. You have your part in this."

The stern tone sharpened his mind. The neighbours could think what they liked. With the Tree in such resplendent health, a green light seemed to spark out of the needles. Billy felt his forearms tingle. Looking down, he could see that the hairs were standing up as though a strong source of static was in the room. The Tree bowed, and Billy looked up to see the four connected gold rings being offered. As he reached forward, the hairs on his arm leant towards the Tree and began to vibrate, making his skin itch. He snatched at the rings. There was a loud crackle and a jolt made his muscles clench at once as though he'd held an electric fence.

"Ow!" said Billy. "What is it doing?"

The Tree remained silent, though Billy read concern on its face. The tight clench of his right fist gradually subsided. He was able to open his hand, which now felt as though it had a bad case of pins and needles. To his horror, he found his fingers locked together: somehow the four rings had slipped over them and were now fixed beneath his knuckles. He could feel the rings tightening on his digits, and started to fear they would continue to close until squeezing them clean off.

"What is this?" Billy turned to the Tree with real fear now. "It's hurting."

"Is it really hurting?"

He paused for a moment. "No. I suppose not."

"You've never seen this device before?"

"No."

"Is the twenty-first century a much calmer place, I wonder?" said the Tree. "Do the police still patrol here unarmed?"

"Well yes," said Billy, thinking this didn't really explain life in the twenty-first century, or answer his question for that matter. "It's a bit more complicated than that though."

The Tree nodded. "'Twas ever thus. At least I think so…"

"Can you please tell me what I have on my hand?" said Billy, trying to conceal his panic.

"Certainly. You have on your hand what was known in common parlance as a knuckleduster," said the Tree.

Billy stared at the Tree. Was his next task an early spring clean?

The Tree drew closer, speaking quietly and deliberately. "It is a weapon. Your next task is to smite your enemy."

Billy looked at the object on his fingers. What had been perfect circles now had raised ridges along the outer side. As he formed a fist, the ridges defined themselves, rising to form weighty studs. This was a knuckleduster with added magical attitude. Whoever was on the wrong side of this would not forget the encounter. Billy flexed his fist uncertainly.

"To smite means to…"

"I know what smite means," said Billy. "You mean for me to have a fight."

"Not I, it is the task," said the Tree, still speaking in low tones. "And smite implies to win a fight. I am sorry."

He looked up, surprised at the gentle words coming from the Tree.

"Why are you sorry?"

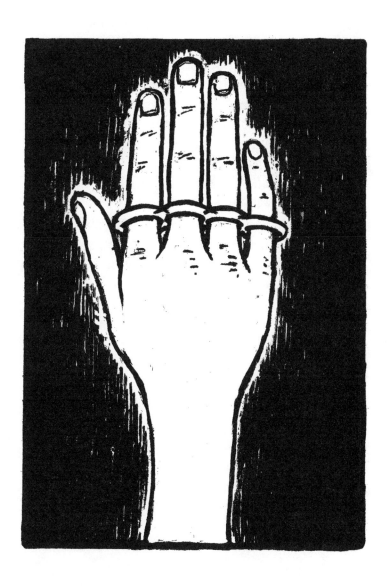

"This task appears to be very much against your nature," said the Tree. "I suspect provoking a fight will feel quite unnatural for you."

Billy knew that he could make a good account of himself if required, but he'd only ever needed to defend himself. Even in the thick of a real fight, no matter how angry he'd get, he would take steps to avoid seriously hurting an opponent. He would use the leverage of his long limbs to pin them down until the fury left them, or at least until a prefect arrived.

"I might not have to provoke it very much," said Billy.

"They must make life difficult for you."

"Well yes, but what with home it doesn't matter that much."

The Tree nodded. "See out the dark days, Billy."

It hopped back into the bucket and fell still and silent.

Robert Lock had sprung into Billy's mind as soon as the task had been uttered. His face, leering from the top of the bike shed, taunted Billy, daring him to take up this challenge. With Robert's relentless abuse, a big fight between them had probably been inevitable anyway. No matter the circumstances, Billy still hated causing people pain. Simply by being clumsy, he'd inadvertently caused a number of injuries to friends over the years. As a child, riding his rocking horse too hard, he had toppled the wooden beast over itself, throwing him to the floor, bashing his knees and jaw. His friend Michael had been sitting in front of the horse, waiting patiently for his turn. The horse hit him so hard in the mouth that his teeth had plunged through his upper lip, scarring him permanently. Billy had sat shivering in the corner whilst his father patched Michael up before taking him off to the hospital. All afternoon he'd remained in the corner, both there and not there. He'd still been in the corner when Michael's mother called around to make sure Billy understood the consequences of his carelessness.

"He's learnt this lesson well enough," said his mother before going into full diplomatic mode. Her hugs had brought him back later that afternoon. He had learned there wasn't much he hated more in this world than causing another person pain. Michael had never spoken to Billy again.

This year had left its mark on Billy, but he hadn't forgotten that old lesson. Now he was going to have to provoke and prevail, inflicting more, perhaps permanent, scars on another. However much Robert's cruel behaviour might justify this action, Billy did not relish the task and he struggled to find sleep.

NOTHING KATHERINE SAID ON THE cycle to school managed to shake him from his mood. Billy was sure that everyone at school would hear about the fight, and he wasn't sure how she would react to his provoking it. In the end, an awkward silence fell between them, which he felt sad about too. He didn't want Katherine to think he was sulking about her asking that they just remain friends. With her imminent departure, this seemed sensible anyhow. It was going to be hard enough losing her to the Gulf as it was.

Arriving at school, Billy looked at the kids milling about before registration. Robert didn't have a bike, so there was no easy way to see if he had turned up yet. Often he was late for registration, with the smell of cigarettes thick on his clothes. The pronounced lump of the knuckles in the outer pocket of Billy's rucksack was making him quite self-conscious. If he was caught with the weapon, he was certain he'd be suspended, perhaps even expelled.

Before he slept he'd taken a closer look at the knuckleduster. Wherever you prodded it the thing was as solid as steel, but when he gripped it, the stud-like appendages would appear. Deeper, in the palm of his hand, the knuckleduster broadened to steady itself. He could also feel a sort of ratcheting mechanism occasionally ticking within it; there was more to this device than he had found so far. Eventually, he'd placed it on the blade of the axe. Should anyone want to attack the house now, they had better be prepared for the consequences. This was a long way from a comforting thought.

Robert turned up a few minutes late, but sporting a black eye which looked so fresh and angry that their tutor, Mr. Rowe, who was usually very calm, gasped in shock.

"What happened, Robert?"

Robert paused, and looked at him whilst waiting for the class to fall silent. He drew back a wide grin, revealing a gap where one of his upper front teeth had been. Billy saw that blood had flown through tiny, ruptured veins in one eye, turning the white area quite red. "I walked into a door, sir."

Mr. Rowe looked both cross and sad. "A door?"

"Yeah, but you should see the state of it."

This raised a healthy giggle from the class. Robert waded through the desks to his chair. Sitting down, he looked over at Billy and smiled. It was so neutral Billy couldn't tell whether it was ironic or a random act of communication. Billy looked down; Robert had been through hell and back, how could he possibly smite him now?

The question dogged him throughout the morning. Despite his cocky reaction, Robert had clearly been in a brutal fight. Thinking about it, Billy realised he didn't know much about Robert at all. There were no brothers or sisters he knew of, no one had ever seen a parent. It was strange now that he thought of it: one of the most notorious but actually little-known people at school.

Then he stopped this train of thought. He was on a quest. He must restore his father to his home. He turned his mind to the kind of conversations children on the playground, particularly younger children, were more familiar having with Robert Lock. The screams, the pleading and the disbelief that despite these pleas the pain was going to continue. Girls, boys, dinner ladies too afraid of a brick through their kitchen windows—all were prey to his psychotic episodes. Billy started to feel on firmer ground; the task had a purpose, perhaps even a heroic quality. Not one person had stood up to Robert, not in a meaningful way. Not in a way that he would find hard to forget, perhaps for many years to come.

Billy slipped his hand into the outer pocket of his rucksack. The knuckleduster jumped onto his fingers, coiling and adjusting for size. He pumped his fist and ran the raised studs against the pocket lining. Robert was going down.

With the decision made, and his courage teetering on stilts, Billy brought the event forward to lunchtime. He had wanted to do this after school to attract less attention, but some deep instinct was telling him it had to happen now. Not blind to his long-held fear of authority or the potential of having a visit from social services, he was also beginning to believe that the Tree was his best, and probably only, shot at returning to a normal life. He had to follow these tasks through. Besides, Saul was having an amazing effect on his mother. She might even be able to stand up to an inspection from a social worker. There had to be worse homes than his, didn't there?

He filed out of the maths class, paying close attention to where Robert was headed. As usual, he had a collection of mates, and kids who wanted to be considered his mates, and as usual they formed a circle around him whilst he got his first cigarette of the break under way. Billy leant awkwardly against a wall, knuckleduster now in his coat pocket, waiting for a moment to make his move.

"What's on your mind, Billy?"

He turned sharply to face Katherine. He was usually delighted when she initiated conversation, but of all moments, not now.

"Nothing."

"Please don't lie to me. You're not very good at it, and I don't like it."

Over Katherine's shoulder, he could see Robert's entourage begin to fade. This was when they headed to the tuck shop to stock up on sweets for the afternoon, the moment Billy had been waiting for.

"I'm not lying, I…"

"Billy. I still want to be your friend. Is this because I'm going away?"

Robert had bent down to do a shoelace up. His mob had moved on to the tuck shop queue where they were pushing other kids roughly out of their place in the line. This was as good as it was going to get.

"This has nothing to do with that. I still love…" said Billy, before putting the brakes on, before remembering he had a smiting to deliver. "I mean, we're still friends. But I have to go now."

Billy moved to walk past Katherine. Her falling face stopped him. This was ghastly, she was going to hate him, but Robert was on the move. "I'm going to have to do something awful. There are very good reasons for it."

He could manage no more. He barged past Katherine, forcing himself to avoid her eyes. He must take on Robert now. It was a matter of twenty feet before Billy had put himself between his enemy and the tuck shop.

Robert looked up, both surprised and amused. "Got a problem, Billy?"

"I do actually." Billy looked down at him, at his black eye and his gormless, gap-toothed grin.

Robert spat out a laugh. "It's your lucky day, Christmas. Trust you to want to have a pop when I look like an easy target."

"I've got a problem with you," said Billy.

"I'm sure you do. I've had quite a bit of attention today, and I know that has got to disappoint you. But I'm in a hurry. I've got to get through that queue. So get lost."

Robert pushed one of Billy's elbows hard and spun him out of the way, walking off towards his friends. The tuck shop queue had become quieter, sensing some potential in the air. Billy saw their faces, a mixture of kids, several looking scared at having been shoved backwards by Robert's mob. This had to end.

Forgetting the weapon waiting in his pocket, Billy ran at Robert and hit him hard, with both palms, square between the shoulder blades. Robert's head snapped back; he'd not heard him coming. His feet tripped and he lurched forward as though his legs had been hacked by the axe. Billy stumbled forward, stamping on Robert's calves and thighs and adding momentum to the fall. It also meant that he was perfectly placed to hear the sickening crack as Robert's outstretched jaw connected with the tarmac. Then silence. Billy, heart pounding and fists poised, stood over him. The tuck shop queue, stunned and silent, already knew what Billy could not see. The fight was over.

"Robert?" said Billy. "Robert, get up."

He leant further over him and his red mist dissolved as he saw blood pouring from Robert's mouth. "Oh, please no! Get up…"

But Robert wasn't getting up; he was motionless and pale against the red tide flowing from his face. Billy began to shake and fell to his knees, stroking Robert's greasy hair away from his vacant open eyes.

"Please, please. I'm sorry."

He looked about the playground in horror. "Please!" His newer, older voice abandoned him for a shrill and fearful one.

There was a rustle behind the tuck shop queue. Mrs. Herringate pushed through the rows of children, alarmed by the silence; the worst sound possible on a full playground. She saw Billy, and then she saw the blood. Her face descended into cold fury.

"Get away from that boy."

Tears were streaming down Billy's face. He hadn't wanted to do this, had he? Not like this. He was sorry, wasn't he? Robert was going to be all right, wasn't he? His mouth opened and shut, but the words wouldn't come. People were looking from him to Robert and back to him. Then from the corner of his eye he saw Katherine, her face ashen, her arms closed. At that, his mind left him, and engaged some automatic mode, which took him from the playground to the bike shed, onto his bike and out of the school gates.

Katherine's scream sounded acute, and the silence that followed terminal. He raced to her side, seeing she had been struck, though he wasn't sure by what, it had moved so quickly. When he dived to the ground, it was clear she wasn't breathing and her neck was at a terrible angle. His own screams overtook his memory of her last...

THE SKY HAD ALREADY TURNED black when Billy realised he'd been dreaming. Relief that Katherine's screams were not real seeped into his cold body. He was shivering violently. Some far-off memory stabbed at his brain but couldn't quite be acknowledged. He was in Higginson Park, at the feet of the statue of Sir Steve. What was he doing here? Where was his bike? Behind the statue; he had cycled here. Then the memory surfaced, and suddenly he wasn't shaking from the cold any more.

Billy retched, throwing himself forward on the grass, but his stomach was empty and nothing came up. Had he killed Robert? Why had he left without making sure he was OK? Billy was confused and disorientated. He needed to know what had happened to him. He pulled out his mobile phone; he had a missed call. He never had missed calls. It was Katherine; one of the four numbers on his phone. But Katherine was only allowed to call her father, no texts or calls to friends. Why had she broken this strict rule? Was it to tell him that Robert was dead?

He forced himself up and began to march a path from the statue to the river, stamping hard so as to be able to think about nothing but the pain. As his shivering began to subside, Billy forced himself to look over his options; a habit he had got into when his mother first began to deteriorate. He had to find out what had happened to Robert. He knew where Robert lived, but thought his would be the last face his family wanted to see. He could go back to school—certain suspension of course—but at least he would know how Robert was, *if* Robert was; there had been so much blood. He looked at his mobile for the time. It was gone five o'clock. He'd been in the park for close to four hours. How was that possible?

There was not much memory past the blood and Mrs. Herringate and Katherine. The school would certainly have called his mother about this. Possibly the police. Probably the police; this was assault at least. Billy thought for a moment about the amount of pain that Robert had dished out, unnoticed by the world. Then he remembered that he didn't know if Robert had survived at all. His best bet was to face his mother. They would have to talk about this. He just hoped he wouldn't be kept from the Tree, that he would not be prevented from carrying out the remaining tasks. Billy got on his bike. He thought about slapping Sir Steve's bronze backside, decided he didn't deserve the luck, then paused and gave one for Robert, just in case.

For once, Billy was glad of the dark. Normally he hated the clouds killing the gentle light from the moon. Somehow that seemed to make cars approach faster, and pass much closer to him. Tonight he welcomed the anonymity it afforded as he cycled back the faster route by road. He began to feel a degree of guilt for his mother. How could she be expected to cope with this? His appearing to go off the rails wouldn't help her recovery at all, dog or no dog. And Katherine, where was she at that moment and what had she made of his behaviour earlier? In the space of a week, she had seen him brought to school by the police, make an uninvited pass at her and now randomly attack a kid at school. He'd never had the knack of impressing girls, but he was fairly certain this would be listed under marks against Billy. She was going soon anyway, well out of this madness.

He turned into Marlow Bottom. The roads were quiet, which was odd. It was Friday afternoon, and they should have been busy. Billy approached the last corner before his house and slammed on both brakes, skidding sideways.

Blue flashing lights ricocheted off the surrounding trees: the police. His heart sank through the road beneath him, and his arms twitched as if about to start shuddering again. Billy doubled the strength of his grip on the handlebars. If the police were there, then they were speaking to his mother. He couldn't let her stand up to that alone. He peddled on around the final corner.

The blue lights blinded Billy as he approached his house. They'd brought a police van; how many officers did they think they needed to arrest him? As he approached his house, the van started its siren and pulled off at speed. Billy jumped off his bike, assuming they had spotted him, but as it roared past he could see it was actually an ambulance. But it had definitely been parked outside his house. His mind began to race.

"Billy!"

A tall man in corduroy trousers and a shabby burgundy jumper was calling his name. Still blinded by the ambulance's lights and deafened by the siren, he peered towards him.

"Billy, it's me..."

His heart gave a huge thump. Had he found his own way home? "Dad? Is that...?"

"It's Katherine's father."

His heart sank as he saw that it was indeed the General. He was younger than Billy remembered, but looked bleak. Something bad had happened.

"Where's Mum?"

"I've taken her back inside. Don't worry, I've dealt with the police. You have to come with me to the hospital."

"Is Robert still…"

"Robert," said the General, "is at home with a sore lip."

Billy's heart took a further, tentative leap. Much more of this and he thought he might pass out again.

"Who is at the hospital?"

"Katherine!" said her father, with the exasperation of one who is more used to asking questions than answering them. "You just missed the police, they wanted to speak to you. She'd cycled over to let you know that Robert was OK. A car hit her as she got near your house." He paused for a moment, blinking. "She flew twenty feet."

Remembering his dream in the park, the world went quiet. Billy saw tears form in the General's eyes, and despite his own coming on fast behind, he couldn't look away.

"She's going to be fine, thanks to you, Billy. If you hadn't destroyed that fence, the police said it definitely would have killed her. Your mother said you burned it down the other night. Why did you do it?"

Billy stood, bewildered and blinking. "It had to come down."

"You're telling me!" said Katherine's father with a shaky grin. "Let's go, shall we?"

Billy didn't need telling twice. He ran to the shed with his bike and slung it in without locking it, before sprinting back down the front path. To his right the charred remains of the fence were smeared across the snow. It had to be where Katherine had landed.

"Come on, Billy," said the General.

IT WAS A SHORT TRIP to the High Wycombe Casualty Unit, but the General broke the silence almost as soon as they were under way.

"I had been trying to get Katherine to bring you over for some time," he said. "We talk about you almost every day."

He looked over at the General in surprise.

"I'm not that interested in hearing what the girls in the playground have been gassing about. I'd wanted to tell you, before all this happened, what a great job I think you've been doing."

Billy looked down; he had been through so many emotions today that he wasn't sure how to take this praise. Only ten minutes ago he thought he might have killed someone, albeit without intending to.

"I had wanted to offer support, though Katherine told me how proud you were. She wouldn't let me come to the hospital without finding you first, she knew how upset you'd been about this Robert boy." Katherine's father stopped the car, pulling in abruptly.

"I don't know the details, Billy, but it seems to me that someone like that is going to find the end of the road at some point. There is never a good time for these things. You have done so much to keep your family together. Working on your own, keeping your head down. Using your instincts to make it through each day, without anyone to let you know whether you're on the right track."

Not knowing where to look any more, Billy turned to Katherine's father. How could he know so much about these things?

"I know you've been through the mill today," he said, matching Billy's gaze, "but I want to thank you. Your intuition has probably saved my daughter's life. Don't stop trusting it. In your situation, I believe you should trust that part of you over anything else."

Billy looked out towards the front of the car. This was as close as he had got to fatherly advice for some time, and the warmth was overwhelming.

"How was Katherine when you saw her?" said Billy.

"The ambulance had already got her on a gurney, or rather a stretcher, when I arrived," said her father. "They said 'walking wounded,' but I need to be sure before I can relax."

The General drove back out onto the road for High Wycombe. Billy let the unfamiliar motion of the car shuffle the tension out of him. It had been almost a year since he had last been in one.

"There is one more thing Katherine had to tell you," said the General.

Billy turned back to him. "What's that?"

"You've been suspended from school till next year."

Billy laughed in surprise, and the General joined in. They both knew it wasn't a laughing matter, but at this point it just felt right.

"YOU CAN GO IN NOW, but only for a couple of minutes," said Katherine's father, looking much brighter for seeing his daughter. "The doctor wants her to rest as much as possible."

Billy nodded and walked into the ward. The curtains were drawn around the other beds. Further up and to the left a sidelight was on and the curtain left partly open. Walking as quietly as he could, Billy approached the gap and popped his head in. Katherine was sitting up in bed, already disobeying the doctor's orders, with a huge grin and a black eye that was even worse than Robert's.

"Come here!" said Katherine, full of impatience.

Billy hesitated, remembering the look Katherine had worn in the playground, but her smile hadn't lost any of its magic, and it drew him in.

"It's OK, and I'm fine," she said. "How did you know about the fence? And I want to know the truth, Billy."

"It had to come down," said Billy.

"It's very bad to lie to patients!"

"Is it?" said Billy, feigning nonchalance. He sat on the edge of her bed. "Look, I've had a bit of an…episode. I don't remember much after, well, after I left school. What happened to Robert?"

"Head wounds always bleed like crazy," said Katherine automatically. "A lot of it was you rocking open the gap where he'd lost that tooth. The school called an ambulance in, but they just cleaned him up and sent him home. He didn't even go to hospital. I tried to call you."

"I know. I was really out of it. I wish you had sent me a text, avoided all this."

"I thought it would be better if you heard it straight from me."

"Are you really going to be OK?"

"I'll probably be pretty stiff. They want to run two more tests. If they're OK, I'll go home tomorrow," said Katherine. "Hoped I might get the rest of term off at least. No one to cycle in with now."

Billy smiled. He'd already forgotten the suspension, though he was gutted to be missing their daily cycle. "Sorry about that."

"You're not going to tell me what's going on, are you?" said Katherine.

"Would you believe I'm on a magical quest?" said Billy, calling her bluff.

Katherine smiled, seeming to expect Billy to break back into a grin. He didn't and just looked exhausted. "Are you OK, Billy?"

He remembered the doctor's orders and smiled.

"I'm fine, and you need to rest."

Then, following his instincts, he leant in and planted a kiss on her right cheek. She leant in slightly against his mouth. It was enough. They had made it through this horrible day. Billy went back out to find the General, wondering again whether kisses on the cheek counted for the task.

WALKING IN THROUGH THE KITCHEN, Billy almost tripped over his mother, who was looking tear-stained and tired. The deerhound was nosing her palms in concern. Billy closed the door behind him. Time to start explaining again. Instead his mother held both her arms out, and he fell into a tight hug.

"I'm so sorry, Billy," she said, to his complete surprise. "You've been so brave. So very brave."

"Mum?"

"It's my fault."

"No."

"I've hardly been here, and now you've been suspended."

It occurred to him that in the last year they had barely touched, perhaps terrified that the other might disappear on contact, leaving them alone. Billy shifted away from the hug, and held her by the shoulders. "You're going to have to trust me for a while longer. This is all happening for a good reason."

His mother looked at him thoughtfully, as if assessing someone she hadn't seen in some time. "When did you get so tall?"

❧ December 20ᵗʰ ❧

Billy woke up to his mobile's alarm, and headed downstairs. The light was casting shadows that danced about the living room. As he opened the door, the Tree turned to him. It was on fire, and dying. He dashed forward to try to help, but it ignited fully in a fierce shower of white flames, its sap crackling as it boiled in the branches. Looking up, he could see the precious candle had melted over the last green needles at the top of the Tree...

BILLY SAT UP IN BED with his mobile whistling. Another bad dream. He'd never felt so exhausted. With legs and arms that wouldn't answer, he knocked over the chair and fell to his knees by the end of his bed, his hands landing only inches from the exposed blade of the axe. He shook his head, grabbed his dressing gown and headed downstairs.

The Tree was already out of its bucket, pacing around the room, deep in thought. Billy walked into the room and flopped into the chair. He used to think it'd be fun being grown up and able to stay up past midnight every night; an entirely overrated pastime, he now concluded.

"How did the fight go?" said the Tree, without breaking its stride.

"Smitten, or smote," said Billy, "job done, suspended from school of course, and Katherine's in hospital. Otherwise a perfect day."

The Tree turned to Billy. "I'm dying."

Billy's tiredness evaporated.

"What? How do you know that? No one knows when they're going to die."

The Tree branched Billy a withering look. "Lots of people know when they're going to die. Please don't start being foolish. I wasn't certain on my visit to Agnes, but it's quite clear to me now."

Not knowing what to say to this contradiction to the other night, Billy simply looked at the Tree. It had already shaped his life so much, and yet he felt he didn't really know it at all. How many centuries had it seen? Was it possible that this would be its last time on Earth?

The Tree hopped slowly towards him. "You have been chosen not only because of your great need, but because you are able to see me at all. I only meet you halfway with the magic."

"Halfway?"

"Perhaps less," said the Tree. "Just let it sink in for now, and for goodness sake, ignore anyone who tells you to stop daydreaming."

"I always have."

"Good lad," said the Tree. "I hope you've managed to put the day behind you, Billy. I think the next task is going to be—steep."

NOT QUITE BELIEVING HE HAD to go out again, Billy cycled down the High Street shortly after one in the morning. Most of the late-opening bars and restaurants had now emptied, and he was able to weave through the stragglers with relative ease. Billy hoped that these late punters would distract any police officers who might have questions about a kid his age being out at this time. That, combined with his suspension from school, would probably make the visit from social services inevitable. The bike had skidded out from under him as he crossed a manhole cover in the street. Black ice had formed on it, quite invisible to the eye. The weather was beginning to chill down again. Billy pulled up by the park railings opposite All Saints Church and locked up his bike.

"Too late, mate. I've turned the fryers off."

Billy jumped at the voice. Behind him, a man rolled down the serving hatch of his kebab van with a loud clatter. Billy paused. He'd expected the man to pop out from a door and drive the van away, but nothing happened. Forcing himself to focus on the task, he took his right glove off and delved into his jacket pocket. Opening his palm to the cold night air, Billy counted the gold rings; still five, all loose this time, thankfully. He put them back, and zipping his pocket, turned to face the church, the darkness clinging to everything.

Billy looked up at the stone figures and heads that lined the edges of the main tower. The architecture was designed to intimidate and from down here it was working. Fearing his nerve wouldn't hold, he marched straight across the road and into the graveyard surrounding the building. Frost was beginning to form on the ladder that ran up the edge of the water tank nestling under the right-hand side of the church. The light ice fell off quite easily under his gloves and boots, and he was soon on top of the large iron water tank.

The tank had a walkway leading around the edge, and he knelt here for a moment. Billy looked out over the Reverend Mike Hayter's gesture to running an environmentally friendly parish. The dark water looked unnaturally still. A layer of ice had formed on the surface. When he touched it, the ice splintered, creating high-pitched notes that echoed around the metal tank.

With his breath caught, Billy turned his attention to the section of roof to his left. The leading edge of the roof was pitted stone rather than tile and looked a good deal more robust. The downside was the downside; a lethal drop onto the gravestones which were packed close to the edge of the church. He took a couple of deep breaths before starting to clamber up the pitted stone. Crawling upwards, checking each stone before putting weight on it, he made steady progress. Each time his brain remembered the drop to the left it reeled sickeningly, but he was able to climb from the stone wall to the ladder above it. The solid iron rungs calmed his frayed nerves and, once his breath settled, he began to climb the ladder.

The rungs ended halfway up the tower. At the top was an old window, blocked up with cemented flint stones, with a ledge a good two feet deep. Billy drew himself carefully onto the ledge. The wall of the tower above the ledge was vertical and smooth, with no edge or lip to give purchase to climb.

He put his gloves back on, and tried to think clearly. The only way inside was through the window. He pushed a finger into the mortar between the flint; to his relief it wasn't as solid as it appeared. Billy gouged between the stones then leant and hammered at the blockade with his shoulder. Gradually, it gave way, falling into the tower with a clatter. He fished out his mobile to use it as an emergency torch. The sudden light made him blink, but he was able to peer into the cavity and swing himself in, relieved to be away from the roof.

Around the tower were open holes with large bells, mounted on huge wooden wheels. On the opposite side he saw a set of iron rungs that led to a door onto the steeple roof. He carefully picked his way past the rubble and climbed the rungs. Billy pushed against the door, hoping it wasn't locked. It shifted a little; it was simply heavy. Shoving the door as hard as he could, it opened slowly, and he stepped out onto the steeple roof.

Immediately, he felt the exposure and proximity of the drop. Beside him the upper steeple reached into the night sky. Billy checked that the door had an exterior handle before letting it close behind him, and began to look for the beast the Tree had sent him to find. A narrow path allowed him to circumnavigate the entire steeple roof. At each corner was a gargoyle which spouted water away from the roof. At the far side of the tower Billy found what he was after.

A separate and far larger gargoyle sat on the edge of the tower, looking up to the steeple. Its face was squat and toothed like a lion, but it had scales etched into it, making it more dragonlike. It was broad and muscular across the shoulders like a large Rottweiler, but the forearms were long. A short tail completed the beast. Brilliant but confusing; why put this kind of work up and then hide it out of sight of the ground?

Billy worked his way around to face the beast, and took off his gloves once more. He fished absently for the five gold rings in his pocket. They chinked against the knuckleduster as he drew them out. He leant forward and knelt before the gargoyle. The paws looked too thick to wear the rings, but somehow he knew they would slip over the claws of the raised right paw without argument. He worked from the outer claw, finding a way to coax each bright ring over the rough grey stone until four of the five had been placed. Billy felt a touch of pride whisper through him. This was how he had hoped his tasks would be. Pitting him against tough obstacles, encountering beasts he had read about in books. Not forcing him into uncomfortable interactions with friends, foes and unknowns alike. He had conquered the tower.

As he felt around for the back claw, he once again looked up at the gargoyle. He had half expected it to break into conversation, much like the Tree had. Perhaps this was simply a task designed to decorate? Extreme decorations, thought Billy, was how you might describe those that had arrived with the Tree. The fifth gold ring slid home. Billy bobbed up from his knees and pressed his back against the steeple, eyeing the creature with its paw now adorned. Moments passed and turned into minutes. Billy uncertainly lifted a foot and gave the left paw a faint kick, not wanting to risk loosening the rings to the right. No reaction; the task must be complete.

He recalled the fear he had faced on the way up, and would find again on the way down. Was this all there was to the task? Billy stared into the grey eyes of the gargoyle.

Breathing deeply, he raised a thumb and pushed it into the right eye of the beast. It was just stone. He laughed, not that it helped him relax much. He turned to leave, rounding the corner to the south side of the tower nearest the bridge.

His heart began to pound. The Tree had told him to keep daydreaming, and an ugly flash had entered his mind's eye. The General had told him to trust his intuition, so he turned back, and retraced his steps to the last turn. It was exactly as his mind's eye had predicted: the gargoyle had vanished.

Suddenly, a blast of foul breath made his eyes stream; the Gargoyle's face was only inches from his own. It must weigh tonnes; how could it move so quietly? thought Billy, before his mind began pumping waves of terror and adrenaline. The Gargoyle grabbed Billy, its left paw closing easily around his entire neck. Instinctively he clung to the Gargoyle's arm with both hands, and felt muscle writhe through the cold stone. Carrying him like a rag doll, the Gargoyle scaled the high steeple, digging in deeply with its long claws. Once settled at the top, it pulled Billy close to its face, its eyes peering through his own into his skull. Eyes still stone gray, but now moving, damp and alive. Billy tried to scream, but the weight of his body was almost entirely on his jaw, and all he could manage was a terrified whimper. Reacting, the Gargoyle screeched more foul breath over him.

Seeming to reach a decision, it spiralled down the steeple, scoring the stone with outstretched claws with Billy bumping and clattering behind, locked in its colossal grip. Pure fear pounded through him, and yet he knew he must not give in. He must survive.

Reaching the edge of the tower, the Gargoyle flung its left arm over the edge, holding him out into the open night sky. Billy's legs peddled at thin air in desperation. The Gargoyle looked at the steeple, then further to the west before looking back at Billy. It drew him closer.

"You will not succeed," it said, in a colder voice than Billy had ever known. The Gargoyle drew him closer still. "She is mine."

It screeched at him a final time the sulphurous breath, nearly blinding him. The paw closed tighter around his neck. He felt his vertebrae being forced apart, and blinding flashes of light filled his vision. With his left arm, he fought to open the zip on his pocket. The Gargoyle increased its grip, a sneer revealing long stone incisors.

The pocket came open and his hand closed on the knuckleduster. He switched it to his right, and the weapon slid on at once. The Gargoyle roared, its eyes widening and grip relenting. Billy sensed a little fear. He let his fury pour through his right hand and the studs appeared, then swam together to form a flat blade, the base expanding against his palm. The Gargoyle screamed again, and flung Billy left and right. He swung his fist back as the Gargoyle continued to fling him about, and managed to aim a punch. Billy brought his knuckles down hard halfway along the Gargoyle's left forearm, and was at once flying through the air. After several seconds, he landed on a section of the tiled church roof, on his back, upside down and sliding rapidly towards the edge. Unable to control his descent, Billy screamed, the Gargoyle's closed fist still gripped around his neck, and severed forearm splayed over his chest. He clattered to the edge of the roof and fell out into the night sky.

There was a faint pressure, a sense of cracking, then sound disappeared entirely. The cold was so complete he barely noticed the immersion as he fell into the water tank. The heavy arm and paw still clinging around his throat made him sink steadily, with pain building in his ears from the pressure of the water. Through the shattered ice he could make out the Gargoyle at the edge of the tank, sniffing at the surface. Once more the paw tightened around his throat, and suddenly Billy needed air. He brought the knuckleduster down hard against the paw. The grip loosened, and he heard a dull roar of pain from outside the tank. Billy struck it again.

He was free, and started to float upwards, his lungs bursting. For a moment, he thought he saw the Gargoyle waiting. He broached the surface weakly, his adrenaline spent, his lungs dragging air in. There was no ladder to help him, but with a last effort Billy hauled his sodden form out of the tank. He lay face down on the walkway. Unable to raise the energy to look about for the Gargoyle, Billy felt the world go black and quiet, the chill breeze sapping any vestiges of warmth from him. As he passed out, he noted that the hand on his shoulder was not made of stone.

Katherine slid further away from him. No matter how fast he ran he could not keep up. He looked down, he was running on ice, why wasn't he falling over? He looked up. She was shouting his name. He redoubled his efforts, but to no avail. Suddenly she turned around, seeing something, spun, then fell and disappeared through a hole in the ice. Billy rushed to the gaping edge, but as he arrived the ice vanished, leaving solid, cold black earth…

"I'M NOT SUPPOSED TO USE this any more," said a voice, "but I figured we could both use warming up."

Billy sat up, no longer dreaming, trying hard to find his bearings. He was still in his clothes, but they were almost dry. The room was very warm, and his boots were steaming in front of an iron wood burner with the front doors open. The room had curtains hanging all the way around the walls. Not curtains, thought Billy, cassocks. A mug was thrust at him. He looked up to see Reverend Hayter, or Mike, as he preferred to be known at the school.

"You're old enough to have coffee, aren't you?" said Mike. "I think it warms you up so much better than plain old tea."

Billy's lips were still frozen, but he managed a small smile of thanks and took the mug in both hands.

"You look a bit better," said Mike. "You had me quite worried there. But I thought, with the week you've had, it might be better if we sorted this out ourselves."

Billy wasn't sure if the relief was coming from the coffee, the heat from the wood burner or the young vicar's kindness; all of it was equally welcome. He could hear outside that the wind had built up, and wondered for the first time since waking where the Gargoyle had gone.

"Did you find me…?"

"In the water tank? Yes," said Mike. "I think this is yours."

Mike drew the knuckleduster from his pocket and offered it to Billy. Trying not to catch his eyes, Billy pocketed the device. As embarrassed as he was to have been caught with the weapon, with the Gargoyle on the loose he was not about to relinquish his only means of protection. Mike sat down at the other end of the sprung canvas settee which he had dragged in front of the fire.

"I heard about school," said Mike. "I'm sorry you've had such a tough time. I'm guessing if I started to ask you questions, you'd find it impossible to explain. So I'm not going to ask you anything."

The relief didn't fade, though, as Billy suspected this conversation wasn't over.

"I was supposed to be made a bishop this year," said Mike. "A city too. Salisbury, amazing cathedral, significant parish. But about eight months ago, I owned up to the archbishop. I couldn't ignore it any more, you see. It got too weird. Seeing all the dead people turning up to people's funerals."

Billy choked on his coffee. This wasn't what he had expected.

"It was like a welcoming committee, with these other people jostling their way to the front to greet the deceased. It's hard enough trying to read a eulogy, without people who had been at the events you're describing from the past picking you up on the things you were misinformed about."

Billy grinned at Mike. "You mean you see ghosts?"

"It's not funny!" said Mike. "I was a rising star for the liberal side of the Anglican Communion. And suddenly the biggest problem the archbishop has ever had to deal with. You see, I couldn't just ignore the fact that I'm having…well, visions. I don't think I'm mad. If I'm not mad, then, given my job, I have to believe I have been given this gift for a reason."

Mike was no longer smiling, and neither was Billy.

"It doesn't feel like a gift, by the way. It feels like I actually *am* going mad, and no one can possibly understand what it's like."

"I think I can," said Billy.

"Can I ask you a question?" said Mike.

Billy nodded.

"How did a three-tonne statue disappear from my steeple? Were there any other people there?"

Billy shook his head. "I woke it up."

"Yes," said Mike, "but not without a fight. It had a hell of a limp when it went past me."

Again Billy struggled not to spit out his coffee. "You saw it?"

"I thought it was part of my, you know, visions. My daydreams?" said Mike. "I wasn't sure whether you had seen it. But then I thought you must have tangled with that hand."

"It's still in the tank?"

"Making a real racket. Keeps scratching and thumping. I don't know what I'm going to tell the verger."

Billy thought fast. "You could tell him it's the cold contracting the tank?"

"Thank you. Yes, I think that might be best."

The two sat looking into the flames. It was a comfortable silence. When he felt that he was dry enough to get home without freezing, Billy spoke.

"I'd really like to tell you more, but I think it's against the rules at the moment."

"I understand," said Mike.

"I'd better go."

"Well, this is my place, as well as God's, and you're welcome here anytime."

"You know I don't believe in God?"

"I figured as much, Billy. That's fine." Mike aimed a large iron key at the outer door of the vestry before passing it to Billy.

He took it, struck once again by the man's simple kindness.

"You can use this anytime, though it gets a bit busy on Sundays."

"Thank you, for this…for the coffee."

"I hope that one day you can talk about it more. I also promised the archbishop no more ghost stories, so I'd be grateful if you'd keep it to yourself."

"Who could I tell?" said Billy with a smile. He gave Mike the mug, put his boots on and made his way out of the vestry.

Too cold even to acknowledge the two police officers who eyed him from the warmth of their car, Billy cycled up the High Street, trying to digest the twists of the last twenty-four hours. He and Katherine were all right. She didn't hate him for attacking Robert, though she probably still didn't understand why it had happened. Robert was apparently in one piece. He had a vote of confidence from the General, and now from Mike, which was more welcome than he had imagined. Odd for a vicar to admit to the things he had. Billy hoped it wasn't some elaborate attempt to feed information into school; he had seemed genuine enough.

Now there was another new player on the field, one Billy thought he could safely label as the opposition. The Gargoyle had been terrifying, strong in a way humans would never be, and brutal, a complete predator, as some humans were quite capable of being. Billy stopped pedalling for a moment as he coasted around the small roundabout at the top of the High Street.

A predator. The thought hung in his mind and then dropped with awful realisation. He started pumping the pedals, spinning his legs as hard as he could through each gear.

The Gargoyle had told him he would not succeed. Then it had said, "*She* is mine," not "*He* is mine." It wasn't after his father. He forced the terror out of his mind and concentrated on taking the straightest line possible. The streets were abandoned, so Billy used every inch of both sides of the road, taking the apex of each corner at increasingly steep angles, closing his mind to the icy patches waiting to grab him. A sliver of hope pierced his mind: perhaps Saul could hold it at bay. The Tree would be inert by now, would it wake and defend the house? Would his mother have taken her sleeping pills? An image flashed before him, of her being carried away, limp, over the one-armed shoulder of the Gargoyle. He sped through Marlow Bottom with his head low, pounding knees almost meeting his jaw on the undersized bike. Reaching High Heavens Wood, Billy turned at his house, rode to the back, dived off his bike and burst through the door into the kitchen.

Inside, the only sound was Billy's exhausted breathing. He fought to silence it. He took a quick look at the still Tree, before turning and making his way up the stairs, fast and silent. He passed his own room and continued along the landing, past his parents' bedroom and on to the spare. Almost not wanting to look, Billy forced himself to push open the door. As he did so, he first saw Saul, sleeping, then his mother breathing evenly, quite asleep. The deerhound's eyes flashed open, and he raised his huge head from his paws. Billy threw him a small smile of relief. Turning back down the landing, then down the stairs, Billy went to have a word with the Tree.

"Wake up." Despite everything, he hated speaking to the Tree when it was still. It made him feel like he was crazy. He shook the branches. "We have to talk."

Apparently the Tree didn't agree. It would not be roused.

"Thanks a lot."

He turned and headed back up the stairs and into his room. After he undressed, he put the knuckleduster back on, and then put the axe across his bed under his pillow. He was no longer wary of keeping these tools in the house;

in a fight where he would be taking on mythic beasts, he thought this fair. For the first time in a year, before getting into bed, Billy made sure his bedroom door was left open. He didn't want to be the last person to answer the front door if it was smashed off its hinges. Lying back in bed, he let the tiredness take him. A small voice spoke up inside his mind, the same voice that had told him to survive the Gargoyle no matter what happened. The only difference was that this time the tones were of quiet pride. He had made it through what had to be one of the toughest days of his life, and he was still in the fight to bring his father home.

THE ROOM WAS BRIGHT WHEN he woke up, the low winter sun bounced off the walls, making him blink as he opened his eyes and checked the time. Noon, how had he slept through his alarm? By not setting it, of course. He had to be more careful now, even though he suspected the Gargoyle didn't operate during waking hours. He listened for sounds in the house.

"Mum? Mum…"

No reply. He hopped out of bed, bashing his toe on the knuckleduster. It must have slipped off during the night. Billy made a mental note to keep it under his pillow in future, though for the time being it remained on the floor. He slung on his dressing gown and ran downstairs. There was a note on the hall table. His mother and Saul were off, out for the afternoon. Well, that was probably for the best. He went into the kitchen and started making a bacon sandwich, realising he hadn't eaten since before his fight with Robert, only a day before, though it seemed much longer. It would be getting dark at around four o'clock. He needed to go and visit Katherine in hospital and be back before the evening drew in.

CYCLING OUT OF HIS DRIVE and turning left, Billy passed the corner and headed out along the bridle-way which led to Lane End. Once in the village he crossed the motorway flyover, and went past the Chequers, a pub where his father used to take them for a Sunday treat. Up and down another two steep hills, where his light bike was a real advantage. As always the dogs from the farm bellowed their ferocious warning, while wagging their tails, knowing as well as Billy that it was expected of them. He got off his bike and walked to the hedgerow, where he placed his bike and climbed the public stile.

He started counting kites. It was a good day with enough heat from the weak winter sun to coax up a few light thermals. The red kites had held his fascination since they had been reintroduced into the area. A huge wing-span and split V-shaped tail feathers made them look closer to small dragons than birds. It had been terrific news to Billy that his imagination had been backed up by science, with birds the likely evolutionary route that the dinosaurs had disappeared into.

On his most successful day, Billy had counted no fewer than thirty birds. Below the birds was the main road, followed by the steep hill forming the other side of the valley. It was impossible not to notice the huge golden egg, which topped a collection of stone buildings on the top of this hill. Once, after reaching this spot while walking off the Sunday roast from the Chequers, Billy had asked his father why they built it.

"To distract people from what was going on in the caves underneath," said Tom Christmas.

Billy's mother rolled her eyes, knowing where this was going.

"Going on in the caves?" asked Billy, his eyes widening.

"Don't you dare tell him," said his mother, smiling despite her disapproval.

"What happened in the caves?"

"Tom. No!"

"What, the Hellfire Club? A great deal of, er, snogging. With nuns too," said his father, avoiding a substantial punch from his wife.

"Oh gross," said Billy, holding his father still, so his mother could land her attack.

"Well, you asked!"

The punches rained from both Billy and his mother. Tom crouched low on the ground.

"Would've been a bit cold for me," he said, with a terrible grin. "Bloody chilly in those caves."

Thoroughly disgusted, Billy toppled him onto his side and walked his mother away in mock horror.

Smiling at the memory, Billy turned and fished his bike from the hedge. He got enough speed from the hill to get him all the way to the main road, and back on his way to see Katherine in the hospital.

BILLY AND KATHERINE MOVED OUT of the ward to a quiet corridor, and sat on spongy chairs which looked out through huge windows over High Wycombe. Katherine was still quite wobbly, and Billy had had to steady her as she sat. Once down, she was straight out onto the thin ice.

"No excuses. I want to hear about this magical quest."

He'd forgotten that a rejuvenated Katherine would be picking over the bones of what he had said and what he had done. He wondered what could he tell her without appearing like a complete lunatic?

"If you're having a breakdown, that's fine," said Katherine. "Dad had one when Mum died. Talked complete gibberish for days, poetry almost. Very un-Army-like. But great fun in a strange way."

He'd also forgotten how blunt she could be when in possession of a large amount of energy and a few facts to run with. At these times there was a side of her that reminded him of the persistent journalists who had followed him in the weeks after his father's disappearance. They had offered him birthday presents for his mother in early January, with cameras running to ensure any clip they caught could make it out onto the evening news. Unlike them, Katherine was decent, but in the way a well-placed punch could be decent.

"How did those tests go?

"Fine. One more to go, and then I should get out this afternoon. Don't change the subject."

"Say I am having a breakdown."

Katherine sat up eagerly. "Oh good, go on."

"And in my madness I had found a way to bring back my dad."

"Nice. Delusional, and timely too."

"This madness made me attempt many difficult things."

"Like what?"

"Like having a bad fight, like having to meet people when I should be in school, and like, well, like trying to kiss you."

"That wasn't your own idea?"

"Not exactly."

"Oh. Well, these tasks don't sound too bad."

Billy pulled his knees up to his chest. "Then there was the fence that I had to chop down."

"Well I'm glad you did that! What do these voices sound like? The ones that ask you to do these things."

For a second Billy thought Katherine was being sarcastic, but looking over he could tell she was just concerned. He smiled.

"I don't hear voices in my head. Well, no more than you do, I suspect," he said, looking back out over the rooftops of High Wycombe. "But the stakes keep being raised."

They sat in silence for a moment. The sky was beginning to grey over and, though he had other things on his mind, Billy began to wish for the long summer days to arrive. The nights were becoming inhospitable.

"I get out tonight. Let me come and help you," said Katherine. "It must be miserable having to do all this on your own."

"You can't even stand up without a hand at the moment."

"I could help you plan what you have to do. It sounds like so much fun."

Billy remembered sliding head first off the church roof with a Gargoyle's paw locked around his throat. It would be nice to have some moral support, but there was no way he wanted to drag Katherine into any danger.

"I think I have to do this by myself."

Katherine looked down, disappointed. "It's not like there is that much time before I have to leave anyway."

Billy had forgotten about that. He was desperate that they should keep in contact after she went away. Perhaps he shouldn't exclude her from this, but wasn't it selfish to do that, knowing that there could be real trouble from here on in?

"Get yourself out of here, and fit, and if there is anything I can bring you in on, I'll let you know."

A huge smile burst over Katherine's face. "I'll start packing my bags."

"I haven't promised any…"

"I meant, I'll be ready if you need me."

❧ December 21ˢᵗ ❧

Billy paced around the living room. His mother had gone to bed early, looking well after her afternoon out with Saul. On the way home, the wind had started to push him off the cycle path and into the road, whipping up from nowhere, and as he looked now outside the window, the leafless pear tree was being pummelled so much that Billy feared it wouldn't last the night. As soon as he was confident his mother was asleep, he had brought down the axe, the cricket bat and the knuckleduster, and was patrolling between the front and rear of the house, leaving the lights off so he could see out as far as possible.

The conversation with Katherine had started to bother him. It had occurred to him that everything that had been happening to him could have been exactly what he had suggested to her: figments of his overactive imagination. He could conceivably have dreamt up the reasons for everything so far. For fighting Robert, for climbing up the church and perhaps hallucinating the Gargoyle, for wanting to kiss Katherine. He knew he was apt to get lost in his daydreams. They were so vivid it was possible he could be spinning this strange tale himself. He stopped and checked himself. Hadn't the vicar seen the Gargoyle too? Hadn't Agnes seen the Tree for herself?

Actually, Agnes had never told him that she had seen the Tree. Perhaps he had imagined her too, but hadn't he seen her all these years, fighting to feed the ducks? Wasn't she known in Marlow as the Duck Lady? Another thought struck him. Katherine had seen the sheet music moving. If Katherine had seen that, then all this had to be real, hadn't it? Billy found himself staring out into the windswept garden at the back of the house.

"Nasty weather," said the Tree.

Turning, Billy glared at the Tree.

"Why didn't you warn me about the Gargoyle?"

"I'm sorry, Billy," said the Tree. "Had I prepared you for it, you might not have survived at all."

"If I hadn't taken the knuckleduster along, my mother would have been burying me right now."

"Oh I doubt that," said the Tree, holding Billy's angry look. "Gargoyles don't tend to leave much to bury."

He took a breath. "I'm sure that would be a great comfort to Mum. Why did we have to release it?"

"The reasons for the tasks are not always clear. It will most likely have some further part to play. But I am glad you prevailed. We should talk a little tonight."

Billy followed the Tree back to the embers of the fire. The Tree propped a branch on the mantelpiece, and Billy sat on the footstool.

"Have you ever wondered if it was normal that you were able to be in two places at once? I mean, that you could be in a classroom taking in the lesson, and also lost in the mountains of your imagination?"

"You mean, as in daydreams?"

These had always felt entirely normal to Billy. Often he was able to stay tuned to the waking world at the same time as daydreaming. He assumed it was a similar process to acting, where part of the mind is thinking logically about the words and the cues, and the other is reacting to the world as if this is the first time the scene has played out. Except in his mind there wasn't a script, and the people he met were so real as to make it hard to believe he was just daydreaming.

The Tree nodded.

"But everyone has those, don't they?"

He thought about it. Both sides of his consciousness went into his imagination. On these occasions, he would be impossible to rouse. These episodes had so worried his mother that he had been to see a specialist at hospital, and had an MRI scan to check that there was no brain damage from his numerous dismountings: the rocking horse, his bike, the apple trees, and the shed roof.

"Not everyone has completely vivid excursions…no," said the Tree.

"I see other kids sometimes, in the daydreams," said Billy, speaking slowly. "But it's not like a dream, we have full conversations. They even give me their e-mail addresses. But I don't have the internet, so I can never try them out."

"I should try stamps next time," said the Tree. "That system seemed to work perfectly well on my last visit."

"But it's just my imagination," said Billy. "Daydreams aren't magic! Not like this, I mean."

The Tree leaned in closer. "Not magic, you say? Whoever told you that?"

"They can't be. They're just normal."

"It's normal to be looking forward, eyes quite open, and you quite awake," said the Tree. "But not seeing the world around you? You can touch the trees, run faster than your form would allow, you can lift your feet off the ground and fly."

He'd never thought of this as anything other than normal. Didn't everyone have moments like this?

The Tree stood up straighter, making Billy look up. "The point is that you have a very powerful imagination. More powerful than you can know. You use it like an infant might use a fully functioning spaceship. To sit in, pretending to escape the world, but never even throwing an exploratory switch to see what it feels like to fly. Over time, if you choose, you may come to understand and use the controls."

Billy was staring into the fire. It was eerie listening to the Tree make sense of his restless mind.

"We Trees don't simply pick the most needy child, like some terrible cosmic equation. There are children in the world that would outscore you on that front. We are *called*. Some part of you that you don't fully understand pulled me into your world. The tasks are, in part, of your own making."

There was nothing for Billy to say. So often when the Tree was awake, his rational mind forgot all the questions he had. Fighting off his stupor, Billy stood up. "So what am I supposed to do with this gift then?"

"I'd call it an ability. A potential ability. This only becomes a gift if you are able to hone it," said the Tree. "In a few more days, I shall be gone. Whether you succeed or fail, this ability will exist; it is yours to explore. But if I have learnt anything about human nature, it is that your memories are short. Patterns repeat themselves throughout history, and lives. With your father back here, will you remember me?"

A ten-foot talking Tree? There was no way that would fade from his mind, would it?

Around the Tree, the walls started to reflect the green pulse of light, which indicated that the decoration ritual had begun. Billy took a step backwards as the Tree leant in towards him. The skates, the bike, the iron bar and the mistletoe remained on the branches, and Billy saw each of them pass his eyes before the Tree reached out with a single stem. It was the replica of his bike. He reached out and picked it up.

"What do I...?"

"It is a keepsake," said the Tree. "Do with it what you will. Tomorrow you must give away that which you have come to value. These possessions can no longer offer comfort."

Billy didn't like the sound of this.

"You must give your bicycle up as reparation to your enemy," said the Tree.

"I can't do that, it was a present!"

"And you must give the dog to Agnes."

"No!" Billy held both hands to the Tree in horror. He hadn't thought that Saul was anything other than a gift to bring his mother around, never contemplating that he'd have to take him away from her. His bike was a gift from his father, perhaps his last gift from him.

"The tasks are not to be questioned, Billy."

"I don't understand. I can't take Saul away from her, she'll sink back down, be depressed again, I know it."

The Tree hopped back to the bucket. "I can only try to navigate a little, Billy," said the Tree, losing patience. "It is up to you to steer. This is about opportunity and faith. But if you'd prefer a dog and a bike, those are choices available to you." The Tree fell still and silent.

"Damn it!" Billy kicked the red chair. He'd hoped he wouldn't have to see Robert again before next term. Now he had to give him his beloved bike. The gift that had been a bit more than his father could afford; which had saved him from countless fights; which had taken him to be with Katherine that afternoon. And Saul. How was he supposed to take away his mother's closest companion, when in one week he had brought her around more than any love he had offered over the last year had been able to? Why did the cost have to be so high? He collected his weapons and trudged up the stairs, stamping his feet as quietly as possible.

PULLING THE COVERS OVER HIS head to avoid the morning sunlight, Billy wondered how long he could put this day off. Losing the bike was a bitter blow, mainly for sentimental reasons, though he wasn't sure how he would get about without it. It was certainly too small for him now, but it had got him out of so many scrapes he was loathe to lose it—especially to Robert. Although he felt guilty about the fight, he wasn't sure that he owed him much of an apology. If you compared the scorecards between them, you couldn't really say that one random act of hostility added up to the legion of incidents that Robert had enacted on Billy and the rest of the school. Then there was Saul. The transformation in his mother had been breathtaking, but he was quite certain that the deerhound's departure would mark an equally rapid return to the crippling depression. Why did the Tree ask such things of him?

"Not the Tree," said Billy, repeating the Tree's words.

But if not the Tree, then who? Was it some dark part of his own psyche that was jealous of the dog's ability to bring his mother out of herself? Or was it some other, as yet unidentified, force? Billy grew tired of his thoughts and threw off the bedclothes. He would deal with the bike first.

It took longer than he thought to walk into Marlow. He'd chosen not to ride the bike ever again, pushing it along with just a hand on the saddle. He decided to go past Boots to the bike shop up the alley, to see how much it would cost to buy a second-hand one that actually fitted him. The owner recognised him, and offered him a good deal if he part-exchanged his old Trek.

"Get you one with a reflector that isn't broken this time," said the owner, trying to be kind. Even with the part-exchange, which he knew he wasn't going to be able to offer, the several hundred pounds needed were more than Billy had to feed his mother and him for the next two months.

Robert's house was one in the rows of ex-council properties that ran up the hill behind the small police station. Billy walked slowly up the hill.

He looked down at the cracked reflector and ran his finger over the outline, in the same way he had when it was new, but with a completely different emphasis. His father had been right. Billy wished with all his heart that he could tell him so. With much pain, he closed his mind to thoughts of the bike, and tried to remember the quest.

The outside of Robert's house was much tidier than Billy had pictured it, with neat rows of edged flower beds lying dormant in anticipation of the warmer months. Billy walked up the drive, trying to hold his nerve. Robert had to get his temper from somewhere, and he hoped he wouldn't have to meet its source. He tapped quietly on the letterbox, unable to find a bell or knocker, and took a couple of paces backwards. Perhaps everyone was out. A glimmer of hope struck him. If they were out, he could just leave the bike with a note on it; the Tree couldn't argue with that. The house was still silent. He tapped gently on the letterbox once more, just to be sure his story would stand up.

The door flew back.

"What the hell do you want?" said Robert, throwing a worried glance over his shoulder.

"I need to speak to you," said Billy, wondering what had Robert so nervous.

"Don't worry, I'm not going to sue," said Robert. "You should go."

"It's not that."

"Who is it?" came a low voice from inside the house. Billy wondered if this was his father.

"No one," said Robert, before turning back to Billy with some urgency. "Just get lost. You won, OK? Everybody saw it."

"I don't care about that," said Billy. "I need to speak to..."

"Robert! Tell whoever it is to bugger off, you're letting the cold air in."

"Just go," said Robert, now moving to shut the door.

Billy held out a long arm, stopping the door. "No. I have to speak to you."

There was the sound of a newspaper being thrown down inside the house, and Robert looked at Billy half angry, half pleading. Billy held the door, not knowing what he'd do if it were shut, but feeling awful for Robert. An arm appeared at the door and sent Robert flying past Billy, out into the cold.

"If you want to chat, close the frigging door and do it."

A man in his early twenties rounded the doorway. He was pale, with dark rings under his eyes. He was clearly strong, having propelled Robert out of the door with some ease, and far too young to be his father.

"Sorry, Alex," said Robert quietly.

"Who is this? Hang on, I know. This is the Christmas kid. The one who gave you the hiding the other day."

Billy took another step backwards, not knowing what to say. He'd left the knuckleduster at home, because he was sure he could make it back before dark. Right now, despite the mess it would make of this guy, he wished he'd brought it as backup. He tried to hold his ground, but there was suddenly no ground between them. Alex had moved quickly and had his face pressed up into Billy's own.

"Heard you did him over when his back was turned?"

Billy didn't know what to say, but this was no rhetorical question. "That's right."

Alex stood up, just taller than Billy, and stared at him for a few seconds. He threw out an arm and grabbed Robert by the collar of his polo shirt. "I prefer to tell him exactly what I'm going to do."

He threw Robert against the wooden garage door, which gave a muted thud, and held a hand over his throat. To Billy's horror, Robert was already crying. He had never seen him cry, and had thought it something he wouldn't ever do.

"Stop it!" said Alex, pointing at Robert's face with his other hand. "Stop it or it'll be worse."

Robert sucked in air and glared at Alex.

"Now, because you didn't listen to me, you're getting two in the stomach," said Alex in a matter-of-fact voice. "You're getting one in the forehead for letting in the cold air, and one in the leg for not introducing your friend."

Billy dropped his bike in horror. "You can't do that!"

Alex turned to him in surprise.

"Don't!" said Robert, gritting his teeth. "Please." He shot Billy such a pleading glance that Billy dropped his raised hands.

"It's good advice," said Alex, turning back to Robert.

He brought back his right hand and hit Robert hard in the forehead with an open palm, slamming his head back against the garage door. Billy looked on despite himself. Before Robert could regain his breath, Alex punched him with his left and then right fist, hard into the stomach. Robert lolled forward, before a boot at his thigh sent him flat to the cold cement drive.

"As I was saying," said Alex, "if you let them know what's coming, the overall effect is that much more…effective." He smiled at Billy before returning inside, closing the door behind him.

Robert pulled himself up and sat with his back to the garage door, his head in his hands but apparently no longer crying. Billy went over to his bike and picked it up. He didn't know what to say, so he just stood there, letting time mop Robert up. Eventually he spoke.

"He's my brother."

"Your parents let him behave like that…at home?"

Robert gave an eerie laugh but didn't reply. There was another awkward silence.

"I came round to apologise," said Billy.

"Your mum trying to get you back into school?"

"No."

"Make sure I don't sue?"

Billy almost rolled his eyes as he thought of the numerous assault charges that Robert had managed to dodge. "Not that either. I wanted to make amends. I thought you might like this." Billy had let a hand drop down over the cracked reflector, and was tracing its edge with his index finger.

Robert looked at Billy, his face clouding over. "I'm not some bloody charity case. We own this place, you know."

"I know. I mean most people do around here."

"You don't need to feel sorry for me."

"It's not that. I'm going to have to get a bigger bike anyway. And I do want to make amends, and stop all the friction between us."

Robert got off the ground and looked more closely at the bike. He put a hand on the taped handlebars. Billy was torn. He needed him to take the bike, but it felt awful having him look over it in this way. Robert took his hand back and looked briefly over his shoulder to the house.

"Thanks, but I can't take it. Alex'd just sell it if I did."

Billy had to think fast. "Well, he couldn't do that if he didn't know you had it. If you kept it somewhere else. Like at Olly's house."

Robert turned this over in his mind. "His mum is pretty OK. I bet she'd let me keep it in their garage."

"There you go," said Billy, pushing the bike towards Robert, and taking his hand off the saddle for the last time. "I am sorry about the other day."

"Yeah, OK," said Robert by way of acceptance.

Billy wanted to ask Robert what had driven him to single him out over the last year, making his difficult time that much harder. But Robert was still nervous about Alex coming back and lifting the bike. Another time, or not at all. Besides, the light was fading and he still had to deal with Saul and his mother.

"You better get that down the road."

"Yeah. Thanks, Billy."

Billy held out his hand, and after giving him a strange look, Robert shook it. With that, he turned and walked out of the drive, trying as hard as he could not to listen to Robert peddling the bike away in the opposite direction.

By the time he'd managed to get back to his house, the bike had actually slipped from his memory. The winter sky was threatening the light, and he still had to persuade his mother to part with her dog, and get back into town to find Agnes. By which time it would be dark, and he'd be on foot and that much more vulnerable to the attention of the Gargoyle.

The house was locked when he returned, meaning that his mother and Saul were out. He looked again at the sky before heading into the kitchen. Unable to do anything else, Billy popped upstairs to his room to collect the knuckleduster, in case he was to be out after dark, then went back to the kitchen. Putting some water on to boil, Billy took pasta from a jar, and then went to the fridge to see what he could find. He hadn't been to the shops since the Tree arrived, disrupting his careful system of buying food. As he was only able to carry a couple of bags on his bike, Billy had got into the habit of building the kitchen stocks up with frequent trips to the supermarket on his way home from school. He realised this was going to be harder now without his bike. It occurred to him that he could probably borrow his mother's bicycle. Not what your average teenager wanted to be seen riding around Marlow on, but a lot better than walking with the shopping.

The kitchen door opened, letting in chilled evening air.

"Give me a hand then." Billy's mother was carrying at least five full bags of shopping.

He looked at her in surprise before rushing to catch the bags. He had learned the hard way that broken jars meant less food later in the week. They piled the bags on the side, with Saul waiting patiently to be let off his lead. His mother bent down, and the dog padded through the kitchen to the hall and began noisily drinking his water.

"Where did you get the money?" asked Billy, a tad wrong-footed by this, and checking to see how extravagant she had been. It all looked sensible enough, although there were more fresh vegetables than he would have bought. The frozen ones were much cheaper.

"In the cookbook," said his mother in a quiet voice.

The cookbook was where Billy carefully folded the notes he collected once a month from the bank. He hadn't known this was common knowledge.

"I thought I could give you a hand with the cooking?"

Billy said nothing. The transformation that the massive deerhound had brought about in his mother had been so drastic, and he was quite certain that his departure would mark the start of another withdrawal from the world. This part was a lot harder than his damn bike. As if on cue, Saul came back into the kitchen and looked at Billy. The day was drawing to a close, and they had places to be. He'd thought about making up a story about his owners wanting to collect him, but knew this would only lead to his mother wanting to meet them.

"About Saul, Mum," said Billy.

His mother stopped putting the canned tomatoes in the cupboard above the chopping board, and put both hands on the sideboard.

"It's time for him to leave."

His mother shut her eyes slowly, before turning back to Billy and speaking with a voice that was only half there. "Leave. But why?"

Billy folded his arms. "He's got to go, I'm very sorry."

"Please, Billy."

His mother put a hand on his shoulder. It shook there a while. Billy would have given anything to keep the happier version of his mother even if it was the dog and not him who had been able to bring her back. He pulled away from her hand and went out to the hall to collect the lead. When he came back, his mother had sunk to the floor with her elbows on her knees and head hanging low. The deerhound had leant forward and was resting his great muzzle, head also down, against her shoulder. Seeing Billy with the lead, he looked up and walked over. His mother was saying something, in the sad way that Billy had gladly forgotten. He knelt down and put his ear close to her face. Gradually, he was able to make out what she was saying.

"I'm sorry, I just thought, he came at Christmas. Perhaps Tom, perhaps Dad, had sent him."

He couldn't bear this. With his emotions at the point of snapping, Billy stood and led Saul out of the room.

"Wait." She climbed up to the counter and fished through the bags of shopping, pulling out four cans of supermarket dog food. Putting them in a bag, she held it out to Billy.

"Sorry," she said.

Billy didn't know whether this was meant for him or Saul. He took the bag, and headed back through the hall to the front door, and on out into the cold night air with Saul trailing as far behind him as his lead would allow.

GRADUALLY, THE WALK WORKED OFF the awful feeling of having let his mother down. Saul had stopped dragging on the lead, which was a relief, as Billy thought he must weigh at least half as much as he, and probably more. Whilst perplexed by the effect the dog had on his mother, he'd been impressed by the deerhound's gentle nature. Despite an intimidating stature and muzzle full of long teeth, Saul had exuded simple, placid assurance. Unable to ignore the failing light any more, Billy started to jog, and Saul trotted alongside, seemingly more comfortable with this speed. Billy suddenly missed his old bike, which would eat up yards of tarmac with each push of a pedal.

As they turned into the park, the streetlights flickered on. Out of breath, he looked down towards the landing area, hoping that Agnes's green-feathered hat would come into view. Ignoring the bronze knight, Billy sped down to the water's edge, then along the riverbank, running over the small humped wooden bridge and carrying on along the path until he was opposite Bisham Manor. With a sinking certainty that he was going to have to trail the streets of Marlow in the dark, Billy headed back along the river's edge. He passed back over the bridge, when Saul stopped dead, dragging Billy to a halt.

Such a deep growl motored out of the deerhound that Billy thought he could feel the rumble through the wooden slats beneath his feet. A notion of Saul being completely benign fell away; his top lip was curled back revealing huge teeth, and the hackles over his shoulders stood upright. Thinking of the Gargoyle, Billy slipped the knuckleduster on. Saul took a couple of steps backwards, still growling and sniffing the air. The deerhound suddenly caught another scent, or corrected his first guess, and turned to face the fields behind the path, yanking Billy around.

By now the dusk was making it difficult to see anything clearly, the fading light robbing any colour from the ground. Some way off, Billy thought he could hear the faintest sound of splashing. A small stream led from under the wooden bridge up into the fields, and a long way off Billy could now just make out a rising wave of foaming water. Saul barked, the first time Billy had heard aggression in his huge voice, and it broke his stupor. At once, the both were running back up the river path. Billy heard a dreadful clattering as they made it past the landing stage, as if something heavy and maybe made of living stone was following him. He was almost certain he could hear the mistimed canter of a beast with a missing leg, but knew that turning back would cost him precious seconds.

This wasn't supposed to happen; people would still be out, shopping for Christmas presents. Perhaps the Gargoyle thought it could catch him before he reached the edge of the park? Perhaps it simply didn't care. Billy put on an extra spurt of speed, yelling at Saul to pull, despite his aching lungs. To his horror, the three-legged beast appeared to his left, skirting the edge of the park. He must have been planning to cut them off at the entrance. Billy hauled Saul to the right and coaxed even longer strides out him. Their only chance of escape was the path by the bridge.

They swung around towards the river path, and he heard the Gargoyle's high-pitched scream. He risked a quick glance back. It was skidding and slipping across the damp grass, desperate to turn towards him, but was finding no grip. Hope surged through Billy. He hit the path at full tilt.

He'd almost made it to the bridge when he heard the broken canter on the gravel path, but now he was bounding up the steps only moments from civilisation. As he made the road, his heart sank; the town was devoid of people. From behind him, he heard an ominous clang, and he knew without looking that the Gargoyle had sprung onto the bridge. He thought briefly of letting go of the lead to protect the dog. But somehow he had to find Agnes, or the whole quest would have failed, finishing him and his mother. Saul had chosen to lead them into the churchyard, and Billy patted his top pocket frantically, searching for the vestry key. He and Saul sped around the far side of the church.

There was a fierce banging above him. The severed stone hand had not made it out of the water tank and was doing all it could to give their position away. Billy dragged the key out of his pocket and shot it home into the black lock. Behind him, those dreadful broken steps were sounding again, chasing him down. He spun the key in the lock and pulled the door open. The vestry was pitch black, but Saul leapt in, and Billy followed, slamming the dark oak door behind them. The key! He'd left it on the other side of the door. In horror, he opened it just enough for his hand and arm and grabbed at the key, fighting to turn it so it would come loose. The key turned and the lock clicked closed, with the door still open, meaning he wouldn't be able even to shut it, let alone lock it from the inside. How could he be so clumsy?

He steadied himself and turned the key back as calmly as he could. The lock retracted, and finally the key came away in his hand, but pain suddenly shot through that arm, almost making him drop the key. Something had grabbed hold of his wrist with such incredible strength that Billy fell to his knees in shock. He screamed in pain, causing Saul to start barking, his huge voice booming

about the room despite the muffling cassocks. He fought to pull his hand through the crack left ajar without losing the key. The grip was too strong, and with the door as it was he couldn't hit out with the knuckleduster.

"Billy, let me in!"

Agnes's voice, but the grip was too strong, surely?

"Please Billy!"

The note of fear in her voice made him falter. More fingers came around the edge of the door—human— enough proof to let him release his grip on the door. It flew back, revealing a terrified Agnes wide-eyed under her green hat. She slammed the door shut, and the room went pitch black.

"The lock, the key," said Agnes, pulling her weight against the door handle. "Hurry!"

Billy's left wrist was still screaming from her grip. He scrabbled in the dark for the keyhole. Suddenly Saul stopped barking. A huge impact on the door sent Billy sprawling back, dropping the key. Ancient dust from between the huge oak planks flew up, making his eyes stream.

Agnes screamed, but her colossal grip managed to hold the door in its frame. "The key, you must lock the door!"

With his eyes now hampered by the dust in addition to the lack of light, Billy simply shut them and sent his arms out fanning across the floor. The big key was easy to find, and hadn't fallen far. Finding the hem of Agnes's skirt, he moved closer and followed along one of her arms to the handle of the door.

Agnes was concerned at his interest in her skirt. "What are you doing?"

Billy tried to get the key at the lock, but she was blocking his way. "Let go!"

"Are you mad?"

"You have to, I can't reach it."

Agnes let go of the door with one hand, and Billy ducked underneath her. The key went home, but he couldn't turn it unless she let go with her other.

"Let go!"

"He'll get in! OW!"

She flew backwards, and the key spun the lock home. Again the door was rammed. The force knocked Billy back onto Agnes, and they fell on the floor in a heap. Another less enthusiastic thud followed, then silence. A full minute passed before Agnes broke the quiet in the room.

"Your bloody dog bit me on the bum."

TWENTY MINUTES LATER BILLY HAD lit the room and pulled the canvas settee in front of the wood burner, the way the vicar had done before. Looking around, Billy had found some small bits of kindling and was trying to relight those logs which hadn't burned through. Agnes and Saul appeared to have made peace. Billy thought it was amazing that Saul had managed to get his teeth through the mass of layers that Agnes employed, let alone have the strength in his jaws to close them.

"Told you we'd meet again," said Agnes. "Sorry about the police, dear, they can make my life very tricky."

"Didn't exactly help mine either," said Billy remembering the faces of the schoolchildren pressed up against the glass. A finger of flame pushed his shadow against the wall.

"Ooh, well done, you," said Agnes.

He sat back on the canvas chair. This was his chance to square his nagging conscience. "Have you still got the pie?"

Agnes looked at him with a touch of fear. "You can't have it back, youngster."

"But you haven't eaten it?"

"I'm still here, ain't I?"

"You know that it's poisoned?"

Agnes let out a shrill laugh, making Saul start. "Poisoned indeed. What a notion. It's a ticket, is what it is. Ticket to see my family. Bit like the Tree is a ticket to see your family. That is, if you're using it for that, and not some damned fool selfish…" She tussled the deerhound's massive head and blinked back a tear or two.

"I'm using it to get my dad back."

Agnes shot him a proud smile. "'Course you are. Was awful that, last year, at Christmas too. You were in my prayers."

"Are your family…dead then?"

"They are. But I'd put most of them in the ground before I took the Tree's juice. The 'lixier. I was born before the beginning of the last century, and I met my husband Frank the year after the Tree came to me. At Christmas too. We had two boys. Jack and John, but they both lost their dad to the First World War. I thought I was smart you see, but if I'd been smart I would of had enough 'lixier for other people. Germans might as well have shot me for the holes they put in me."

The wood burner began to crackle as the flames woke the sap in the half-burnt logs.

"Well, Jack and John grew up determined to be like their father. Army took them both, dressed them, married them, and when the time came, buried them too. The Second World War left Jack's wife a widow, but orphaned John's twin girls. Orphaned 'cause a house fell down during a raid in London. Fire brigade had thought it was safe, a house two doors down had been hit, and then theirs tumbled. But the twins, Jill and Jenny, survived."

Billy shifted uncomfortably. He thought that if that lot had happened to him, he'd be tempted to eat the damn pie. He was at the end of his tether after holding together a house for a year.

"Well then I had to take the 'lixier, even though I knew it would mean I was likely to see both the girls die eventually."

"Couldn't Jack's wife have helped?"

"She thought I was cursed. Seen the rate I was burying them, and even tried to take the girls. What Jack saw in her I never did understand, but such is the way of course."

Saul laid his head on Agnes's knee.

"War took them all, Billy. I held on as hard as I could. Jenny went into the Army, trying to prove me wrong, trying to prove her dad right. Trying to make a difference. She was in Kuwait almost a century after I was born. Nobody would say exactly what happened because it was to do with…intelligence." Agnes was not ashamed of spitting the word out. "Intelligence and another fallen house. They should have had Jill there too. She knew at once, and well, she wasn't really there without her twin. Was all but gone with Jenny not there. Her heart took pity."

Agnes got up and grabbed another log, turning it over and examining the concentric rings. "So you needn't think you're poisoning me, young man. I'd say knowing too little of some things, and too much of others has done that, and I'm grateful that my reward for trying hard to love a few people a lot is that my time of passing is at least in my own hands."

With a last look at the log, Agnes pushed it slowly into the embers, and watched them take the wood over. Then she sat and put an arm around Billy. "Don't confuse my tale of woe with yours. Measuring misery is the errand of fools, and we are not fools." Agnes looked over her shoulder to the empty room, ensuring the cassocks were still empty. "Has the Tree told you about our gift?"

"He's told me that it's a good thing to daydream."

"Is that all? But there's such little time!"

Agnes took one of Billy's hands in her own; it felt soft, but still so strong. He hoped she wasn't planning to squeeze it; his wrist was bruised already, matching the welts on his back. "Have you ever wondered if it was normal that you were able to be in two places at once?" said Agnes.

"I talked about this with the Tree, but it's just imagining things."

"Just imagining, is it? You think that is so easily done?" said Agnes. "Why, it's imagining that drives hope, it's imagining that gets problems solved. Take me. Took imagination to get me to believe I could bring up two girls at this age, and I've been this age longer than most."

He looked at her in confusion. "It already helps me with hope, I don't' see what else it can…"

"But we ain't just talking about hope now, Billy. If you learn how to use it properly, well, it can take you places—and I mean take you. Your body won't even need to breathe."

Across the room, the lock on the door rattled and then fell, allowing the door to open. Billy could hear voices through the gap.

"I'm telling you it's kids, look at that door. *That* is vandalism."

"I have got eyes, you know."

Billy stood up and turned to face them: an elderly lady and a man whom he recognised as the verger.

"They've had the wood burner on again and moved the couch."

Billy went to speak, but Agnes caught his eye and put a finger to her lips, before pointing to her left. Billy clapped his hands over his mouth to stop himself screaming. He was still on the couch, or someone who looked just like him, all shins and elbows, eyes glassed over, but apparently awake. But still he was standing in front of the wood burner. He took a hand away from his mouth and looked closely at it. The hand appeared quite solid, but the light was passing straight through him, and he no longer cast a shadow. He looked back at Agnes, who smiled and threw him a cheerful wink, and he blinked.

He was at once back in his body, in one piece. Someone was screaming.

"Verger, we've got squatters!"

"We're not squatters," said Agnes, turning and eyeing the prim choir lady. "Squatters don't have keys."

"They're the ones that forced the door."

"But it was still locked," said the verger, not wanting to intervene between the two wilful opponents.

"They let themselves in," said Mike, entering the vestry from the church door. "I have loaned Billy a key as part of our after-schools programme."

"But our last vicar never ran an after-schools programme," said the lady from the choir, a mite dismayed.

"I'm sure that is true," said Mike. "Now Billy, I did tell you Sundays would be busy."

Agnes took Saul's lead, and began to make for the door.

"Happily, you're both in time for the evening service," said the vicar, smiling and opening his arms widely to ensure that Agnes knew she was included. "You may take this door to the church."

Agnes looked at Billy, who shrugged; he didn't relish this any more than she did. The alternative of going back outside and perhaps being ambushed certainly didn't appeal. Mike spoke to Billy as he crossed the room.

"I could give you a lift home, after the service?"

"Yes, please," said Billy and gave Agnes a slight push towards the door. Saul trailed behind them.

"The last vicar never let dogs in the church," said the lady from the choir, in a small voice.

"Oh," said Mike. "I'm sure that is true too."

BILLY AND AGNES SAT IN the pews near the back of the church.

"How did you do that? Get me out of my body, I mean."

"I didn't do nothing, youngster. What you have to understand is that your imagination is the most precious thing you have. The one thing you can always rely on."

Billy frowned, not really understanding what she meant. "What will you do about the Gargoyle?"

"Oh, well. Saul, is it? Saul and I will take care of each other," said Agnes. "I'm a bit more worried about you, it's you he has a taste for."

"Well, I don't really know how long it will hang about," said Billy, watching the choir file in. "Did you have something like the Gargoyle when you had the Tree?"

"Goodness no, never seen anything like that…"

A silence fell between them. Mike began the service.

Agnes shifted uncomfortably on the pew, looking for the exit. "I don't really belong here, Billy. Cut my ties to it a long time ago."

Billy wanted to go with her, but she shook her head and nodded at Mike who was watching them from the altar.

"Don't worry about me, I won't be eating that pie just yet. We may well see each other again. But not, I suspect, until you bring your dad home."

With that, Agnes took advantage of the noise of the congregation as they stood for the first hymn, and whisked herself and Saul out of the church. Seeing them go, Billy suddenly felt quite alone, albeit surrounded by about ninety parishioners. His mother would not be in a good way when he went home, school was not even there as a distraction and the only person he could really discuss what was happening with had just walked out the door.

"I TAKE IT YOU DIDN'T like my sermon?"

In truth Billy hadn't really been listening to the service. He'd been taking advantage of having to stand up from the pew at various times during the proceedings, each time seeing if he could leave his body behind. He'd thought it was nice of Mike to mention thoughts for those in hospitals, and those lost, but he still wasn't sure if he was having his buttons pushed.

"I told you. I don't believe."

"Which makes you an excellent judge of how my sermon came across. Well, what about the marks on the door? Can I take it that it was our one-armed friend?"

"I think so."

"I told the verger it was me."

Billy turned to him, smiling. "You did?"

"Told him I'd hit it with a ladder while inspecting the water tank," said Mike. "You see I did have things to apologise for, even if they were in the best interests of all."

Billy gave a small grin. "Thanks."

"Now, are you going to tell me about this," said Mike, "or am I going to have to wait till our stone friend eats one of my choir?"

"I'm afraid it's going to have to be after Christmas," said Billy, looking out of his window, and beginning to wonder whether Katherine was out of hospital yet.

A couple of minutes later, they pulled up outside Billy's home. Mike waved farewell and headed back to town. Billy turned and walked up the path to the front door; bikeless, dogless and wondering what state his mother would be in.

THE KITCHEN DOOR REVEALED A tableau of the scene in which he had taken Saul away, minus his mother. The door unlocked, he knew she was in the house somewhere and, rather than disturb her, he set about tidying the strewn bags of shopping and half-abandoned cooking. After the twin kicks of giving away his bike and letting his mother descend into herself, he welcomed the routine of tidying the kitchen. This much he could manage. Bags went with other bags to be recycled. Food that could be used again, the fridge. Tins to the cupboard. Surfaces wiped. Pans washed, wiped and away to the drawer. This chaos he could manage, easy effort rewarded by the pleasure of seeing the results, and the hope that it might please. A sound was coming from the hall.

Billy turned the lock to the kitchen door. He would not be out again tonight, unless the Tree made him go.

The sound from the hall was still there, paper on paper? He turned off the kitchen lights, checking once more before doing so that his work there was complete, and followed the source of the sound.

The door to his father's study was open; this was clearly where the sound was coming from. He pushed the door open further. His mother was kneeling at the green leather sofa under the window at the front of the room. Spread over the base cushions and arms of the grand sofa were many pictures, some colour, some black and white. They were photos of his father. The last time they had looked at photos of him together, they had been trying to locate a good likeness for the police. Neither of them had been inclined either to look at, or for that matter to take, any more photos since then. His mother looked up; she had been crying, but didn't look too sad.

"See what I found?" she said, holding up an old black and white photo.

Billy dipped down to take a closer look. It could have been a photo of him, but the picture was of his father. The likeness was staggering, he'd clearly outgrown his clothes, and the unrepentant smile and knee raised on a footstool told the world that he didn't care a damn if that was the case, or who knew it.

"He's got my legs."

"You mean you've got his," said his mother, smiling.

She went back to the shoeboxes of photos, pulling, checking, then discarding them on the sofa, setting herself a feverish pace.

"What are you looking for? I might be able to find it," said Billy.

His mother put one hand over the box, whilst checking another photo in the other. "I'm fine, I'm just sure it's here."

Billy brushed a few of the photos off the nearest arm of the sofa and sat whilst his mother continued to work away. Perhaps she wasn't just going to sink back now? An older photo came up, and she grasped it with both hands, eyes running over it.

"Got it."

Billy got up and knelt behind her to look over her shoulder. "What is it?"

"Just look."

The photograph was one of the oldest they had, and beginning to crack at the edges. It showed a Christmas scene, a family dressing a tree with paper chains; the type his grandfather had once shown him how to make. Two children were at the tree, helping an older man to decorate, but off to one side was what his mother had been searching for. A younger boy was burying his head between the paws of a large Scottish deerhound. The similarity to Saul was striking, and the inference to his father clear; he was the youngest of three children in his family.

His mother turned her head towards him a fraction. "Do you see, Billy?"

Not knowing quite what to say he simply rested his own head on her shoulder, letting more weight fall on her than he had intended.

"I'd forgotten about this picture. But you see why he could have sent him? As a message?"

"Anything's possible, Mum."

His mother tilted her own head back. "You're certain that Saul had to go?"

"I'm afraid so."

His mother let out a sigh, put a hand up on Billy's head, then stood slowly and left the room, taking the photo with her. Alone again, he looked at the collection of old photos for a few moments, but it was less enjoyable on his own. He sorted them by colour and returned them to the shoeboxes before locking the house and taking himself to bed.

☙ December 22ⁿᵈ ☙

He was running, sprinting over ice again. Looking ahead, he saw his father still there, just out of reach, unable to answer his calls, making eye contact then slipping further away. He could make out an arm around his father's waist; it was made of stone. Billy dropped to his knees and made progress by slamming the knuckleduster into the frozen water and hauling himself forwards. But he was too late, his father was being taken beneath the ice, and just as Billy made it to the edge, there was no ice, only earth...

HE WOKE UNCOMFORTABLY, HIS ARM being shaken by the Tree. "You were having a bad dream."

Blinking, Billy tried to assess his surroundings. He was already downstairs, stretched out on the couch, but how did he get there?

The Tree sounded faint and far away. "You sleepwalk, Billy."

Well that wasn't news. A number of times, he'd woken up in the airing cupboard, once or twice in the car. Normally, his father had simply turned him around and sent him back to bed. It had been another good reason to keep his bedroom door shut.

"All those we meet walk in their sleep from time to time. It's preparation."

The Tree still sounded strange, its voice arriving in shards. Billy felt he must still be half asleep. He stood and stretched, trying to shake himself awake. He turned back to the Tree; something still wasn't quite right about it. As the Tree turned in its bucket, Billy let out a low moan of horror. Almost half the branches were missing or burnt. The Tree looked as if someone had set upon it with a blowtorch.

There were peeled strips of bark from the main trunk where branches had been torn, exposing bare wood beneath. The ends of the branches that were left were covered in ash—the remains of torched needles. If this had been an ordinary Tree, Billy would have felt sorry for it; knowing it was far from ordinary, he was wracked with the pain he imagined it felt. The Tree groaned slightly as it tried to rise from the bucket, then overbalanced and fell into the room. Billy was there just in time to prevent a hard landing. He caught the candle before it fell and placed it on the mantelpiece.

"What happened? Was it the Gargoyle? I thought it couldn't get into the house."

"I wasn't in the house today."

"Tell me what happened."

"It's difficult to say," said the Tree, as if it had no air to speak with. "How did you get on?"

"Enough of that. It's done," said Billy. "What can I do to help you?"

The Tree paused, struggling to get up, and then fell back with a groan. "You better go and get that axe."

Billy hesitated.

"Do you want to help or not?"

He was upstairs and back down as fast as he dared, knowing that if he slipped on the stair the axe could easily gobble a foot. The Tree had managed to turn and was now leaning against the red chair, clearly desperately ill.

"What do you need me to do?"

"Whittle, Billy. This ash is from magic and rather poisonous. You must take all of it off, even if it means losing branches. Do you know what whittle means?"

Billy was pretty sure it meant holding the blade at an angle and taking small cuts or slices, but that would be tricky to do with the huge blade. "I think so."

"That's very encouraging. Please start."

"Won't it hurt you?"

"There's no choice about this," said the Tree. "For either of us, actually."

Leaning into the Tree, Billy grasped the axe close to the blade with both hands, trying to control its angle as much as possible. The axe had cleaved a gatepost the other night, he was fairly certain it would simply fall through the slender trunk of the Tree. Working from the top, he cut away the blackened bark, praying the Tree would not flinch. "Say something, would you?" Billy's hands were shaking from the focussed effort.

"What?"

"Distract me," said Billy. "It's in both our interests."

The Tree moved its eye and mouth above the burned area, and looked at Billy. "If you're sure it will help."

Billy nodded back. He was feeling nervous and so that much more apt to make mistakes.

"Well, I can tell you about my day, I suppose," said the Tree, looking up at the ceiling, and away from the axe. "I had been having a nice chat with your father, and... OW!"

Billy had nicked a perfectly good branch in surprise. "Sorry! But you spoke to my father?"

The Tree looked back at him with a degree of concern. "You said talking would help."

"It will, please go on," said Billy, returning to his work.

"Well, as I said, I was spending the day reminding him, well reminding part of him—the same part that you lose when you daydream, or that walks you when you sleep—about you, actually."

Billy marvelled at this news. The Tree had spoken to his father. He was definitely alive, somewhere.

"Still quite lost, though very moved when it came to you. As though it were a big hole in front of him, which he'd been stepping into all the time, but unable to see or recognise," said the Tree. "Then we were interrupted. It found us."

Billy tried hard to focus on his task. "Where were you?"

"Between," said the Tree. "Yes, I think it is best described as between. It is hard to find people when they are between. Your enemy has some skill."

"My enemy: just what *is* it?"

"I think a better question is: what does it want? I know it of old, of old rumour that is, but my mind wanders so far these days that I forget where I have placed some older memories. I hope..."

Billy looked up in concern at the silence. "You hope?"

"I hope I haven't kept the memory in any of the branches that were lost," said the Tree. "That would be unfortunate."

Catastrophic was probably closer to the truth, Billy thought, turning back to the task. He still hadn't worked out the Gargoyle's part in this strange battle, but he feared pressing the Tree might make the answer harder to find. He'd now cleared about a third of the blackened branches, but so far it had been the easier ones.

"I do remember a legend amongst our kind, that the last of us would face a terrific foe," said the Tree. It seemed to sound better now some of the burnt bark was removed. "I put up a good fight though, I think you'd have been proud."

Smiling and a little surprised at this, Billy looked up at the branched face. "You didn't happen to take the other arm off, did you?"

"Well no, I..." the Tree paused, looking at Billy as he worked the heavy blade. "That was you?"

"It was."

"Well, that is encouraging. Perhaps we're not finished after all."

He looked up at the Tree. "We're not finished? What do you mean?"

The Tree groaned and started to shake; he hadn't worked fast enough. Taking the axe in one hand, he ran the edge more firmly down the entire length of the trunk. A roll of bark, like spooned butter, curled up before his eyes. Now able to see an entire length of the Trunk without bark, there was a clear line where black sap was rising and, Billy presumed, killing the Tree. Looking closer, he felt certain of this: as the black sap rose, it was splitting and bloating the wood. His mind sent out panicked messages. If the Tree died, so did his chances of recovering his father.

With his hands shaking, he brought the axe down hard at a point six inches above the line of sap. The blade fell easily through the trunk and buried itself into the floor. The black line continued to rise in the four feet of trunk that Billy had severed, fizzing as it spat though the fresh cut. The foul fumes which came off brought back an instant memory for him: the breath of the Gargoyle. He wished he'd managed to punch it in the neck rather than the arm.

Where the sap boiled out of the cut, it fell and put holes like cigarette burns in the carpet. Billy picked up the rancid section by a branch and took it to the fireplace. With the axe, he fed the spoiled wood to the fire. Almost at once, more smoke arrived than the chimney could cope with. Coughing, Billy dropped the axe and grabbed the top six feet of the Tree. He ran into the hall, slamming the door behind him. Resting the Tree on the stair, he turned it around, looking for a face, but was unable to find one. A terrible thought hit him. Had he killed the Tree?

"Hello? I'm sorry, I just didn't know what to do."

It was always horrible talking to the Tree when it was inert, it felt ridiculous, but this was different and much more frightening. He thought fast and took the Tree upstairs.

A few minutes later, he was sitting in the bath as the shower poured down over them both. Kneeling forward, he fought to fit the plug. He was sure that to survive the Tree must drink. Now soaking wet, Billy jumped out of the bath and dashed back downstairs to the kitchen, where he found the strange yellow bottle that contained plant food. Back in the bathroom, Billy squeezed half the bottle in, then the other half for good measure. He climbed back in the bath and sat down, still in his pyjamas. In their house, it was impossible to get anything other than lukewarm water from the cold tap. He just hoped that lukewarm wouldn't be too warm for the ailing Tree.

When the bath water was a foot deep, he turned off the shower and surveyed the room. The place was soaked, worse than if he'd attempted to give Saul a bath. Billy felt exhausted, too exhausted to withstand the blow of the Tree dying. He stood and listened to the water dripping from the Tree's branches. It was over ten minutes before he noticed that the water was now only ankle deep.

"Thank you, Billy," said the Tree, sounding exhausted but much stronger.

"You're alive!"

The Tree branched a weary smile. "For a few days yet, thanks to you."

FOLLOWING INSTRUCTIONS, BILLY GRABBED THE Tree's bucket and headed out into the front garden, past the pear tree with the gate, to the ashes of the fence. Here he filled the bucket with the damp ashes before heading back inside. The Tree was in the living room surveying the embers of its carcass.

"I'm sorry about that," said Billy.

"Oh don't be, I'm more than happy not to be dead," said the Tree. "Did the velvet sack make it?"

"Covered in black sap, I'm afraid I put it on the fire."

"Good lad. No use once poisoned."

Billy rubbed handfuls of ash into the open areas as the Tree had described.

A contented face observed Billy. "There are some centuries when I would gladly swap all the ancient magic on Earth for the wonder of a pair of hands."

"Except nothing that these hands do can ever bring my dad back," said Billy, leaving the remaining ashes in the bucket for the Tree to bed into later.

"Well, that is both true and not true," said the Tree. "How could you complete the tasks without your hands?"

He looked down at his hands. His oversized paws had joined in his year of crazy growth. Until this point, he'd regarded them as unwitting aids in his general clumsiness. Now that they had seen him through most of the tasks, and had rescued the Tree, he viewed them with a touch more pride. They were becoming tools.

The Tree wound the surviving lights around itself, taking care not to disturb the precious decorations. Billy looked at the room and realised that the carpet looked terrible. This was the second time the axe had been through it, and now large burns meant he'd have to pull it up. The room still stank of Gargoyle breath, and Billy presumed the smoke that had filled it was to blame. It was going to be impossible to keep this from his mother.

"Perhaps we don't have to worry her about this," said the Tree, reading his thoughts. "Why don't you pick up the axe?"

Billy's brow furrowed as he stooped for the axe. Of course she was going to see this; she was depressed, not blind. As he stood back up, he knew the Tree was working again, the room was full of static charge raising the hairs on his arms.

"I think you'd better step outside of the room for a moment."

He took the Tree's advice and went to the stairs, laying the axe on the bottom step. Back in the living room there was a faint hiss, and Billy turned to see that every dust particle in the room was being drawn into a gathering whirlwind. Even the sap was coaxed out of the rug. Billy's clothes were still soaking wet, but before his eyes he saw a faint mist being drawn from him, all the moisture joining the weather in the living room. As the mist met the twister, tiny internal lightning bolts flew up from the carpet, crackling fiercely. Now quite dry, Billy felt the dust being drawn from his father's study and the staircase whip past him like sand from a windy beach. Just as slightly heavier material was threatening to join the mêlée, the twister began to move, its footprint snaking across the carpet until it reached the fireplace, and shot up the chimney, dragging the fetid embers with it.

Billy walked back into the room, relieved at the hours of work and explanation he'd been spared in a matter of seconds. The carpet looked as if it had been laid that morning, and the room sparkled and smelled of nothing but fresh pine.

"We'd better keep you from Mr. Dyson," Billy said. "He'd want to know where your bags were."

"I haven't packed anything," said the Tree. "Merely sent it beyond oblivion."

"I see," said Billy, not wishing to explain himself. "My mistake, but thank you. That was a lot of cleaning you spared me."

"I fear this is not nearly enough to repay you. Never in my whole history has a child, I mean a young man, saved me. Thank you, Billy."

Billy dropped his gaze. Compliments from the Tree were a rare thing.

The Tree hopped away from him. "Let's see if this works, shall we?"

At once green light poured from the branches, brighter than it had ever done before, making the Tree cry out in surprise. Its needles crackled and stood out taut; it began to unfurl new branches. Again Billy felt the static ripple over him, sending shivers down his spine. Beyond doubt, the Tree was back. Bowing forwards, Billy met the branch, which handed him the mistletoe.

"Quickly Billy," said the Tree. "Put it back in its pouch."

Looking about the room, Billy saw the pile of velvet pouches sitting on the windowsill. The mistletoe had started to writhe in his hand almost immediately, although it didn't seem to be growing. He pulled the nearest pouch open and popped it in, closing the drawstring tightly. Once inside, the mistletoe continued to wriggle about, as if he'd captured a mouse.

"From here on in, it will be harder to keep the tasks from those uninvolved," said the Tree, hopping back into its bucket. "Try to keep focussed on each task, and remember at all times, this is about faith."

"But what am I supposed to do?"

The Tree threw Billy a strange look. "People tend to use them to get kisses at Christmas, but you have completed that challenge already."

Billy tried not to blush.

"Mistletoe is a parasitic plant. Given a chance, this piece will multiply considerably. Take it within the boundaries of the park, but on no account let any spread beyond."

With that, Billy was left alone in the spotless living room, with the animated pouch hopping about with increasing impatience. Tying the neck as firmly as he thought possible, he slipped it into his dressing gown pocket and headed up to bed.

IT WAS AN ODD FEELING to wake up knowing he was meant to be at school, and knowing he wasn't going to be. Unwelcome until next term. Billy sat in the upstairs window seat above the front door, still in his dressing gown, hoping to catch a glimpse of Katherine. He was kicking himself about letting the landline, the house phone, go unpaid. It had proved a blessing at first—no more earnest journalists and no more false alarms from the police. The last call from the police had been for his mother, who had been taken to the mortuary at High Wycombe General Hospital to see an unidentified body. This had been the second such occasion, and Billy thought it was this which burst her remaining hope; he thought perhaps the last body had looked a lot like his father. But now, with no working phone, he had no way to check how Katherine was doing, so he kept his eyes fixed on the end of the road.

He had not slept well. The mistletoe had fidgeted under his pillow until he had thrown it to the far corner of the room. He then thought he could hear it creeping about on the carpet. Getting up he found it on the landing, where it had snaked an arm around one of the bare wooden banisters and was busy fixing a strong grip. The mistletoe had proved to be as parasitic as the Tree had described; splinters of wood from the banister came away with the greedy plant as Billy prised it off. He tightened the draw-string, and put it in a plastic bag for good measure, then hung it from one of his bedposts. It had then rustled in irritation at this treatment throughout the remainder of the night. But at least this way Billy knew where it was.

With bleary eyes, Billy saw the children from his end of the lane make their way out and towards school. They were happy, and with good reason; this close to Christmas, there was no risk of them having to do any schoolwork. Gradually, the flurry of activity trickled away. Billy hit the window ledge in frustrated realisation. The General would have given Katherine a lift. After all, her bike had been wrecked on Friday night. The remains were in his shed, next to his mother's bike. Perhaps, given that they were now leaving, she would have been kept home anyway, as there would be a great deal to pack up.

His mother was still in the spare room, the door next to this window, but he had heard nothing since getting up. He was certain she was still in bed, as before. He looked up the hill towards Katherine's house. Nothing was coming down the road. He sighed and went back to his room to dress.

With the mistletoe still rustling as he threw on jeans and a jumper, Billy wondered what he should do. The Tree had surely been hinting that it knew that he hadn't really kissed Katherine. Was he to succeed in every other task, bar that? That wouldn't be enough, and though he felt closer to the Tree after last night, he didn't kid himself that it would allow him a pass, or near miss, on any task. But how would he get close to Katherine now?

Forcing himself into domestic mode, Billy shut the door on his room, with the mistletoe still suspended from his bed, and headed out of the house, planning to restock the kitchen. After a couple of experimental turns around the garden on his mother's bike, he found he was now too tall for it. He went back to the shed and put the saddle up three inches. Katherine's bike lay in three pieces on the floor. The bike was quite dead, and she was fortunate not to be on equal terms. At least his mother's bike had a basket, and while that would be ghastly to have at the school bike shed, it was a welcome thing when you wanted to gather in food for Christmas.

It was well after lunch by the time he returned. He'd come back into the house glowing from the cold air. Having stowed the groceries away, he took off his hat and headed into the house. As he passed the living room, he saw his mother, with an outstretched hand, touching the Tree. She was still in her dressing gown, but didn't look too unhappy. After a while, she looked around and caught Billy's eye.

"I thought the tree was taller this year?"

Billy stepped into the room. "It was, but it had started to go bad, so I took a little off the bottom."

His mother looked around the room, seeming lost. "It's so clean in here. When did you find the time to do this?"

"I got up early," said Billy. "No school, remember?"

His mother nodded, gave the room another glance, and then headed back upstairs. Giving the Tree a wry smile, he turned and followed her up the stairs.

"Did you take my bike out?"

"Yes, Mum."

"What happened to yours?"

Billy paused for a moment; he hadn't thought she would notice. "I got too big for it. I gave it away."

"You gave it away?" said his mother, turning on the landing. "But your dad gave you that. It cost a lot of money."

Billy took a moment before responding. "Someone is trying it out. If they like it, then they'll pay me for it."

His mother turned back to her room, parting with such a quiet voice that Billy could barely hear it. "It never occurred to me that you'd sell it at all."

Lacking an explanation he could share with her, Billy turned back to his own room and turned the handle. The door wouldn't open. He tried it again, turning the round handle fully both ways. He could hear his mother lying down on the bed, but her door wasn't quite shut, meaning she could hear him too. He leant on the door harder.

Nothing. Wedging a foot against the banisters he used his full weight on the door, though as quietly as possible. It gave a little. A strange smell hit him, like uncooked cabbages. He risked another shunt, and the door came free, not falling open, but allowing steady pressure to open it.

As he feared, the mistletoe had made its way out of the bag and gone searching for bare wood. The door frame had been nearest, his bed being made of iron bars. The mistletoe had entered behind the joints which made the frame, swelling it so much that it had prevented the door from opening. But now it was out of the bag, pouch empty. How was he supposed to get it out of the frame?

Infuriated, Billy grabbed the axe from the foot of the bed. Hoping he could get an edge of the blade into the door frame, he took the axe in both hands and turned back to the door. As he did, there was a hissing noise from the frame, almost like faint screaming. He took another step towards the frame; again the sound came. Puzzled, Billy pulled the axe above his head, looking as if he was preparing to swing. There was no mistaking the scream this time, faint though it was. The frame wobbled in front of him and gradually the mistletoe crept out. Using its stems as limbs, it pulled itself out of the frame, and then turned, pressing back against the wall as if terrified. Intrigued and smiling, Billy laid the axe down. The mistletoe appeared to calm itself, though it remained pressed against the wall.

"Hello there," said Billy. "No need to be frightened."

He took the velvet bag and untied the neck. The mistletoe began to shrink, stems slipping back into themselves and white berries popping into thin air, until it was small enough to fit back into the pouch. He held the neck open and placed the pouch in front of the plant. Slowly, it crept forwards and climbed inside.

"Thanks," he said. "It won't be for long."

Grinning a little at this odd exchange, Billy pulled the drawstring closed, but didn't knot it, by way of compromise. He put the axe back at the end of the bed next to the knuckleduster, and headed out of his room. His mother had remained in bed, despite all the noise. He suspected that she would still be there when he returned. He went downstairs and left the house by the kitchen door.

Back in the shed he busied himself changing over the lights from Katherine's bike to his mother's. With the saddle at the right height, he was able to use his long legs properly and found he was able to make decent progress, albeit slower than the speed he was used to on his road bike. An arm of mistletoe with a single berry poked its way out of the pouch and over the edge of the front basket, apparently curious to know where it was off to. Billy was relieved the basket wasn't made of wood, in case the mistletoe got peckish again. As he cycled the long way, alongside the river, it got quite excited by the number of trees, and he tucked it back inside the pouch, just in case.

Along the High Street, the shopkeepers had put Christmas trees up above their shop fronts, tipping out and forming a guard of honour. The white lights in the trees flickered in the fading sun. People bustled, taking advantage of the extra day without children to buy remaining gifts. The determined shoppers had a desperate, even anxious, edge as they hunted down ever greater numbers of gifts and trinkets. Weaving through the mob, Billy kept a protective hand over the basket. He remembered that the Tree had warned him that the tasks would no longer be easy to keep from outsiders, and he wondered exactly what this meant.

Rounding the wrought iron gates of Higginson Park, he hopped off the bike and chained it to the bars near the playground. Velvet pouch in hand, he walked further into the park. Large trees lined the main pathway down to the river. The park was moderately busy, and Billy recognised the reds and yellows of his school uniform over by the cricket pavilion, the smokers' corner. Billy looked over at them a while before turning back to the path and picking a tree close to the river.

He took the pouch and opened the neck with some caution, expecting the plant to spring out. Nothing happened, not even a peeking berry. Looking more closely, he could see the small sprig quivering in the bottom of the pouch, perhaps shaking with fear. Suddenly it burst out of the pouch, turning it inside out. The shaking had been more like rapture. It launched itself onto the tree and sank its stems into the bark. The vampire of the plant world, thought Billy. After watching it for a moment, he turned back to the cricket pavilion. The group was splitting up with the failing light. Thinking of what lay waiting at the other end of the emptying park he started to head off towards the gate.

"Hey."

Billy turned to see Robert cycling towards him on his bike. It fitted him perfectly, which was pretty galling. He turned back at the tree, where the mistletoe had already grown enough to hang from a branch.

"Billy," said Robert, out of breath and reeking of fags. "I was hoping you'd be here."

Billy shuffled his feet, not sure of the ground that now existed between them. "How was school?"

"Crap, of course. Wish I'd been let off too."

Behind Robert, an older couple were starting to take an interest in the mistletoe.

"Do you?"

"'Course I do. But that's not what I came over for. It's about your mate, Katherine."

"Wasn't she in school?"

"No, but…"

Billy looked at the cracked reflector on his bike, trying to focus. "Her dad kept her back home to pack?"

"No…"

"Well what?"

"I'm trying to tell you. She passed out. Last night at home."

Billy grabbed Robert's jacket. Was he joking?

"Where is she now? At home?"

"I don't know. I just thought you'd want to… I thought we were all right now?"

Billy let go of Robert's jacket, reeling backwards, as images of the Gargoyle filled his mind's eye. *She is mine*— had the Gargoyle meant Katherine?

"Are you all right?" said Robert.

"No, I mean, I've got to see what…"

Robert was looking over his shoulder, causing Billy to lose track of a sentence he never quite had. "You know that plant you were sticking in that tree?"

It was over a hundred metres to the cricket pavilion. "How could you see that from over there?"

"I've got good eyes. And that bloke has just nicked it."

Billy turned to see the old couple walking away with the mistletoe. He shot a look back at the tree; there was still more of it there, enough to keep growing. He turned back again. "Thanks, Robert."

Robert shrugged and cycled off back towards the pavilion.

Billy turned away, his thoughts full of worry for Katherine, but also concern for the task. The mistletoe was about to leave the park against the Tree's instructions. He fired up a bit of anger. "Hey! Yes, you. Stop!"

The old couple turned back towards Billy, who was jogging towards them.

"You can't take that, I just put it up there!"

The old lady frowned at him. "You can't own mistletoe. And there hasn't been any in Marlow."

The husband rallied behind his wife. "It's Christmas, everyone should have mistletoe at Christmas."

He knew that he was talking to the type of Marlow resident who answered to nobody. The lady looked over her nose at her husband, who blinked at Billy, daring him to respond. Billy was torn between spending time dealing with this and finding out about Katherine's condition.

"I think it would be a bad idea to take it outside the park," said Billy, and turning, walked back up the path to where he had locked the bike. He didn't need to look back to know they had exchanged a smug glance, before heading off to the car park. Well, he had completed the task, and given them fair warning. He took the bike and walked it up to the gate. It had been awful to see his bike with Robert, but it had been good not to have the usual round of abuse.

Billy cycled slowly up the High Street, unsure if he should head up to Katherine's house, the hospital or his own home. A misplaced noise grabbed his attention. Not sure whether it was the loud screams or the high revving engine that filled his ears first, Billy threw the bike against the parked cars to his left. Tyres now screeching above the engine noise, an old, gold Mercedes flew past him with its bonnet lifting. It swerved left and right, hitting the cars on either side of the High Street before clipping a huge kerbstone. The powerful car shot up in the air, spinning to its right, before landing on its side with a crash and a huge shower of sparks. The rear wheels continued to power around, until the engine gave way with a loud bang, making the people nearby scream again.

Already sure he knew who was inside the car, Billy followed the crowd of people who rushed to see what had happened. A man was warning people to stay back in case the fuel tanks leaked. Ducking past him, Billy clambered to the side of the car, just as somebody was hauling green foliage out of the car.

"Mistletoe!" said the man. "Must be a hundred weight of it. It's all over the windscreen and everywhere."

Billy spooled away from the car with his heart pounding. This task was certainly getting noticed.

An eager voice piped up from the crowd. "Are they dead?"

Running back to the bike, Billy didn't want to know the answer.

"I think so!" said an equally eager onlooker.

Why hadn't he just ripped it out of their stupid, greedy hands? He forced an image of a comatose Katherine into his brain. He needed to focus. At least the Gargoyle wouldn't risk going through town with all these crowds. He pushed the bike past the crash and crowds, before hopping back on and heading away from the High Street. Katherine. He had to find out what had happened to Katherine.

Billy passed his house as fast as the bike could go. Leaning into the sharp corner, he tried to hold onto as much speed as he could. At least at night, he could see there were no cars approaching. The reason for the speed was the brutal angle of the hill. He used to have races with his father to see who would get off and walk first. When he first got the road bike, he'd put on the pedals that were designed for racing shoes, and attempted the hill from a standstill. The hill was so steep that each time he hauled upwards with the specialised shoes, the front wheel would lift up, making him feel as though he were about to tip over the back. This time, he would accept nothing less than completing it in one go. His legs, already complaining from the furious pace with which he had left town, now started to howl. Ignoring them, and filling every inch of his lungs with cold night air, he stared at the tarmac a few feet in front of his bike. As long as it kept moving, he wouldn't fail.

The hill didn't relent easily, giving way in stages, each releasing the pressure in his legs a little more. Sweat poured through skin taut with the cold air. Katherine's house wasn't far. If her father's car was in the drive, he'd know they were in; if not, it meant riding on to High Wycombe and back to the hospital. He rounded the last corner, and bright security floodlights from Katherine's drive blinded him. He cycled steadily up into the thick gravel, eyes low, until he could move the pedals no more. There were three cars in the drive, her father's and two he didn't recognise. Looking past the floodlights, he could see there were lights on in the house; they had to be here. He approached the smart, bricked cottage, and pulled back the black knocker on the white door.

The door flew open before the knocker could fall. Katherine's father hadn't even seen Billy, and was still in conversation with a man he was showing out. The

General looked much more imposing in his uniform, and both men seemed tense. As he turned to Billy, the General eyed him, not surprised to see him there, but not entirely pleased either.

"Come in, Billy. Through to the kitchen, on the left."

Billy went in. The men continued their conversation behind him as they went outside. The kitchen was warm and much bigger than theirs at home, with an Aga oven at the far end beyond a battered pine table. Billy headed for the warm stove and stood against it, letting the heat wash painfully back into his hands. Above him, a drying rack carried the General's underpants. These polka-dotted boxers were not what Billy expected a leader of fighting men to wear.

"I don't think Katherine would thank me for letting you see those." Billy jumped about three feet. The General was back, and still not smiling.

"I wasn't, I mean…"

"Did you hear anything that was said after I opened the door?" said the General. "Anything at all?"

"Not a thing," said Billy.

"Did you recognise that man?"

"No, I… No."

"That's what I told him," said the General. "Damn fool thinks you're a spy."

His mouth opened, then closed, then opened. "He thinks what?"

"That Billy, was the Foreign Secretary of the United Kingdom, and apparently you evaded two secret service personnel on your way in." The General gestured to a chair for Billy to sit in, and took another himself. "I'm just glad they weren't looking after me."

Billy sat down, relieved to see some of the formality leaving Katherine's father. "I thought it might have been a doctor."

"No. How did you find out about Katherine? She said you didn't have a phone at home any more."

"We don't. Robert caught up with me in the park, after school."

"Given up fighting you, has he?"

Billy smiled. It wasn't just confronting Robert which had brought about that change, but he didn't mind the General thinking so. "He didn't have any details. What happened to her?"

He could see tremendous worry cloud over the General's face. "She didn't wake up this morning. Just kept sleeping. I let her rest, thinking it would be good for her, till it became obvious this wasn't normal sleeping. Then I called the doctor."

"Are you taking her back to hospital?"

"The doctor thought it better that she stay here just now. She's locked in sleep but stable, and here she won't catch any bugs. My sister is upstairs with Katherine now. Another day, and if she's not awake, then we go back to the hospital."

"He had no other ideas?" said Billy, feeling weak.

"No, nothing concrete. Blood pressure, heart rate, everything points towards sleep."

Or dreaming, thought Billy. There didn't seem to be anything else to be said, though he wondered what the Foreign Secretary had been doing here in Marlow. That was almost like the Prime Minister popping in for tea; it didn't happen.

"They don't still expect you to go the Gulf?"

The General gave a weary laugh. "World events don't stop because some poxy general's daughter is sick, Billy. They're offering to let me pass but…"

"But what?" said Billy, not meaning to be quite this blunt.

"But what? If I did, then I would let my men and all their families down, by not doing what I happen to do much better than most people."

Billy had never encountered such confidence before. He would never want to confront this man, who could park his personal feelings in such a way.

The General saw Billy's reaction and shot him a smile. "So are we agreed? You won't run to the press and tell them about my boxers, or anything else you saw here?"

Billy laughed, relieved to be on firmer ground. "Can I see her?"

Katherine's father pushed his chair back and stood. "Give me a moment, I'll see if the room is ready for guests."

Billy moved over to the kitchen window, his thoughts suddenly pulled back to the crash in the High Street.

The General came back down the stairs. "You can go up now, second door on the right."

Billy nodded and went past him.

"Make sure you talk to her, Billy. The doctor said it was important."

AS HE APPROACHED THE DOOR, it was already opening. A lady at least ten years older than the General came out, leaving the door ajar.

"Ah, you must be Billy," she said, smiling. "Katherine has told me so much about you."

Billy raised his eyebrows. Surely she hadn't just woken up?

"Before this happened, Billy," said the General's sister with a tired smile. "Go on in. I told her you were coming."

HE WAS STRUCK BY HOW tidy Katherine's room was compared to his own. Sleeping, she looked peaceful but pale. Her hair had been washed clean of the ashes from the fence, and lay neatly to the side in a loose ponytail. Her eyes, one bruised purple, were still. In fact, Katherine was very still indeed. Billy moved around and sat down beside her, making the bed rock so she would move.

"So, I think I caused a car accident today. Possibly killing two old geezers too. Well, one geezer was a she. Made a real mess of the High Street."

Katherine, apparently, wasn't impressed.

"It was the mistletoe, you see. From my quest. The Tree said it had to stay in the park. Except I couldn't hang about and sort it out, because I heard about you. And there's this Gargoyle that's been chasing me near there too. Perhaps you've seen it?"

She must have missed it.

"Well, you'd know it if you did. It's really bloody scary, and stronger than that deerhound we had. He's gone too. With the old Duck Lady. Did you know her name is Agnes?"

Not in the habit of asking the crazies their names as it only encourages them, Katherine declined to comment.

"She's very nice actually. A bit mad, but then she's had this really tough life. And she had the Tree too. But a hundred years ago. I know, you'd think that would make her much older than she looks."

Well, naturally.

"But it's the magic. It's real, you see. Very real, like pain and luck. And now I'm worried. I'm worried that the

Gargoyle might be after you too. So if you see him, run. Run like you're in a room that is catching fire, and don't look back. Do you understand?"

Katherine gave no indication that she hadn't understood.

The General's voice boomed from downstairs "Billy…Billy!"

Billy spent another moment just looking at Katherine, then left the room and rushed down the stairs. Katherine's father, looking concerned, stepped to one side to reveal two policemen.

"Something's happening in town. Apparently these officers think you might have been a witness. Is that possible?"

Billy thought he knew what might be happening. But how had they traced him here, and what did they know about the mistletoe?

"There was a big car accident in town. I was nearby."

One of the policemen spoke. "We need you to come and corroborate some of the facts."

The General looked at Billy. "I can come down with you."

"That won't be necessary," said the other officer.

Katherine's father turned back to him. "I'm sorry, I wasn't speaking to you."

Billy intervened. Katherine needed cover, and he would have to deal with this alone, somehow. "Please, you're needed here."

The General pulled a card from his wallet and gave it to Billy. "If anything gets out of hand, call me, and I'll be with you in minutes."

ONCE OUTSIDE, BILLY ASKED IF they could take his bike down with them. They agreed, aware of the fairly useful card in his pocket. The police Volvo was not the sluggish family car it appeared. He dug his fingers into the sides of the seats. They were driving hard, at one moment on the brakes, the next using all the straight-line speed the car would give them. Already they were approaching the bottom of the hill, and the ninety-degree bend. Billy clutched the grab handle in the ceiling. A minute later, they had left Marlow Bottom and were heading into town. Joining the High Street, they turned left, and parked in the causeway in front of the park. Billy got out of the car and was rooted to the spot, staring at the park.

Mistletoe poured over every tree he could see. It tangled through the iron railings, snaked underneath the paving stones and made it difficult to see far into the park. Clumps of white berries pitted the mass of green. It was moving and still growing. His heart pounded. This was now very public indeed. The police officer gave him a nudge, and they turned and walked up the High Street. As they approached the scene of the accident, the acrid smell of recent burning filled Billy's nose. They skirted the firefighters, who appeared to have just finished damping down the crashed and burning car, and two or three others nearby that must have got caught in the flames. Things had clearly escalated since Billy had left the scene. Why hadn't he just taken the mistletoe off of the old couple?

"Full of burned plants," said one of the firefighters to the approaching police.

Although Billy heard him, he wasn't looking at the car. The nearest ambulance had its rear doors open. There were two bodies in the back, one with feet sticking out from underneath the blanket. Billy suddenly froze. The foot had flinched. He heard himself groan, but as the sound left his mouth, it echoed back out of the ambulance with an older female voice. The woman sat up, the blanket falling. It was the lady from the park, sooty but uncharred. "You! It was you!" Her bony finger pointed directly at Billy. Beside her, her husband sat up as well.

"You!" he said, fighting the restraints around his waist. "It was your mistletoe!"

The police officer looked at Billy, who had looked away, face clearly crimson in the flashing lights. "What do you know about this, then?"

Billy had no answer for him. A paramedic arrived to see what the noise was about.

"Get the police!" the man cried.

"Sit back down," said the paramedic. "I've already told you once."

"You shut up," said the man, who then shot a look at the police officer. "Hey you! Detain that boy."

"I don't think that will be necessary," said a voice from behind the ambulance. Mike Hayter appeared, looking concerned.

"I was afraid these two would end up causing an accident," he said to the police officer.

The faces in the ambulance fell, speechless.

"Really getting on a bit," said the vicar to the paramedic. "I feel awful, I should have spoken to them about stopping driving, but you know it's the only way they could leave the house."

"Are you completely mad? That boy...why he..."

The paramedic closed the door on the enraged pair. As the ambulance drove away, Mike turned to the police officers.

"Quite a mess," said the vicar. "I understand they only just got the old couple out. Now what did you need with young Billy?"

"He was spotted leaving the scene, and fitted a description from…"

"…from the couple in the Mercedes? I see. Where were you off to in a such a hurry, Billy?"

"My friend Katherine has fallen into a coma. I was seeing how she was doing when they arrived and brought me back down…"

"I see. Well, do you think you need anything more from Billy?"

The police officer was stumped. "I think I'm going to have a word with the accident investigator. If you're in a hurry for your bike, Billy, the car is unlocked. I may be a little while."

Billy looked up at Mike with huge gratitude, and they walked back off towards the church and the parked cars. As he recovered his bike, Mike studied the mistletoe.

"Any chance that this is to do with you, then?"

Billy stood by his bike and swung the boot down. He felt hugely indebted to the vicar, but still reluctant to tell him the full story. "It's not about trust. I just can't risk it. There is too much at stake. Sorry."

Mike looked at Billy, then back up the High Street. "Do you think it'll spread?"

"It's a parasite," said Billy. "As long as it doesn't find anything else to eat, it won't be able to move."

He swung his leg over the bike and looked back over at Higginson Park. The noise from the High Street was beginning to subside. "I shouldn't go in there. It's still loose."

He cycled away, leaving Mike staring at the park. At least he hadn't left him without fair warning.

HIS MOTHER WAS IN THE kitchen when he got home. She was bending over the sink; her right hand was bleeding. She barely noticed his arrival and was doing nothing to stem the wound. He bundled his coat off and bent to inspect the cut. It wasn't as deep as it first looked, but was still worse than he had hoped.

"How did it happen, Mum?"

His mother had the signs of recent tears. "I broke one of the Christmas glasses."

He looked down at the sparkling chips in the sink. The glasses were by far the finest in the house, and had been given to his parents by an elderly aunt, who had passed them on with an uncharacteristically chilly warning. Be very careful, she had said, the glasses represent you and your future family; you break them at your peril. His mother had lost one of the six in the move to this house. Thereafter, she had failed to conceive Billy for another five years, despite trying as soon as they had moved in. After he was born, his father had brought the glasses out, despite it being July, not Christmas, to toast his son. Billy's uncle had dropped his flute, despite dire warnings from his father. He'd then managed to keep it secret until the following Christmas, even contacting his mother's aunt in an effort to replace it, not believing his wife's superstition, but fearing its effect. Now they were down to three.

"Why did you bring them out?"

"Well, we didn't use them last year, so I thought I'd give them a clean," said his mother. "I just hope that wasn't Tom's glass."

She took a deep breath, as Billy dabbed the finger with kitchen roll soaked in antiseptic.

"Dad isn't dead, Mum," he said, concentrating on his work, "and he never believed in the glasses thing."

"No. But we never did have another baby. I miss him so much," said his mother, before inspecting her finger.

Billy put the lid on the antiseptic. "He will come back."

But his mother was already leaving the room.

He wished he could tell her about the tasks, but even if that were allowed, would it be fair to raise her expectations? The kiss was still a moot point. This sent his mind back to Katherine's room. He wondered how long the doctor would let her stay at home. Perhaps she used an Army doctor? He hoped that didn't mean she could be shipped out to the Gulf. Stuck on a plane, unable to wake even to pop her ears. He set about picking up the pieces of shattered glass which were big enough to handle, and placing them in the box.

⊰December 23rd⊱

The familiar fatigue, more akin to being asleep than awake, followed him out of his bed, down the stairs and into the living room. The Tree was already up, despite the fact that it was only six minutes past midnight, pacing up and down in front of the dead fireplace.

"Evening," said Billy, flopping into the red chair by the bucket.

"Morning," said the Tree, still deep in thought.

Leaving the Tree to pace, he let his mind drift. Thoughts of Katherine entered his mind. *She was still sleeping, but as he called her name her eyelids fluttered, reacting to his voice. He put out a hand, at first reaching for her face, but then falling away to pick up her hand that was suddenly made of pine needles.* Billy jumped.

"Katherine," said the Tree leaning over a blinking Billy. "You have a friend whom you love, whom you wish me to help recover."

Billy leapt out of the chair pushing past the Tree. Find Katherine?

He shook the sleep out of his head.

"What do you mean, find Katherine?"

The Tree shifted from side to side. "I have to confess, we have a problem."

"What problem?"

Hopping over to the mantelpiece, the Tree bent down and examined the fireplace. "We might have been a little premature in getting rid of the poisoned ashes."

"Why does that matter?" said Billy, dreading the answer, but determined to hear it.

"It appears that when you chopped away the poison, we lost the area where I stored the memories of this task."

Billy fought to control his fear, and his temper. "Your task was to return my father, who disappeared a year ago last Christmas Day."

"Not the girl?"

"No," said Billy, now doubling his worry. How bad was Katherine?

The Tree raised branched eyebrows, then hunched down, again concentrating with great intensity.

"You had found him!" Billy was now unable to contain himself, and advanced on the Tree. "You told me he was alive and safe."

"Did I mention where?"

With that, Billy had both hands around the trunk of the Tree, ignoring the scratches. "I saved your life last night, and now you don't even remember the task."

"I am certain shaking me will not restore the memories."

"Then what?"

"My tag, my import tag," said the Tree. "Do you still have it?"

Letting go of the Tree, Billy went over to the pile of velvet pouches still piled on the windowsill. Underneath the pile lay the import tag, which was as big as his open palm. He picked it up. On one side there were the words *Imported: Christmas Tree & Decorations (12)*, on the other an inked drawing, a logo of a Christmas tree.

"Nothing," said Billy. "There's nothing on here."

"Show it to me," said the Tree. "Please…"

Billy held up the side with the words "Imported…" on it. The Tree looked back at him.

"Anyone can read that. Turn it over."

Billy flipped the tag over.

"As I thought," said the Tree. "An ancient map."

"A map?" said Billy. "But it just looks like a tree."

The Tree peered down at the label. It began to glow, and Billy looked closer. The ink bubbled up and sat for a moment on the surface of the cardboard tag, then sank back in, this time not in the shape of the tree, but in a perfect line drawing of the British Isles. A dot of red ink blinked from a point just west of Scotland. The Tree looked over the label as a naval officer might look over a new chart. As it tilted the card back and forth, the ink sloshed across the material, revealing a smaller scale, close-up version. Indeed, the map was now showing a moving three-dimensional approach to what appeared to be a series of islands. Names such as Oban and Tobermory flashed in front of him before the map crossed over more water and appeared to halt over an island called Rum. The island had mountains to the north and south, and the map drew in closer still to a southern range with a peak, which had a pool below. Near the top was what looked like an albino deer. As the picture drew close, the deer looked up, directly at Billy and the Tree.

"Senga."

The Tree dropped the tag, and the image snapped back to the logo. Looking shaken, the Tree hopped back to the mantelpiece.

"What was that creature?"

The branched eyes of the Tree were searching for something; eventually it turned back to him. "This is unorthodox, Billy, but I need you to come with me."

Billy looked back at the Tree. "Come with you where?"

"Rum."

BILLY WAS WEARING TWO SCARVES and his father's spare overcoat.

"Warmer."

"You want me to wear more?"

"Yes. Do you own any hats?"

Fishing deep within the drawers in the hall, Billy pulled out two skiing hats belonging to his parents.

"Both of them, and another set of gloves," said the Tree. "The extremities are most important."

"How cold is it on this island?"

"Well the peaks are about two thousand feet up, and catch the proper cold winds from the Atlantic. But that isn't the reason I need you wrapped up."

With the last pair of gloves added, the Tree judged Billy ready, and they left the house by the front door.

"How is this going to work?" Billy had seen the Tree shoot into the air once before, and he didn't fancy his chances of being able to hang on if this was the proposed method of transport. The Tree leant over him, shaking slightly, and a few green needles fell onto Billy, sparking as they touched him. At once, his legs started to feel less stable; a giddiness took him over.

"What is this stuff?"

"To help you relax on the flight," said the Tree. "Don't relax too much though, and whatever happens, don't let go."

Billy thought this might prove to be a tall order with two pairs of gloves on. He crossed his knuckles over a pair of branches. He looked up at the Tree again, stomach lurching with the loss of balance.

"So we're going to Scotland?"

"The Western Islands, yes."

"Not too fast, eh?"

"Look down, Billy."

They were already drifting over the roof of his house. He doubled his grip, fear and surprise bringing fresh strength. They were also accelerating; the lights below grew smaller, the air grew colder. Glad of the layers against the brutal cold, Billy was surprised by the lack of drag from the Tree. He'd expected to have his arms ripped out of his sockets and to be buffeted by high winds. In fact, he was drawn by the gentlest force, and it was not the wind, but the chill of the air that made his eyes blink.

"How long will it take?"

The Tree branched low eyes to speak with him. "Hold on tight."

The Tree accelerated violently into the night sky, testing his arms and nerve further still. Pools of artificial lights, cities, began to creep under them, then a long motorway snaking north. Billy could make out the line of the west coast, chopping in from the north of Wales, becoming the western edge of England. Ahead of them a wall of cloud rose from the ground, obscuring the rest of the land below. The Tree pulled ever upwards, above the level of the clouds, and suddenly Billy had the sensation of skiing as they twisted about the peaks of glacial cloud. Exhilaration washed the worry of his father and Katherine out of his body and he started to revel in the journey. He had one task: hold onto the Tree. This he could manage.

They were climbing again, now quite high above the cloud base. The Tree peered ahead, searching for some detail. The moon was close to full, and bright enough that Billy could still see the colour of his clothes.

"There it is."

They were descending; the Tree was aiming for a small twisting hole in the cloud. As they fell out of the sky, Billy felt his legs rise up from underneath him, until he was diving, still clinging to the trunk of the Tree. They sank through the twisting hole like water disappearing down a drain pipe, and though the night beneath them was pitch black, a river of moonlight from the gap above led them down. Below him, Billy could see a collection of islands, but it was already clear which one they were headed for.

"Rum," said the Tree.

The island wasn't as small as some in the vicinity, and Billy recognised the mountains to the north and to the south from the label. Below the range on the north-west side was a pool of water, which was still enough to let him briefly glimpse their reflection before they were spinning around once more to the western edge of the southern range of mountains. As they drew closer, they could see the shape of a white deer, lit in moonlight, head up, calling to the night sky. Its voice was like the sounds of wind and rain through leaves. And now the Tree was answering the deer, calling back in the same leaf-washed tone, drawing them together. Then another sound, like low thunder, came from the ground below. It was a vast

herd of red deer, approaching the peak of the mountain in a huge spiral that would close about the albino.

Before Billy could take in any more, his feet were scuffing along the ground. It took four or five steps for him to plant his feet underneath himself, but once he let go of the Tree, his sense of balance left him entirely and he fell flat on the ground. It was as though he'd spent the last hour spinning in one spot.

Between the uncomfortable revolutions of his head, he made out the white deer nuzzling the Tree, still conversing in the strange language. The deer was odd in other ways as well. Where antlers might be, there were branches that looked like those of an ash tree, its bark catching the moonlight; and as the deer raised its hooves, he saw roots pull up easily from the boggy ground and paw at the Tree. His brain gave up fighting the spinning and confusing images. He lay back and shut his eyes.

"Billy, this is Senga," said the Tree.

Forcing one eye open, Billy looked up. The Tree and the white deer were standing over him. "I can't get up."

"It will pass," said Senga. The voice was female and rich. "You were not designed to travel in this manner."

"I really had no choice," said the Tree. "I am sorry, Senga."

"It is done, and there is no purpose in looking over paths which have now passed," said Senga, before turning back to Billy. "Rest a moment longer, little one. I must attend to Teàrlag's injuries."

The Deer turned back to the Tree and examined the base cut that Billy had made. It shook its head and called out in the leaf language to the herd of deer which now surrounded them. Two large stags came forward. The Tree appeared to be protesting their presence.

"Don't you think you've travelled far enough for one night?" said Senga, laughing a little, before motioning the stags in. They walked forward, shoulders a foot apart, and bent low to collect the Tree.

Billy still couldn't stop his head from spinning, but he faced where he thought the Tree's voice was coming from.

"Teàrlag," he said, getting used to the unfamiliar name. "That joke you wanted. How do you kill an entire circus?"

"I'm sorry, Billy?" said the Tree, losing all semblance of his grandfather's voice.

"Go for the juggler."

Teàrlag frowned above the two stags, then broke into a small grin. "I get it!"

The deer set off down the mountain towards the pool. The low thunder let Billy know that the whole herd was pouring down the mountainside as one, following wherever Teàrlag had been taken. He struggled to his feet so as to be able to see them, but only managed as far as his knees, before resting on all fours, trying not to fall back. Senga walked over to him, her hooves swished as light roots pulled up through the deep bog. Billy managed to kneel, and found Senga looking at him with clear intrigue.

"Have we met before, Master Christmas?"

His head still spun, as he tried to focus on the deer, with the wooden antlers and the female voice. "I think I'd remember if we had."

Senga began to shiver, and then shake as would a wet dog. She stopped momentarily before throwing Billy a wink. "I think it's good manners to look away. But I won't tell…"

The shaking returned, more violent than before, and Billy was unable to look away. The blur of white that shimmered before him betrayed glimpses of a human form emerging. Words floated out in that strange language, and the moon redoubled its light on the hilltop and on Senga. Out of the blur, a human hand reached out. Billy caught it and clung on. The hand looked and felt like bark. She increased her grip, and his dizziness evaporated. The crescendo of white shaking subsided and he looked on, somewhat embarrassed to be standing in front of a naked female form. Senga's skin was still white, but with the luminescence, and black pitting, of a silver birch. The last details of her deer features fell from her face as she looked up at the moon, and from her fresh scalp poured light willow branches, stranding like loose dreadlocks, and falling forward over her shoulders and chest. Looking down, Billy could see that she now had human feet, though he felt certain that if she moved white roots would be exposed. What manner of creature was this? Senga drew in a sharp breath, galvanising this new form. Her eyes remained as black as they had been as the deer; she looked at Billy, assessing the tall boy.

"Not where you imagined you would be tonight?"

Billy was still uncertain where he should and shouldn't be looking. Senga was otherworldly beautiful, but wasn't it weird to feel attracted to something that, by way of mildest explanation, was other? He was lost for words, and scrabbled in his mind for why he was here at all. Not to fall into those deep black eyes, certainly. He let go of her hand.

Senga smiled. "Why thank you, Billy, your reaction is charming. You may relax a little if you understand I am really rather old."

Beneath his layers, Billy flushed, and sent his eyes down to the peaty earth below. He remembered what had brought him here: the Tree, he'd cut the Tree and lost the part that knew the whereabouts of his father.

"What choice did you have?" said Senga. "Lose the Tree, lose your father and perhaps a lot more. And thank you, Billy. I have known Teàrlag a considerable time, thousands of human years, and I should have been broken to lose her."

He paused a moment to let the shift in gender settle in. It was so hard to think of the Tree as anything other than "it." "She said that this was the last visit, that after me she would die, and she was the last of her kind."

Senga looked back at Billy. "That is not her fate, not yet. I sense this has some way to play out yet, and that she has some further part in it."

"I have a friend, Katherine, who I think has got caught up in this," said Billy, shifting his weight to move his frozen toes. "She sort of featured in a couple of my tasks. Only now she can't wake up."

"Saved by another task, yes?"

Billy nodded. The fence.

"Only now the enemy has shown interest."

He nodded again. "It wasn't direct, it didn't name her. I thought it might be my mother."

"Or Teàrlag?" said Senga.

Billy nodded, still adjusting to the notion of Teàrlag being female.

Senga took a couple of steps, to watch the deer carrying Teàrlag to the pool below. "Or me."

Billy didn't know what to say. He knew he was having a rare glimpse at the structure behind the centuries of the magic Trees, but he didn't know how to weigh the complications of this other world with those that he faced at home. *We're not fools, Billy*, a memory whispered. *Don't measure this.*

"Teàrlag will have told you, and it is true, you help to weave all this, Billy. It is why she came to you at all. She will have told you to look to your dreams for guidance, for direction, yes?"

"Well, yes," said Billy with a touch of frustration. This had the distinct tone of one of Teàrlag's statements, which would seem full of promise, but give none of the answers he needed to move on with certainty.

"And to show faith in the tasks?"

"Yes, and I have," said Billy, gathering some resolve, "and it has been pretty bloody tough."

Senga was gone. Then she was at his shoulder, whispering at his ear. "Tougher than being sliced in half like Teàrlag?"

She drew a fingernail across his belly. Somehow he felt the cold finger; it had passed through the seven layers of clothing. He gasped. Senga looked steadily at him. It was clear that she meant no malice.

"The Gargoyle is seeking to foil the mission of the magic you have encountered. Put simply, we have failed. We sought to improve the world through offering a degree of skill and knowledge to certain humans. It was supposed to endow stewardship of this world. You can see, it is obvious to all, it has not succeeded. The Gargoyle seeks to take independence and use those Chosen to sow dependence. The consequences would be bleak for my kind, and yours."

Senga looked up again at the moon, and Billy watched the light roll over her silver skin.

"Part of steering though life, especially human life, lies in completing the matters within your control before you tackle those without."

Billy let a thought escape; what might she know about the finer details of human life? He knew she'd caught the thought at once.

Senga raised an eyebrow. "More than you might imagine," she held out a fist. "Did Teàrlag speak to you about the miracle of hands?"

"She did."

Senga upturned the fist and opened it, revealing the S-shaped iron bar. It stood out in the moonlight against the white grain of her palm.

"This bar is the spoke of a wheel in the weir, the dam at Marlow. It is not a task to be undertaken alone, and the effects will be dramatic. Be prepared for anything."

"But what about the Tree—Teàrlag, I mean?"

"If we are able to find your father, she will return to you. If not…"

"There's an 'if not'?"

"If not, there is deeper magic we can employ. Be assured, Billy, we will not abandon him, whatever the cost."

Senga drew close to him again. "You should know this. Your father did not leave of his own accord. He did not get lost."

Billy was rapt. Answers were beckoning.

"He was taken. Taken by the enemy. Of whose ranks you have seen but one."

"There are more?"

"Looking further than the challenges you know could jeopardise your father. Teàrlag did not lie. She needs you to complete your tasks, or we are powerless. Do you understand?"

Billy nodded, absorbing this piece of the riddle before returning to his responsibilities. He focused on his own task. He had the iron bar, but the weir was now some considerable distance away. "How do I get home?"

Senga looked at him once again. "It does seem like a long walk now, doesn't it?"

"Short flight?" said Billy, betraying a strong desire to repeat his earlier cloud-surfing exploits, though perhaps without the after-effects.

Senga laughed and shook out her willow locks, revealing so much silver bark that Billy forgot any detail of anything remotely connected to clouds or flying. He breathed in as she stepped towards him, the roots from her feet whispering.

"Now, while I'm sure you've been nothing but truthful with Teàrlag about your performance of the tasks, there is an area where your benchmark may not have been…overly ambitious."

She was still approaching, willow hair now rolling back over her shoulders, leaving Billy without anywhere to look. He took a half step back, but she had already put an arm around his neck. As her mouth connected with his, he swore he could make out a million different colours in the black of her eyes. He'd expected her lips to be cold, but in fact they banished the cold from him. As he had felt her hand over his belly, he now felt her chest against his own. And he knew, in the depths of his bones, that he had not kissed Katherine.

HE OPENED HIS EYES, WAKING in his own room. The kiss was still with him, and he was wracked with sudden guilt. It wasn't as though he'd had a choice. He'd had half a thought that Senga had meant to send him home when she had advanced on him; even if he had not been too clear on the specifics of how it might work. As he thought now of bedridden Katherine, Billy wondered if he might have dreamt the whole thing. Had he slept through the night and missed meeting the Tree? Horror flew through him and he leapt out of bed, smashing all the toes on his right foot. With a howl, he looked down to see the large iron bar lying beside his bed. That hadn't been there last night, so this wasn't a dream.

Nursing his aching toes, he took stock. The Tree had got hurt, but they'd coped. He'd flown to Scotland, and probably seen more than anyone else had seen throughout all the previous years this had been going on. Moreover, he had another task, another physical task that he could take on. He hopped around the room, picking up the assorted garments from the night before. Had Senga seen him undress, or had he vanished before her eyes? It was then that he remembered that he had certainly seen her, well, down to the bark. And then he remembered Katherine, felt guilty again, and limped out of the room to get the bog mud off him.

In the shower, the mechanics of the next task began to weigh on him. The massive weir was known to be dangerous, its ferocious water capable of sweeping even the best swimmers to their deaths. Before the winter snow, Marlow had had a torrential autumn, and the biggest locks in the dam were close to breaching point; but this wasn't the problem. The problem was going to be approaching the weir at all. It was practically inaccessible from either bank. They were going to need a boat. But in order to be a "they," he needed another. Billy got out of the shower.

HIGH HEAVENS WOOD WAS BUSY. With school finally over and Christmas Eve approaching fast, the street bustled with parents rounding on children, reminding them of presents hinted at and chores promised, and the sliding scale that existed between the two. Billy noticed that he didn't feel he had to look away from their glances any more. In some ways, with the Tree seriously damaged, he was more exposed than ever, but it felt so good closing out the few remaining days. He pedalled his mother's bike as fast as he could out of High Heavens Wood to hit the hill on Ragman's Lane with all possible speed.

He pulled into Katherine's house, wondering how he was supposed to receive a kiss from Katherine to match the one he had experienced last night. He knocked on the door, and almost at once Katherine's aunt opened it, blinking in the light.

"Billy, is that you?"

He stepped forward into the shade of the porch. "Hello, I was hoping to hear how Katherine is doing?"

"It's been quite a night. You would have got a call, but Andrew said you didn't have a phone."

It felt odd to hear the General's name, but he was hungry now for this news of the night. "What happened?"

"He woke between midnight and one and rushed into Katherine's room, swearing that he'd heard her voice. I mean, I told him he was most likely dreaming, but he gave me the old line about his training not leaving him."

"But why did he want to phone me?"

"Well, it seems Katherine was calling out your name. I think you'd better come in. He said you were to go and try to speak to her as soon as you came." Katherine's aunt took Billy's arm and pushed him upstairs. "Try to surprise her. Don't worry about being too polite."

"HELLO KATHERINE."

The room was brighter than at the previous visit. At some point, the doctor had visited again. Katherine now had a drip feeding a clear liquid into her left arm. Despite that, he sat down heavily again, so as to shake her and let her know she wasn't alone. When he started talking to her like this, it was a bit like talking to the Tree when it was in its natural state; he had to remember that despite appearances there was a sharp intelligence deep within.

"So. You're going to be stubborn about this. Well, that's fine. At least I know it's still you in there. Taking no one's advice but your own. You should know that a girl has been showing some interest in me."

Katherine showed her indifference by refusing to move.

"Not the kind of interest that I could just make up either. Impressive, full-on, real stuff," said Billy, before moving a bit of Katherine's hair that was annoying him. It felt soft and warm and human compared to the willow. "I think you'd have liked Rum. It's a bit muddy, but they have mountains, and sea and hundreds of deer. The Tree knew the deer. Did I mention the Tree? Anyway, the Tree has a name, Teàrlag. It's a bit confusing, because it sounded like my grandfather, and now I have to think of it as a girl."

Katherine seemed to be getting a bit bored.

"Speaking of girls, the person who we went to see, who was actually a deer for a while, is called Senga. The good news is she thinks we can still find my dad. Which is nice, 'cause I'd hate to go through all this, and have all of you go through this, and it all be because I'm mad. Which is what it will look like if he doesn't show up in two days' time."

He poked her on the shoulder; she was still ignoring him.

"So I'm sorry I kissed Senga, but I really didn't think I had a choice. Walking back would have taken forever. I know you probably feel like you're a long way from home too, but I think if I keep going somehow this will bring us all back, in one piece, in one place, ready for you to leave with your dad."

She was looking paler than the last time he was here. Perhaps they were keeping the window shut in order to keep her warm? Could people in a coma shiver? He looked over to the door. It was ajar, but there was no sign of her aunt. He couldn't kiss her like this; he knew the difference now. At some point, his father's fate was going to hinge on whether Katherine had woken up or not, but if he focussed on what he couldn't achieve now, they would all be finished. Instead, he made to leave, turning to face her as he approached the door.

"Katherine," he said loud enough to wake anyone sleeping in the room, "you're going to have to wake up. I'm getting offers from other girls, and some of them are very tempting. Besides, I'm intending not to sing at all next year, and I believe that means you owe me a kick in the…"

"Well said, Billy!"

He leapt in shock. Katherine's aunt was beside him at the door.

"I told Andrew she needed some plain speaking, and…well, that was putting it plain," said the aunt, giving his arm a squeeze. "Let's let her think on that for a while."

With that, she guided a red-faced Billy out of the room and back downstairs to the kitchen. There was a plate of biscuits waiting there, and he was glad of the breakfast and distraction.

"Don't be embarrassed. When this family isn't on display, the language is pretty frank. She needs something to give her a chivvy."

"Do they have to go to the Gulf?" Billy knew it was a question he couldn't ask of Katherine or her father.

The aunt looked back at Billy. "I think you know a little of the determination they share. I do know this is tearing Andrew apart, and that he'd hoped not to have to leave the country till Katherine was at university. But events are fast overtaking him."

Over the last year, he'd lost his stomach for news. It was enough to keep on top of everything in his own world; more than enough. There was talk at school—talk of fear, talk of terrorism—but he'd simply had too much to cope with to worry about how the world was turning.

"I have to go, please keep talking to her."

"I'll tell her you're out searching for a date."

Billy blushed again. "You know that we're not... We're supposed to be just friends."

"Really? The way Katherine spoke about you I was always sure there was more to it than that."

He thanked her as calmly as he could for the biscuits, and tried to leave the house without looking like he was floating on air.

IT WAS LATE MORNING AND instead of rolling back down Ragman's Lane, he turned left out of the drive and headed for the main road and then Winchbottom Lane. Here there was, arguably, an even steeper hill, without the death-inducing ninety-degree bend at the bottom. Enjoying the breeze and the two red kites which circled above him as he flew down the hill, he allowed himself to feel a moment of excitement at the thought of Katherine speaking about him with warm words. He knew this was a long way from the real world, but the hill was so steep that he felt he could outrun reality, just for a while.

ALL SAINTS CHURCH WAS BUSY holding a Christmas bazaar, so Billy was able to slip into the graveyard that backed up onto the weir without raising any suspicions.

He looked across to the park, saw that the mistletoe had engulfed the trees and was sending out exploratory arms through the iron railings. At night it was easier to believe in anything, and he hadn't had many daytime indicators of his adventures. He began to wonder just how big the next task would prove to be. Senga had said that the effect would be dramatic. Did she mean just for him, or for the public at large? She'd also said he couldn't do this alone, though with Katherine still out of action he was going to have to do his best.

He approached the water's edge behind the church. It was one of the days where you didn't even have to look for the falling edge of the weir. It could be heard. The water was dark and fast moving, carrying vast power before meeting the hundred-metre-long weir which consumed that energy and converted it into sound and spray.

Nearer to Billy, where the water was relatively calm, a wooden boat about ten feet long was chained and locked to a great iron ring in the bank of the river. The boat had been forced hard against the side, and its black rubbing strake was leaving marks on the concrete bank. Alongside a lock a huge chain went underneath the boat without appearing to be attached. Billy wondered if another boat had simply sunk to the bottom of the river.

"A present from my predecessor," said Mike, making Billy jump. "Sorry, I thought you'd heard me coming."

Collecting his stomach and his thoughts, Billy tried to appear calm. "Kept it here in case any of the sermons went badly, did he?"

"I've no idea, but I'll bear that in mind," said Mike, smiling.

It occurred to Billy that he might be able to ask the vicar to help him. After all, he'd offered nothing but support, asking for nothing in return. He also had the advantage of being able to see some of what was happening. Billy couldn't articulate why he didn't feel ready to trust him completely. Perhaps after this was all completed and there was nothing left to risk, then he could. From beside the church, a shrill voice started calling out, "Vicar! Vicar!"

"Whatever I did last time around, I'm paying now," he said before covering his mouth in mock horror at his blasphemy. He turned to walk back to the church. "Four-seven-two."

Billy frowned, confused. "What?"

"If you need to borrow the boat. Four-seven-two," said Mike, dragging his feet along the path.

Billy grinned; he hadn't noticed that the boat was locked. "Thanks!"

"I know, I know. You can't tell me. Dress up warm. There's a storm coming."

An icy wind rolled across the graveyard. It was as if the vicar had woken an ancient winter from its slumber.

THE SECOND TIME BILLY LEFT his home that day, he looked like he was set for another flight to Rum. He needed to cycle, so he only had two pairs of trousers on, but he'd managed to locate his father's skiing goggles, and these were proving an excellent screen from the wind that had picked up since his earlier outing. He'd duct-taped the black iron bar to the frame of his mother's bicycle to make it look a bit more like a man's bike, with a cross-bar. He had the knuckleduster zipped into a breast pocket. He'd thought about bringing the axe too, but was scared of losing it overboard, or of the Gargoyle taking it from him. The thought of the Gargoyle loose with the axe in its one good arm made his blood freeze.

He rode slowly into Robert's drive and placed the bike as quietly as he could against the garage. Without giving himself time to check his courage, he knocked firmly at the door. Robert opened it, and seemed confused to see Billy.

"I thought it was polite to ring before you dropped around."

"Don't have phone," said Billy through frozen lips. "Can I come in?"

"Alex is out."

Billy took this as a yes.

"What are you dressed for?"

"Funny you should ask that. I wondered if you wanted to come and open up the weir." Billy had a notion that this is what the wheel might do. Opening the weir and emptying the river. Hence the attention it would attract.

"Open the weir? Why?"

"Well, you know, for the hell of it. For a laugh."

"But it's bloody freezing out there."

"I know that, but it'd be great, wouldn't it?"

Robert looked at him, checking that he had heard him correctly. "To open the weir?"

"I think that's what it does. I've got this old iron bar, and a boat by the church."

For a moment, Billy thought he saw a smile breaking on Robert's face; then it changed.

"I can't. I'm supposed to cook for Alex tonight."

He looked about the kitchen. There were empty packets, but no sign of a meal in progress.

Robert read his mind, and looked a bit afraid. "I know. I've looked everywhere. I can't find anything."

Billy frowned, then started to open cupboard doors. Over the last year, he'd learnt how to rustle up meals from random cans, fruits and vegetables which had never been in close contact before, or probably since. However, this was looking bleak. There weren't the usual base things like half-empty pasta packets or cans of tuna. Just empty cardboard, and the odd jar of out-of-date sludge. Not good. From the corner of his eye, he could see Robert looking out into the darkness. His brother must be due home soon.

"It's always like this," said Robert in a voice Billy could hardly hear. "Like I ate everything that was here…"

"Ha!"

"What?"

Billy held up a stock cube. "Sorted. Bring me anything from the freezer." He fired up the largest hob, pulled a large frying pan from the bottom of a cupboard, and emptied the cube into it. An open pack of butter was by the toaster; he added a wedge of this to the stock cube, trying not to wonder how long it had been there.

Robert came back, still looking worried. "Prawns and peas. That's it."

"That's fine. Don't suppose there's any wine anywhere?"

Robert's face brightened. He left Billy with the prawns and peas and disappeared again. The new ingredients went into the pan and steam filled the kitchen. Soon Robert was back, with three red wine bottles in various states of near emptiness. Billy took them without hesitation, added them to the mix, along with a dollop of ketchup he'd coaxed from a forgotten bottle.

"We need bread," said Billy, shaking the spitting pan.

"There was some pita bread in the freezer."

"Perfect. Get it."

Billy dropped the pita into the toaster.

"Thanks," Robert said. "You've no idea what a beating I was in for."

Remembering Robert's head being smashed against the garage door, Billy thought that he might, but just nodded. With that, the kitchen door flew open.

"You never told me you were bringing someone over!" said Alex, grabbing Robert by the neck.

Robert's feet skittered underneath him. "Just to cook, Alex, just to cook."

Billy stared into the pan, stirring like crazy at the red and green stew.

"What is it?"

Billy thought fast. "Tom gai soup. Fresh from the pan."

"Sounds foreign. I hate foreign."

"It's Thai."

"Oh. Well, OK then."

Alex let go of Robert and sat at the table. Robert rubbed his neck while Billy served up the soup with pita bread on the side. Robert looked up as Alex dunked the bread in and slurped the soup back. He looked at them both, to one, then the other.

"It's all right I suppose," he said.

"All right?" Robert took a step forward.

Billy looked at him in horror; this was the time for an honourable retreat, not to make a point. Alex turned back to him, of course.

"Yeah. What were you expecting?"

"Perhaps a thank you?"

Billy started to inch towards the door. He'd done his best here, but Robert was bent on destruction. Alex took another step forward.

"Hmmm. Thank you for keeping a roof over my head?"

They stared at each other, Billy waiting for the bowl to fall, and the beating to begin. Eventually, Alex lost interest, and turned his attention back to the soup. For an instant, Billy saw a flash of rage in Robert, and thought he was going to charge after him. He stepped forward and put a hand on his shoulder.

"Come on. Let's get out of here."

Robert turned, still combusting but under control, and nodded.

OLLY'S HOUSE WAS QUIET, LEAVING Robert without a bike. As it was downhill most of the way Billy ferried him on his, standing on the pedals and letting him sit on the seat. The cold breeze was a welcome distraction from the temperature and tension of the kitchen. As they glided down the quiet High Street, Billy had most of the road to himself. With the shops shut and the weather turning much colder, people seemed to have decided to head home earlier than usual. He pulled up outside the church and, having rolled Robert off to one side, began to push the bike up the path. Robert looked up at All Saints tower with some confusion.

"I thought we were going to the weir?"

"That's right, come on."

Robert followed Billy, looking around the unfamiliar graveyard, clearly not happy to be there. Billy turned to make sure he was keeping up before putting the bike against the sidewall of the church. He unwound the tape around the bar from the frame of the bike and swung it over his shoulder. It was only a short walk to the wall but, from the noise of the weir, Billy could tell that the flow of the river had increased. The surface of the river had uncomfortable folds, like an overused bed sheet. He swung his legs over the edge of the bank and onto the boat, leaving the iron bar on the side of the wall. The boat itself was made of heavy oak, and proved quite steady. It had two sets of seats, or thwarts, as his father would have corrected him, and a separate rudder and tiller at the back. A heavy chain was attached to the bank and then disappeared somewhere underneath the boat.

Robert was looking over the wall at him. "Is that thing safe?"

"So far so good. Pass the bar over."

As Robert clambered in, Billy stowed the bar and turned his attention to the combination lock which tied the boat to the wall, looped through the large iron chain that disappeared into the water.

"Billy?"

He was wrestling with the gummed lock. "Hang on."

"It's just that…"

"Give me a minute, will you?" said Billy. The lock hadn't been moved in some time, and the last number wouldn't fall.

"I think it's quite important."

"Got you!" said Billy, falling back into the boat, open lock in hand.

"Where are the oars?"

The boat reacted to the news by spinning in the nearest eddy. Billy looked around the boat. Robert was absolutely right, no oars. Billy shot an arm out to the chain, and with their combined strength, the boat turned in alongside the bank.

With the boat no longer fighting them, Robert was able to sit back on the seat. "You hadn't really thought this out, had you?"

Billy looked down into the dark water. Robert was right, but he didn't want to admit it. Hadn't his instincts and determination got him this far? He then thought about his fading mother and the absent, broken Tree. Perhaps things weren't in such good shape.

"What are we doing here, anyway?" said Robert.

This was no easier to answer. Billy had to think fast. "It's in a bit of old Marlow legend. This bar completes a wheel in the weir."

"To do what?"

"Well, that's what we're going to find out."

Robert gave Billy a look to see if he really was being as vague as that. How could he begin to explain that, on this flimsy reasoning lay, perhaps, the life of his father? Turning back, Robert was looking towards the weir, back to the wall, and then out to the weir once again.

"What is it?"

Robert went to the front of the boat, and examined the prow, running his hands over the turning block. "I don't think this boat was made for oars."

"It's got holes for the rowlocks."

"Yeah, but look at them, they've hardly been used. Can you see that chain, just above the water level on the weir?"

Streetlights painted the water orange, making it hard to pick out detail. "I dunno, maybe. Are you sure?" said Billy.

"I've got good eyes," said Robert. "I reckon it's the same chain as the one that runs underneath this boat. I think it was supposed to be a sort of chain ferry. Perhaps for whoever used to open the weir?"

Billy had to admire Robert, not just for his eyes, but also for his thinking. That would explain a lot. Perhaps the chain could also guide them into the place where they were supposed to add the iron bar. He shot him a grateful smile.

Moving the chain proved hard work. With a massive effort, they lifted a few links over the turning block at the front of the boat. Robert, shorter and wider, was able to pull the chain more easily and took over. As the pace of the chain quickened, it became clear he had been right about the way this boat was meant to move. Billy was glad of the company, and surprised by Robert's resourcefulness. By the time they were halfway across the river, they were really moving. And to his relief, the area was completely deserted, as the heavy chain was making a real racket.

As they drew closer to the wall of the weir, he began to doubt the chain would act as a guide for placing the iron bar. The chain ended just above the water line, but there was no hint of the wheel that Senga had referred to.

"Getting close now," said Robert.

A car passed over the bridge. White lights broke through the orange gloom, revealing the full length of the mighty weir, with huge wooden posts rising like turrets. The temperature was still falling, but the cloud cover was thick and oppressive, as if it were about to thunder, making Billy's skin shiver and itch at the same time. With the crossing almost complete, he risked standing up. The chain was now clean out of the water and Robert barely had to pull on it at all, just letting the links fall through his hands. Another car passed over the suspension bridge, making Billy jump.

"They can't see us," said Robert. "The bars of the bridge are in the way."

Billy looked back at the weir, cross that it was he who needed calming. The chain didn't end, but dropped through an iron loop, down into the water. Here, the weir was higher. As they approached it, Robert appeared to be getting ready to jump.

"Where do you think you're going?" said Billy. "It's going to be as slippery as hell."

"It won't be that bad," said Robert, and made the point by leaping the last couple of feet onto the wooden topside. "Told you."

The boat followed him, bumping into the side of the weir. The water was actually calmer here, and the boat seemed happy enough to sit there. Billy peered over the front of the boat, looking for a clue as to the whereabouts of the wheel. All he could see was weed-covered concrete. He pulled on the chain, but it simply held; there was no more give in it. What if he was supposed to swim down the chain? The wheel might be deep below the water. The thought of trying to swim in the dark through unseen currents that wanted to throw him under the weir scared him silly. He was a good swimmer, but that was really asking for trouble. However, no other option presented itself. He had to learn to trust his instincts; surely that was what this was all about? This time he couldn't tell if his instincts were leading him towards or away from swimming down the chain.

"Pass the bar."

Deep in thought, Billy had failed to notice that Robert had not been idle on top of the weir. A slim trapdoor was now lying open and he was flat on his front, with his right arm delving deep into the weir. Billy was displeased with himself; he was hardly covering himself in glory here.

"I think I'm supposed to do this bit," said Billy, feeling every bit as clumsy as he sounded.

Robert looked up in confusion. "Don't be stupid. I'm right here, I can feel a kind of cog, with a missing place for that bar. Pass it over."

He was outgunning him at every turn: the chain, how it worked with the boat, and now the completion of the task. It was only the tiniest part of Billy's mind that spoke up: wasn't this just a bit too easy? He shook off his doubt along with his ego and passed Robert the bar, and then made to join him on the wall.

"Look, there isn't enough room. Just give me a minute."

Robert took the bar that he had placed by him and transferred it to his right arm, once again delving into the guts of the weir. He looked up, eyes widening. "Got it!"

There was a dull clank from inside the wall, then Robert yelled out and looked up at Billy in horror.

Billy leapt to his feet. "What is it? Is your arm trapped?"

"It just fell away."

Anger flashed through Billy; they couldn't afford to mess this up. He took a step towards Robert. As he did, there was another dull tone, quieter and deeper.

Robert gave a soft whistle. "That was a long drop, this thing is really deep."

Before he could reply, they both heard another, mechanised noise, rising up through the trap door and from under the water itself, which had begun to spit and froth. The sound rose then fell and the water settled back. Then, from somewhere deep within the workings of the weir, they heard a sound like an enormous metal lock falling into place. The chain started to move in Billy's hands.

"Whoa!" said Robert. "You'd better get up here."

Billy shook his head. "No. I think you'd better get back in the boat."

The chain, which had begun by spooling slowly out like a fish nibbling at a line, now gathered pace. Within the weir, the sound of paddles turning through water began, as though a steamboat was approaching. Robert realised where the sound was coming from, and looked over to the far side of the structure. He looked back at Billy with disbelief.

"Waterwheels. The weir's sprung loads of 'em. At least six."

"Get back in the boat!"

"You get out of the boat."

Billy looked back at the chain, and towards the church bank where it was joined. He wondered how long it would take before it ran out of slack, and what might happen when it did. Before he could think further, there was a massive cracking sound. Robert went pale; the noise had definitely come from the weir, and Billy was sure that he must have felt that through his feet.

"I think I'll get back in the boat now," said Robert, moving at once, hopping past Billy to the seat with the tiller to steer.

"Get the chain out of the turning block," said Billy, looking back at the graveyard wall. The chain had started to become visible through the water. Whatever was pulling this was doing so with great force; the chain must weigh tonnes. "Now would be good."

Robert, seeing the chain clear the water, didn't need telling twice. "Get it out of the front too."

The fairlead had a decent grip on the chain, and Billy was trying to twist it out. It wouldn't come, and he could feel the tension in the chain increasing every second. "Give me some slack."

Robert looked up and dropped the links in his hands. "Too late. Get this side of the chain!"

"What?"

"This side, this side. Get this side!"

Looking up, Billy could see what Robert meant; if the chain snapped tight, he would be pinned and crushed against the boat. The boat lurched around, its aft being dragged sideways through the water.

Robert was on the right side of the chain. "Move, Billy, now move, move, move!"

At the last moment, Billy managed to duck as the chain snapped tight above him. He could feel the water churning with the paddles through the bottom of the boat. As he sat up, the world seemed to sway. No, not the world, the weir. It was beginning to rise up out of the water, fooling his perspective. The boat was still being pulled sideways in the water, but as the wall rose, it exposed the mechanics responsible for this feat. A series of waterwheels were providing the power, spurred on by the massive amount of water passing. A mixture of concrete and heavy timber arms was falling into the space left above the waterwheels, tumbling and sealing against the water.

Billy saw the chain continue to tighten as it was lifted into the air. He realised that one of the waterwheels was winding the chain in, like thread on a bobbin. He had a flash of understanding. It was supposed to be a brake, a limit to stop the weir from rising too far. But the wall by the church was old, and the pressure of the water driving this mechanism had to be immense. He realised he wanted them to be well away from the chain if it decided to let go.

"We've got to go," said Billy. "Right now."

Robert looked back at him and pointed at the chain above their heads. "With what?"

With the weir climbing behind them, there was no way for them to escape other than swimming, which would leave them even more vulnerable. Moving together, they kicked the boat away from the weir and stuck their hands over the side, trying to paddle the heavy boat away from the danger area. Billy fought hard against the water. At least with the water blocked against the weir, there was no more current to fight, just a sort of static boiling which had no particular direction.

A huge metallic report from the far side of the river told them they were too late. Looking up, they saw the colossal chain rear up like an angry cobra. Behind them the waterwheels accelerated, increasing the noise and rate of ascent of the wall. The chain arced like a bull-whip before plummeting back to the river. Spotting its trajectory, Robert let out a scream. A split second later, the gnarled end of the chain bit into the prow of the boat, sending splintered wood in all directions.

Like a hooked fish, the boat skipped and spun about, nearly throwing them both into the black water. Now free of the brake chain, the weir was rising with colossal speed. Looking over his shoulder, Billy saw the unseen weir climb above the neighbouring locks. He looked back towards the church. The water level had climbed into the graveyard, and was still rising. This wasn't magic, this was an ancient device designed to flood Marlow.

The boat lurched again. The slack on the chain had now run out.

"Hold on," said Robert, winding his arm underneath the seat.

The chain hoisted the boat out of the water, and as the waterwheels continued to turn, pulled it quickly into the air. Billy found himself standing, shaking, next to Robert, clinging to the seat as the boat turned gently in the air.

"Should we jump?"

Billy shook his head. In every boat-related disaster story he had seen on television, no matter how wrecked the craft looked, it was the people who left their vessel that ended up as fish food. Some seconds later, he knew the boat wouldn't be getting much higher in the air. The old wood of the prow creaked with the strain. It gave quietly and the boat fell straight down. For a second, Billy thought it was going to land the right way up, but it bobbed and stumbled before pushing them into the water headfirst and covering them.

Billy popped up, spitting out gobs of black river water. He'd floated up underneath the upturned boat. It should have been pitch black but with the prow ripped open, light crept into the space.

Robert was already there, coughing up his share of the River Thames. "Great idea, Billy, let's go out and drown ourselves."

He had a fair point. This was too much to ask of an old friend, let alone a recent enemy. However, yelling at each other was pointless.

"Get over this side," said Billy. "We can kick the boat back."

"Upside down? Why don't we just swim for it?"

"Too far, and you don't know what the flooding water will do. We've got to stick with the boat."

Robert bobbed underneath the seat to get beside Billy. He seemed to have found his old temper. "How high do you think the river will flood?"

"I don't know," said Billy, wondering why that fact bothered him. "Well, over the bridge, I suppose."

"Brilliant. Fantastic."

"What's the problem here?" said Billy, momentarily oblivious to the upturned boat and the rising water level.

"You're not the only person in Marlow avoiding the police," said Robert. "I don't want to spend Christmas in social care."

This opened up more questions than Billy could deal with. Without another word, they both started to kick, pushing against the submerged seat. To their collective relief, it began to work. The boat was moving, and even better, they could make out their direction through the shattered prow.

"It's working," said Robert, sounding cheerier.

Billy upped the pace, and Robert matched it.

"Go for the church, that will have the shallowest landing point."

Robert looked through the prow. "I don't think that's going to be a problem."

Looking closer through the split timbers, Billy could see he was right. They were basically just steering now, as the water was pouring around the wall and then back towards town, and they were approaching the church at speed. He hoped Mike hadn't been planning a late service, as the floor of the church would certainly be underwater by now. The speed picked up again, and now they were almost holding on to the seat as the boat dragged them along.

A blinding pain shot up Billy's right shin. It felt like he'd been bitten by stone, and his thoughts shifted to the Gargoyle. It was made of stone, surely it couldn't swim? Robert yelled out and looked down into the water.

"You too?"

"Yeah, bashed my leg on something really hard," said Robert, still peering down.

Billy was already fishing into his pocket, hoping that the knuckleduster hadn't got lost in all the chaos. It hadn't, and remained in his zipped breast pocket.

"Gravestones," said Robert softly. "We're only walking on the tops of gravestones."

Billy felt the boat lift on another rising wave of water, and now they were far enough above the slabs not to risk their legs any further. Billy was struggling hard to see through the open prow. He had a nasty feeling that the boat was heading towards the park, where he'd last strayed into the path of the grey beast.

"I think we should drop off the boat," said Billy.

Robert now had an arm over the seat trying to hold on in the fast-moving water. "If we leave the boat, we'll be swept away."

It was clear Robert was right, but it didn't stop Billy's heart sinking, as passing oak trunks confirmed they were now in Higginson Park. This task was beginning to rumble out of control. What was it Senga had said to imply that this one was going to get noticed? He couldn't quite remember, but thought that the strange creature was a master of understatement. This was the biggest event Marlow had seen for many years. All the riverside properties near town would be flooded, as well as probably all the shops in the High Street. He imagined the punters streaming out of the pubs, trying to move their cars before the wave made them simply turn away and leave the vehicles to the tender mercies of the insurance companies.

The boat swung hard, slewing them to one side, before loud bangs could be heard on the outside of the hull. They were hitting fixed objects again. They lurched, and a wide shaft of metal plunged through the open prow. The higher end of a seesaw had caught the boat, stopping it dead. Now the water was trying to pull them from underneath the boat, but with the metal seesaw they had much more to hang onto. Within a minute, they had both clambered around so that whilst still under the boat, most of their weight was supported by the seesaw, eliminating the risk of being taken by the river.

"I think we made it," said Billy, puffing with the exertion.

Robert looked back at him with an exhausted smile.

The first crash made them both yell in shock. The second plunged the boat down deep into the water, making them hold their breath momentarily underwater, before it bobbed back up.

Robert looked across at Billy, stunned. "What the hell was that?"

Billy thought he had a good idea, and was already fighting the zip on his pocket. The wood splintered between him and Robert, and the remains of the left arm of the Gargoyle burst into the boat. Robert cried out as a piece of wood struck and stunned him. The stone arm withdrew. Try as Billy might, the zip wouldn't budge. He kept at it, hoping that it hadn't been bent at some point during the task. It gave an inch and he sneaked a finger into the pocket, trying to snag the knuckles. Above him he could hear stone claws scrabbling for purchase on the slippery hull of the boat. His index finger slid over the knuckles, but with the first pull he knew the gap in the zip wasn't wide enough. Robert murmured something to him. That was good; if he was murmuring he was also breathing. This time, the good arm of the Gargoyle punched through the hull much closer to Billy. After it had withdrawn its fist, it forced its mouth into the hole, and roared, spraying sulphurous fumes over them both.

This brought Robert around in a hurry. "What the hell is it?"

"Really bad news," said Billy, fighting with the pocket and the knuckles.

The Gargoyle's arm fell closer to Robert, catching him with both wood and stone this time. He moaned, in a weak way that scared Billy. Having made three holes in the boat, the Gargoyle now seemed to be trying to rip out slats lengthwise, peeling back the wood to leave them open to attack from its jaws. The knuckles finally released themselves from the pocket and snapped around Billy's hand, and as he made a fist, the flat blade snapped out of the metal. The boat lurched down once again, sending him sprawling into the water under the boat. He looked up and saw the Gargoyle's left stump in the gaping hole it had made. Before he could find his feet, the right paw was in and grabbed Robert around the neck. The Gargoyle looked briefly at Billy, almost grinning, and was then gone, dragging its prize behind it.

Full of guilt and fury, Billy roared and found his feet. He had to dip underwater to get out from under the boat, but once out, the water was just below waist height. A noise coming from the water took his attention deeper into the park. The Gargoyle was making slow progress on its hind legs, which was good, but it was also dragging Robert underwater, and that wasn't good at all.

"Get back here! Coward!"

The Gargoyle stopped and turned back to face him. He was still holding Robert under the water, and was watching Billy's reaction to his companion's weakening struggle. Billy paused, eyeing Robert and the Gargoyle alternately. He gambled, letting all expression leave his face. He shrugged his shoulders. What did he care if Robert drowned? An unpleasant sneer snaked across the Gargoyle's face. It raised an eyebrow; it knew this game. Billy fought to keep his face neutral. He relaxed his fist and let the flat blade fall back into the knuckles. Moving slowly, the Gargoyle raised its right arm, lifting Robert out of the water. Robert half spluttered, half screamed in fear. Still, Billy remained impassive. The Gargoyle looked from Robert to Billy and then back to Robert, then just as slowly as it had raised him, it pushed him back under the water.

"No, Billy, help, please…"

The water took his voice. Billy knew the strength of that arm; the other had held him over the church steeple with almost no effort. He also knew that this time the Gargoyle wouldn't bring Robert back up. He screamed and rushed at the beast as fast as he could through the waist-high water. The Gargoyle walked backwards, still holding Robert underwater, moving quickly. Billy knew that it wouldn't get tired, and already wading through the water was sapping his remaining strength. The Gargoyle was beginning to increase the distance between them. Billy yelled in frustration. He had dragged Robert into this, and he was going to get him killed.

Then, something stopped the Gargoyle; for a moment, it was clearly distracted. It stooped, this time dragging Robert, screaming, from the water. His arms were wrapped around a fence post. A half-drowned Robert had somehow managed to slow the beast.

It was enough. Billy didn't hesitate, but leapt onto the Gargoyle's right shoulder, struggling to weaken his hold on Robert. It swung at him with the stump of its left arm. It connected and he was lifted clean out of the water, before falling down hard on his hands and knees, spitting the water out, gasping for breath. As Billy scrambled back to his feet, the Gargoyle plunged Robert under water again. But this time Robert had a lungful of air, and strength enough to lock his arm around the fence post again. In its effort to drag him away, the Gargoyle once again pulled him out of the water.

"Get him!"

Prepared this time for the left stump, Billy ducked beneath it, and slammed his knuckled fist into the Gargoyle's ribs. Its roar of pain poured sulphur over them both. Robert roared back, and suddenly realised he was free. He turned, planning to fight the beast with Billy.

"Get back, get back!" Billy shouted. "Just run."

And now the Gargoyle advanced on Billy, eyeing the knuckles, but baying for blood. It meant to finish him. Stone claws sprang out of its right fist, and Billy felt his stomach sink. This wasn't going to be pretty. With speed beyond belief, the Gargoyle was on him and struck, back-fisted, with its good arm. Again, Billy was knocked up out of the water, screaming in terror and pain. As he found his feet, he knew it would be only seconds before it was on him again. He heard the rush of forced water and looked up at the stone eyes intent on killing him. Suddenly, the Gargoyle stumbled, struggled for balance and then fell roaring at Billy's side. He didn't waste the advantage and brought a huge sweeping punch down on the beast's head.

Through the knuckles he felt a crack and a shudder. It had been a blinding punch; perhaps fatal? It raised its head again, looking confused. Billy yelled and swung his fist again. Again a fissure spoke through the knuckles: this stone would split. And now the Gargoyle roared, and tried to stand and walk away, instead stumbled again. Robert surfaced behind it, holding up the wires of the fence. He'd snagged the Gargoyle's legs, and was using the strength of the metal to hold it at bay.

"Kill it, Billy! Kill it!"

And Billy was on the Gargoyle again. But it was still fast and it turned, grabbing him again by the neck with its right arm, and flipped him straight underwater. He saw Robert jump on its back, only to be shrugged off with almost no effort. Turning back to him, the Gargoyle began to crush his throat, and then pushed its huge head underwater to stare at him as it shook the air from his lungs. Terminal lights danced in front of his eyes; he was running out of air and energy fast. Robert jumped back on the Gargoyle, and the beast flinched for an instant. It was all Billy needed. Remembering the line of the fissure, he punched the flat blade of the knuckles into the beast, along the snout. This time he didn't need to feel the crack open. He could see it.

The Gargoyle pulled back, lifting Billy from the water and up into the air. It screamed in fear and pain, and it was finally the sound of the scream that split its head in two. One half peeled away, leaving the other twitching and flinching and trying to function. Billy felt the grip on his throat release and he fell back into the water, all energy spent. He heard the beast scamper around, lost and probably unsure whether it was dead or alive. And now Billy was moving, being dragged back through the water, towards the entrance to town. He looked back and saw that it was Robert who was pulling him away from the noise, and the pain and the remnants of the fight.

AS BILLY REGAINED CONSCIOUSNESS, HE found that Robert had dragged them onto the bonnet of a silver Range Rover, allowing them to sit clear of the water. Above them the clouds continued to darken, and the breeze was picking up, shaking the branches in the park.

Billy looked over at Robert, who was beginning to shiver. "Thanks for getting me out of there."

"Thanks for killing it," said Robert. "I can't believe you were able to hit it so hard. I'm bloody glad we didn't have that fight properly now."

Billy hated to think what would have happened if he had attacked him with the knuckles; he probably would have killed him. "Are you sure it's dead?"

"It looked like it was wandering off to die," said Robert. "What was it anyway? It felt like stone, but stone can't move like that."

How was he to explain this? "It's a mythical creature, a gargoyle, but I don't think you can tell anyone."

"Who the hell would believe me anyway?"

They sat with their backs against the windscreen. Billy felt a surge of relief at the completion of the task, but even more at the prospect that he'd seen the last of the Gargoyle. Robert didn't seem in the mood for asking any awkward questions, but now Billy had one of his own.

"Why would you go into care if the police caught up with you?"

Robert took a breath and frowned. "'Cause there's no one at home to look after me. Both my parents disappeared six months before your dad did."

Despite his exhaustion, Billy felt his attention gripped. "But I never heard about that."

"Nobody cares," said Robert, his voice even. "Not about another low-rent family which has fallen apart. Happens all the time, it isn't news."

"But you must have let someone know. You tried to find out what happened?"

"There's two possibilities. Either they disappeared like your dad did, with no reason," said Robert, looking sick to his stomach, "or my brother did them in."

Billy looked at him in disbelief. That couldn't be.

"He owed a lot of money to the wrong people. After my folks disappeared, those people stopped coming around. And Alex became…"

"…Alex."

"Yeah. I know how it sounds, but I've gone over everything."

Billy didn't know what to think. His own mind had imagined hundreds of scenarios to explain what had happened to his father, some of them a lot more outlandish than Robert's bleak theory.

"Stay right where you are!"

They both looked over the road to the churchyard. A lone police officer was wading through the sunken grave-yard across the road.

"Were you two on the weir tonight?"

Billy looked at Robert. He only had one more task to complete, he mustn't be caught. And even if he did now trust Robert, how could he ever explain this in time?

Robert looked over at him, seeming both weary and almost relieved. "I know something is going on," he said. "I'll take this one. Just wait a minute before you start to run."

Billy had no clue what he meant. Robert stood up and offered his finger and a grin to the police officer, whose face turned sour, then turned back to the car. Before Billy even had a chance to move, Robert raised his right foot and brought it down hard on the windscreen, cracking it from top to bottom.

Billy rolled forward, shocked. "What the hell are you doing?"

From across the road, the man in blue bellowed something pretty unpleasant. Without answering him, Robert simply lifted his foot and stove in the windscreen, completely covering the interior of the Range Rover with thick chunks of broken safety glass. He looked at Billy. "Let him come for me before you run."

With that he was off, running over the line of car roofs that led up to the High Street.

Unsure who to chase, the police officer turned to Billy. "Stay right where you are. I've got your description, so you won't get far."

With that, he continued to wade through the water after Robert, who had an amazing head start. As soon as the police officer had made it to the roundabout at the bottom of the High Street, Billy slid off the bonnet of the car into the water, and waded across the road. As he did, blue flashing lights arrived at the top of the High Street. Robert was silhouetted briefly on the roof of one of the cars. For a moment, Billy stopped, wondering if there was anything he could do to help. Then he remembered his tasks; he still had a chance to save his father. He turned and waded as quietly as he could up Station Road, the elation of the victory over the Gargoyle eclipsed by the wrench of leaving Robert to his fate.

By the time he got to Glade Road he began to wonder if he was going to make it home at all. The wind had whipped up, and it had begun to rain. He had thought it was too cold to rain. Why wasn't it snowing? He pushed his chin down into his bony chest and wrapped his arms tight about him. Growling through his big teeth, Billy focussed on the pavement, still looking over his shoulder for the dreaded blue lights. The water here was only knee-deep, and he thought the police might risk a patrol car to catch the boy who had flooded Marlow.

As he turned onto Little Marlow Road, he knew this was no ordinary storm. He could see the edges of the ever-green trees catch the rain and freeze instantly. Long wind-swept icicles were forming on lampposts, and the surface of the pavement had become treacherous. He'd left the lipped edge of the flooding behind and was now rattling with the cold. He shook his head, and ice particles fell out of his hair. A memory surfaced from a geography lesson where he'd learned about ice storms. If this was what they were like, Billy thought, the Canadians could keep them.

Turning into Marlow Bottom provided relief because it meant that he was probably clear of the police. They would likely be dealing with the twin problems of flooding and severe storms. None of this mattered much to Billy now. His trousers, soaked from the task, were now crunching each time he moved. He'd already lost pain, or any other sensation from his legs, which made walking like trying to balance on low stilts. The scrap of comfort he took was that he was just one task from completion. Billy held onto that thought all the way back to his house.

For the second time in as many days, Billy plunged into the bath fully clothed. His ice trousers briefly miti-gated the hot water, but the inevitable pain followed almost at once. Too exhausted to fight it, he simply laid back, grimacing, and let the frozen muscles scream as they unwound in the steaming bathtub. As it became easier to move, he pulled the sodden clothes off, fumbling at the buttons with gnarled, tired fingers. Large welts rose from just above the knuckles on his right hand. Smashing solid brass into stone had taken its toll. He was sure that by tomorrow it would have seized up properly. For the first time since making it home, he began to wonder whether Robert had been given a chance to warm up yet.

Another thought struck him. He hadn't checked to see if the Tree had returned. Jumping up out of the bath, ignoring the howls from various muscle groups, he threw a towel around his waist and limped downstairs. The bucket was still there, but there was no sign of Teàrlag.

"What are you doing? You're dripping, Billy."

His mother stood in the hallway, concern breaking through her grey bubble.

"Having a bath, Mum," said Billy, sidling past her to the stairs and checking that his towel was safely arranged.

"The Tree has gone."

Billy started up the stairs and away from the questions. "That's right. Mr. Shaw has taken it back for repairs."

He knew his mother was looking after him, probably with disbelief, but he also knew that in all likelihood within another ten seconds or so, she would withdraw again, probably for the rest of the evening. He wished that Saul was still here to comfort her and bring her out of herself. He paused by a window at the top of the landing. Outside the wind howled, trees froze and icy rain mixed with clumps of snow.

❧ Christmas Eve ❧

The mobile woke him at the stroke of midnight. At once, he was aware of two things: he was warm again and in tremendous pain. The latter made itself known when he reached out to stop the whistle of the mobile alarm. The pain started in his right hand, which was predictable enough, but as he twisted, it followed through his back, hips and legs. He had been sleeping in full pyjamas, dressing gown and slippers in order to restore his core temperature. He loosened the belt of the dressing gown to let his back relax, allowing him to sit up. Even though Teàrlag's absence had played heavily on his mind, sleep had found him with relative ease. Now, despite the stiffness and physical exertion, he felt mentally restored, and ready to take on the final task, whatever it proved to be.

Standing in the living room, Billy poured his fresh mental energy into watching the clock as it ticked around to twelve minutes past twelve. The Tree had not returned, but as long as it was back before the usual time, then he could just accept the task, take it on and wait on the doorstep for his father on Christmas Day.

The clock on the mantelpiece swung past twelve past twelve. Billy turned and observed the empty bucket. With his energy waning, he thought there was nothing else to do but turn and head back to bed. As he did, dark thoughts gnawed at him. What if Teàrlag was too ill to return to Marlow Bottom? Senga knew full well that he hadn't kissed Katherine. Had she forbidden her from returning? What if Teàrlag had died? There was nothing to do but hope that tomorrow the Tree would return.

BILLY CHEWED ON COLD TOAST. It had got cold because he'd kept nipping into the living room to make sure that the bucket was still empty. His mother had come down and felt his forehead. It was clear he wasn't looking his best, and he'd not managed to find a decent excuse for his swollen, angry-looking right hand. It was for this reason he was having toast and not cereal, toast being relatively easy to eat ambidextrously. His mother came back down with the thermometer. He rolled his eyes, but accepted the glass tube. It felt like the old days, with the lines between them more clearly established. As he waited for the thermometer to register that he didn't have a fever, his mother left the kitchen, before returning with an old white box. It was the box which held the Christmas glasses.

"I've made a decision, Billy," she said with her hands shaking. "For us. I think it's time we both moved on. I know I've been very hard work this year."

Billy rolled the thermometer out of his mouth, not liking the tone of this one bit. "No Mum."

"I have, I know I have. But now we're going to move on, because we can't carry on for another year like this."

She lifted out one of the glasses and held it up to the light, watching the colours being split by the crystal, before raising it high above her head. Realising she was about to smash it into the sink, Billy dove forwards and caught her arm as it swung down. Pain flashed through his bruised hand but he held it there until she stopped pushing. He looked around, trying to catch her eye, but she just looked out to the hall, not wanting to connect.

"Don't, Mum. Please. Just give it till tomorrow. I think we ought to give him a year."

"Most of the set is broken, anyway. Billy, I have to stop pretending. I think we need to stop pretending."

"I haven't been pretending," he tried to shift so he could take the glass. "Not once, not yet. We have to give him a year."

His mother slowly relinquished her grip on the glass. "How did you get so strong?"

Billy took the glass and placed it back in the box. He turned to find himself alone in the kitchen. If he managed to find a way to complete the final task, well, then there was a chance that he could relight those eyes the way Saul had briefly done. His father could manage that, and within a day there was still hope he could put them both together again. He put the box on top of the cupboard, out of easy reach of his mother, and continued to chomp through the toast.

The missing bike was bothering him; they'd had anti-theft numbers etched into the frames. If the police found his mother's bike, they'd be able to trace it back to their house in no time. If it happened to be the police officer who had tried to collar him with Robert, he'd be sunk.

Though sunk probably best described the bike's current condition. With no Tree, and no task, he thought he'd soak up some time seeing how the town was coping. It would also give him a chance to pass Robert's house and see if he had made it home.

It was snowing heavily when he walked out the front door. The light was bouncing off unfamiliar edges and angles, filling Billy's eyes and making it hard for him not to smile at the difference made by the fresh covering. The first few steps confirmed that the ice storm had made the perfect bed for the snow. Billy locked his legs trying to control an unplanned skid, the snow collecting around his ankles finally stopping him.

The first snowfall in the days leading up to the Tree's arrival had seen a barrage of kids forming snow battle formations. Today, he had to negotiate several hotspots and demilitarised areas on his way into Marlow, which he managed with varying degrees of success. The instincts of a thirteen-year-old swam up within him. They felt odd; he hadn't had much time to spend on being a kid of late. But given he was in no particular hurry, he spent time helping a couple of kids who were pinned down by a larger gang. Billy took more than his fair share of hits to help the younger group on their way, getting booed by the larger gang when their prey was set free. Billy just smiled at them, and sent impressive volleys of snowballs back by way of reply. It was nice to have a practical use for his ridiculous limbs.

Halfway to town he turned up Oak Tree Road, towards Robert's house. He had never thought of him as quick thinking or courageous before, but last night had changed that completely. Understanding what had happened to Robert's parents also put their history in perspective. He hoped the police hadn't complicated things with his brother, but it was difficult to see how they wouldn't have. As he approached the house, the lights were out, with curtains open. Several knocks at the door confirmed that no one was at home. Billy returned his hands to his pockets against the cold.

"Hey Billy."

Robert had appeared from nowhere. He was leaning against a car just outside his driveway. Inside the car was a woman Billy didn't recognise. Smiling, he ran up to the grinning Robert.

"What happened to you?"

"I got away! They were so slow it was easy."

"Really?"

Robert shrugged and smiled. "Not my first time at avoiding arrest."

Billy felt a huge weight lift from him. "I'm so glad you're not spending Christmas inside!"

"I'm not spending it here either. Alex has disappeared, so Olly's Mum is just bringing me around for fresh clothes. I'm staying over there until the New Year."

Billy smiled and slung an arm around his shoulder.

"Gerroff!" said Robert, but he couldn't disguise his smile.

"Thanks for last night. I'll never forget all you did."

"Don't suppose I will either," said Robert. "What is next for you?"

"This and that," said Billy. "If I'm lucky, I might get a Christmas too."

Robert looked straight at him. "If you need any more help, you only have to ask."

Billy smiled. "I think I'm on my own from this point."

Olly's mother honked the horn and then waved an apology to the boys.

"I think I've got to go," said Robert.

"Merry Christmas."

Robert looked a bit more serious. "Yeah Merry Christmas, Billy. But you watch your back, OK?"

Billy raised his eyes, nodded, and walked on towards town.

AS HE MOVED CLOSER TO the High Street, it was clear that nothing like normality was returning. Large unmanned roadblocks sat pointlessly, preventing non-existent traffic from approaching unusable roads. The ice storm had been brutal, freezing over the flood that Billy and Robert had created. As he stepped onto the lip of the frozen flood, he expected to hear the shrill creaks of cracking ice, but there was no sound at all. The ice had frozen fast and deep; no ordinary storm this. He cut down Glade Road, and then Station Road, retracing his steps from last night.

The level of the frozen floodwater had crept up slowly until it began to swallow cars, and street level was now about the same height as door handles. Billy tried to imagine what it would be like attempting to open the front doors of one of these houses. If they did manage to open, would they see a rush of water, or a clear cross-section of ice?

The town was busier than Billy had expected, but this was good news, as more people meant more cover. Breakdown recovery teams walked up and down the High Street, explaining with amazing patience that "recovery to home" was impossible when the car was encased in four feet of ice. Halfway down the High Street, a tall woman in blue and white Lycra had pulled back the roof of her purple MG convertible, and was waiting patiently for the next free breakdown crew. She was sitting on the folded canopy, staring dejectedly at the block of ice that was the interior of her car. Billy wasn't surprised to see people dressed this way in Marlow, regardless of the weather; rowers tended to appear oblivious to the elements, and she had the look of a professional. As he passed her, she answered her mobile with a Scottish accent.

"Yes, I know I'm late for training. No, I'm not ill... Well, you know my medals? Yes, the Olympic ones. I left them in the car last night and you won't believe what has..."

Billy walked past the rower, feeling no small pang of guilt. He looked along the street to see how others were coping.

The shops were making a brave attempt to stay open. Standing in their doorways, shopkeepers were taking orders from customers at the step, retrieving goods out of the shop and passing them up to the new street level. There was a happy noise from the customers as they dealt with the unusual conditions and chatted about how they would not be put off simply because of the weather. The shop owners were smiling and shaking hands with them. Despite feeling responsible for the trouble, however unintended, Billy had to admit that compared to the previous day, when people were fighting each other for every potential present, this felt a lot more like Christmas. You could practically taste the goodwill.

As he moved on towards the bridge, he turned his attention to the police. With both residents and businesses inside the flood-berg, it wasn't practical for them to cordon off the town. Instead, they patrolled up and down the High Street. Nearer the church, three officers were paying close attention to an object on the ground. It struck Billy that it might be the body of the Gargoyle, encased in ice. Poor Mike would have to answer difficult questions about how it came to leave the steeple of his church. He made his way towards them, while staying out of their line of sight.

He realised what the police were guarding as he drew closer. His mother's bike was locked in the ice, rear wheel up to the sky, as if it had fallen from a plane and smashed through the pavement. Why was the bike so interesting to them? It seemed suspicious that with the High Street full of some of the most expensive cars in the country, it was his mother's bicycle that needed three police officers to look after it. His stomach sank further. The identification etchings; it would take them no time to work out where he lived.

"Lost something, Billy?"

Mike appeared at his shoulder, continuing his knack for making him jump.

"My mother's bike," said Billy, glad of the cover he offered.

"They seem quite interested in it."

"Don't they."

"If I sort this out, you're really going to have to start telling me what is going on."

"I'll tell you tomorrow. I can tell anyone after tomorrow."

Mike looked at Billy. "I can't very well stop helping you at this point. Come on."

Billy felt a surge of gratitude for the vicar as he followed him across the road and towards the waiting police.

"Ah, you've found my bike," said Mike opening his arms wide. "I was certain it would be at the bottom of the river."

"*Your* bike you say, vicar?" said the oldest police officer.

"That's right. I'd left it beside the church last night, I'd thought it was gone; can you get it out?"

The police officer looked at Billy over Mike's shoulder. "By the church last night, you say?"

"Well yes, I was actually...well, I was in the pub when the weir broke."

"We'd had reports of two boys riding a bike like this, and another of two boys on the weir before it went," said the officer. "And as you can see, this bike hasn't been locked." He took a step towards Mike and Billy. "And this bike is a woman's bike."

Billy was approaching real panic. He had one task to complete before finishing, and the last thing he needed was problems with the police.

Mike put on his broadest smile. "I think you'll find that most vicars prefer these bikes. It's the uniform, you see? Makes swinging your legs rather tricky. And as for the lock, I always let God decide who needs the bike most. And well, it hasn't strayed far." The officer was somewhat deflated by this. Mike put a shoulder on his arm. "Perhaps you could see your way to trying to free it for me? I'd really be grateful. I have rather a large beat myself, and this is my busy season."

The officer regained some of his civic instincts. "We'll get it back for you, vicar. Just give us a few minutes."

Mike led a dumbstruck Billy away from the scene, and they paused outside the gate of the church.

"That was really slick."

"All part of the service," said Mike with a smile that quickly slipped away. "I see my boat has gone."

Billy suddenly felt awful. He hadn't even thought of this, and after Mike had offered him the combination too.

"I hope all this," said Mike, nodding over his shoulder at the High Street, "is worth whatever it is that you are up to."

Unexpected tears threatened Billy's eyes. "I hope so too."

"Just tell me about it sometime. I have had strange things happen, I won't judge you."

"I know, I believe you, I just don't think I'm allowed to. Not till it's over," said Billy. "But I will then, I promise."

"You still got your key to the vestry?"

Billy nodded; it was hidden with the knuckles and the axe.

"Next time you're passing, you can pick up the bike. I think I had better take it for now."

Billy nodded and smiled at Mike, not knowing quite how to thank him.

"And Billy?"

"Yes?"

"Merry Christmas."

AS BILLY WALKED HOME, THE sky became black and Marlow became whiter still.

He opened the kitchen door, enjoying the warm air on his face. He shook his head, sending snow left and right. His feet made an unpleasant grinding noise on the stone floor. Billy assumed he'd caught a piece of flint in the tread of his boots. As he looked down, he saw how wrong this was. Shards of broken crystal were strewn over the floor. The empty white box on the side confirmed his fears. His mother must have come back down while he was out. He felt sick. He knew his father hadn't believed in the glasses, but for his mother to do this after he'd begged her not to made him feel wretched. He went to the cupboard, took out a dustpan and broom, and began to sweep the bright splinters into the empty cardboard box.

"Billy? Is that you?"

He didn't look up, but kept sweeping.

"Billy?"

At her quiet moan, he did look up. She was clutching at the door frame, wide-eyed and unsteady. He realised instantly that she hadn't broken the glasses.

"But you said we were to keep them?"

Billy held up the brush in shock.

"I didn't do this!"

Another thought hit him hard. If neither of them had done this, then who had been in the house? There was no way the glasses could have worked themselves over the edge. Besides, the box was open on the sideboard, top facing upwards. Someone would have had to take them out one by one. But who, or what? Billy pushed past her, into the living room. There was the smell of pine needles, but no Tree. He turned and ran upstairs to his room.

Snow blew in through the open window, and without hesitating Billy lifted the blanket covering the axe, knuckleduster and key. To his huge relief, they were still there. He slipped on the knuckles and paused for a second, thinking hard. The Gargoyle might have survived after all. "She is mine" could still refer to his mother. But if it had got in the house, without himself or Teàrlag here, why hadn't it simply taken her then? Billy shut the window, and then checked all of the upstairs rooms. There were no signs of intruders.

He slipped the knuckles off his hand, though only as far as an easy pocket, and headed back downstairs. After checking the study and living room, he found his mother in the kitchen, finishing the sweeping that Billy had started. She lifted the box of crystal shards and looked into it, tilting it this way and that. From the doorway, Billy saw the reflected light from the shards play off his mother's eyes.

"It's OK, Billy. Really. I mean, I was going to do the same this morning."

This wasn't fair. "I didn't do this. I'd just got in when you came down, and they'd already been smashed."

"It really doesn't matter."

"It matters that you don't believe me."

His mother turned to him, now failing to hold back her tears. "I believed you this morning, when you said we should give Tom a year, and we should not smash these glasses."

Torn between fury and pity, Billy knew his only defence at this point was to let her believe what she pleased. He didn't look up when she walked past him, or for several minutes afterwards.

SITTING ON THE RED CHAIR next to the spot where Teàrlag no longer stood, Billy was thinking about his mother's accusation. He hadn't gone back upstairs, preferring to keep a floor between them. It was now after six, and he was certain that she wouldn't be back down until the next day. The knuckleduster remained in his pocket, though he was beginning to doubt that the Gargoyle had been through the house at all. If it had, he was sure there would be telltale signs, such as a large hole in the wall, to give it away. Perhaps he hadn't put the glasses away carefully enough? The loss of an item that could be traced back to the day his parents married made him feel terrible. All he could do was try to focus on the tasks, on his chance to return his father, but without the Tree how could he be set a task? His eyes were fixed on the slow-burning candle on the mantelpiece; the flame was small but constant.

Time drifted and his thoughts turned back to his father, to the time he'd been sitting in this chair waiting for him to return with the milk. On that occasion, the clock had also ticked slowly; the relentless beats marking the impending descent of his family. His mother kept coming in from the kitchen to peer through the large living room window; growing ever more concerned, making sure that he hadn't taken the car, making sure he hadn't said anything of significance.

The questions would soon come thick and fast, from many more people than just his mother. It would still be some time until the awful questions that he would pose himself began to arrive. Was his father with another woman? Had he left them for another family? Had he been run over? Was there a ditch left in Marlow that he could ride past without checking for a scrap of clothing— or worse, a scrap of him? Each question would ratchet the reality of his absence another notch. It was that which sank his mother. He could see the unanswered questions reach up from the ground and bend her back with their impossible weight. He had decided it was up to him alone not to sink, and keep them from the streets, until his father was found, one way or another.

The Tree had changed everything, and while it hadn't been a comfortable ride, his hope had been ignited with the candle. Hope had been his enemy in those early days, with each false lead becoming a bitter betrayal. It was only now, at nearly nine o'clock, that he began to fear the hope which had returned with the Tree. Hope had pushed him into so many situations in the last few days, and it was focussing and chasing that hope which had helped him survive. The candle was supposed to echo his faith, and now, drawing close to it, he noticed how little remained. He'd survived so much in the time that the wax had become flame. Now he just hoped he would get the chance to attempt to complete the journey.

By ten o'clock, Billy had a route that he was following to mark time. Each rotation took about a minute and a half. Therefore, he would complete seven rotations and the clock would have moved just over ten minutes. The silence was driving him insane. He'd tried humming, but hearing the silence broken only by his own voice was actually worse. So, the rotations became his method, stopping once outside the back door to check the sky, and then at the front for the same reason.

He was coming out of the kitchen when the knock at the door came. Billy paused, frozen; this was it. Another thought held him: Gargoyle or Tree? There was no pane in the door, and no window with a vantage point. He had to open the door to find out who was there. A second knock came, quieter and less sure. Billy checked his pocket for the knuckles, before the door opened.

Katherine stood, pale as the snow around her, blinking in the light. Billy's smile welled up, amazed to see his friend awake. Almost at once his relief at seeing her was replaced by the strong sense that something was not right; she appeared to look straight through him, and it was only the rarest of occasions that she failed to greet him with her smile. She was dressed up well, in a grey duffel coat and gloves, but while Billy had to look through the steam of his own breath, nothing came from her own mouth; she must be frozen. Perhaps the coma was still having some effect on her?

Katherine took a step back and squinted at him. "Billy, is that you?"

He turned off the light; perhaps it was that. "You're awake?"

"I'm not sure. I was told to come here, bring my skates and to give you these."

Katherine held out the tiny decoration skates to Billy and, despite his concern for her, he felt relief wash over him. This was how it was going to happen.

"Did a tree give you these? Have you met Teàrlag?"

Katherine looked over her shoulder at the road. "I don't know, I'm not sure how I got here."

Billy put his smile back on. "I think we're supposed to go skating."

"In the park. That's right.

"Come in while I get changed."

"I think I'm supposed to stay outside."

Again, this didn't seem like Katherine, who was always keen to get into the least visited house in Marlow Bottom. He pulled back the door in case she changed her mind, and then headed in, sprinting up the stairs. He was sure that by trusting in the task he could bring Katherine back.

In his room, he put the key Mike had given him and the knuckles in his zipped pocket, grabbed the axe, and tied the strap of his old school satchel to either end of the axe handle. Then, on a whim, he went to a cupboard on the landing. Reaching for the top shelf, he pulled down his father's gnarled fleece and put it on. He'd done this before and found the smell of him so real, and the reminder so painful, that he'd ripped it off in shock. He returned to his room, wrapped a smaller towel around the axe head, and slung it over his shoulder. If he came across the Gargoyle tonight, he would make sure it would be for the last time.

At the open door, he tried to contain his sense of panic when he realised that Katherine wasn't there. He headed into the garden, dragging the door shut behind him. As his eyes adjusted to the dark, he saw that Katherine was underneath the pear tree, looking up at the sky. He walked through the snow, feet crunching, but not getting her attention. For a moment, as she began to turn, he thought he could see straight through her cheek. The moment passed, and he put it down to her pale face matching the snow-covered branches of the tree. She held up the small decoration for Billy, not questioning how he would put them on, which again was quite unlike the Katherine he knew.

"These are for you."

"Well, you've already got yours," said Billy, pointing at her shoulder bag.

Katherine frowned at the bag, and then at him. "I think we have to go."

"To the park," said Billy, not feeling great about taking his friend anywhere but back home.

He led the way down the path, with Katherine following a few feet behind. As he slung the laces of the decoration over his shoulder, he felt the familiar gain in weight and size for the last time.

THE WALK WAS AWKWARD. EVERY time that Billy slowed so that they could walk side by side, Katherine's pace fell to almost nothing. If he stopped she stopped, gazing up at the sky. So, he'd walk on and eventually hear her steps making time with his. After a while, he took to looking up, if only to see what held her attention. He only noticed when he stopped walking that the clouds above him were racing faster than he'd ever seen before. As they drew nearer to town, even though the power here was out and the streets were dark, it was definitely getting lighter. The whistling clouds were now only whispers, and low in the sky a bright moon began to cast long shadows. They reached the edge of the frozen flood on Station Road.

He couldn't believe how quickly Katherine managed to put her skates on. Having discarded his hiking boots at the edge of the flood, Billy discovered that though the skates had grown, they were still not quite big enough These were supposed to be his magic skates, not some dreadful parody of Cinderella, with him now cast as an ugly stepsister. Over his left shoulder, he heard ice meet metal. He looked over to see Katherine skate up the road and away from him.

"Hey, wait for me!"

He didn't want her to disappear on her own, though he was pleased to see some of her natural impatience returning. Billy growled and pulled at first one boot, then another, until they each gave way. He knew skating wasn't going to be as easy as Katherine made it look.

It also wasn't as hard as he had feared, though he thought he must have looked pretty strange, hands moving from car roof to car roof, with a poorly hidden axe over his shoulder. His worst fear was that when turning into the High Street he'd face the police, but the High Street was abandoned. He began to risk a few feet without a car roof and felt both warmth and a sense of anticipation. After all the trials he'd faced, this one, the one he got to spend alone with Katherine, now beckoned.

At first he feared he'd lost her, and he struggled to catch up. He followed the skate tracks up the High Street and away from the bridge and the park. Katherine was looping around the roundabout at the top of the road, once forwards, once backwards, once turning between both. Billy was so mesmerised by her movements that he skated into the thick end of a lamppost, sprawling over to one side. He picked himself up, careful not to roll his head back anywhere near the teeth of the axe. Katherine hadn't noticed and simply kept making her turns, each new in some small way: a small jump, a turn of her hand.

Judging his speed better, Billy fell in behind Katherine, though still unable to match her easy loops. The roundabout was pierced at the centre by what looked like a small Egyptian Needle. He hoped that they would find a natural rhythm and he might even be able to hold her hand, the missing task ever on his mind. However, in a short time, their loose orbit of the roundabout became erratic. If he put his hand out now he'd send them both flying. The roundabout wasn't large, and soon he felt a light dizziness. With the surrounding drifts of snow and colossal icicles, he was reminded of flying through the clouds with Teàrlag, only here he was steering, albeit badly. Looking up he saw that Katherine had stopped and turned, and to his delight he saw that she was applying the lipstick he had given her.

Not knowing how to slow the skates, Billy back-peddled and immediately found himself sitting down hard. He looked up, and to his amazement, saw a small red smile begin to break from the right side of Katherine's mouth.

"Not as easy as you thought?"

Billy struggled to his feet. "I never thought it was," he said, before falling back in a heap.

"Oh no?" Katherine took two short steps towards Billy, stopping just inches from him with a sharp skid. She offered a hand to steady him as he got back up. To his delight, she didn't take it back once he was standing. Instead, she started to lead them around the roundabout with her cold white hand. The only thing missing was that brief glimpse of her smile.

"You had me scared, you know," said Billy, hoping to coax her back. "Do you remember me speaking to you while you were out?"

"I heard you," said Katherine. "It was like you were in another room, but I heard you."

Billy smiled; she had heard what he had said and she was holding his hand. He would bring her back, he knew he would. The chill from her hand had started to creep up his arm, though he wasn't inclined to let go. Besides, each time he took on the cold, more of the girl he knew returned.

"Did you speak to my dad?"

"A bit," said Billy. "We get on, I think. But he's under a lot of pressure. Did you know there was a minister in your house? A government minister, I mean."

Katherine didn't seem to react to this. "I heard my aunt, but not my dad. She would talk about you."

"She seems really nice," said Billy, now looking down at his arm, which was beginning to ache with the cold. "Loves you to bits."

"Loves you to bits," said Katherine, the faintest smile returning. "Yes, that's what she said. I didn't know whether she meant dad or you."

The coolness in Billy's arm was now balanced by the flush of his cheeks, but still he didn't let go of her hand. Katherine broke off from their rotations and led Billy down the High Street. Skating like this, able to match her pace and stance, he felt more confident. The afternoon snow had buried the street so deeply that it felt as though they were skating down the base of a shallow valley. At the end of this dell, the arms of the suspension bridge rose out of the ice, but before they reached it, Katherine steered them right and into the park.

With the bright moon now higher, sharp shafts of light pierced the tree and mistletoe canopy, laying a mottled shadow over the fresh snow. As they swung arm in arm beneath the trees, it looked to Billy as though they were lit by a natural strobe. They slid out from underneath the blanket into the open park, towards the statue of Sir Steve—who was so buried in snow Billy couldn't have slapped him for luck if he'd felt the need, though at this moment he felt he had enough going his way. He could see Katherine returning. At odd moments, she would glance left or right, with that familiar curiosity, but it was like a wave that would subside, leaving him alone again. Each time she left, he drew the cold up his arm a bit further.

Katherine tugged him about, and now, really getting to grips with the skates, Billy was able to follow without his heart rate skyrocketing. He realised as she led them across the park that she meant to take them out over the frozen river. This scared him for two reasons: he assumed the ice would be thinner there, and if they fell through the river would be merciless, but also it took them closer to where the Gargoyle had appeared. He pulled back, but Katherine held firm, and he was so happy to see her old resolve that he parked his instincts and went with her. She looked back at Billy with a familiar glint, and began to accelerate.

When they were skating side by side, Billy towered over her, but as she pulled forward their shoulders levelled out, and it was all his long legs could do to keep up with her. With the wide track of the entire river, there was nothing to stop the speed from increasing. There were no warning cracks sounding underneath, as they crossed the line of the river bank, and he was then able to allow his brain to focus on staying upright.

"Come on Billy, faster!"

"This is fast!"

And now the bars of the suspension bridge rose out of the ice before them, and to Billy's dismay, Katherine shook off his hand to lean low and make a turn through the bars and back onto the High Street. He made the turn, with a degree of elegance that he didn't have on land with shoes, and looked to see where she was headed. Katherine had simply coasted, but now turned and started to skate backwards. She was suddenly pale again. He pushed his skates forward and took up her hand. This time the cold ripped into him, pouring up his arms, but he didn't care. They both needed this; he was releasing Katherine from the effects of her coma, and she from the shackles of the task. He had just skated as he thought he'd never be able to. He could never have achieved that alone.

Katherine looked up at his hand, his arm, his face, and swayed back towards him into the living world—more than enough to justify the striking pain that had now reached his shoulder. He turned left and led them back into the park. Here, Katherine swung around in front of him, skating backwards, allowing him to steer. Once again, they were engulfed by the mottled moonlight. Katherine's eyes locked deep into Billy's, as if she was seeing through and into him, and he stopped doubting.

The kiss was fuller and richer than kissing Senga. Billy's brain poured out a stream of endorphins so strong that for a moment he could not tell up from down. Katherine drew him closer, still locked in the kiss, as they spun out through the trees and onto the river. The cold began to prickle through his shoulder, to his neck and then down into his chest. He was torn, he could taste Katherine, feel the warmth bubbling though her, but a deep shiver at his core warned him that he could take no more of this cold kiss. He broke it gently, resting his forehead down on hers, their noses touching.

Katherine flinched, once, then again, and looked up. Then left, then right. Billy couldn't move his right arm at all, his neck was frozen, legs like lead.

"Billy?" Katherine sounded herself more than ever that evening. "How did I get here?"

He realised she had just woken fully from whatever had forced her prolonged sleep. Billy tried in vain to speak, but his throat was frozen, and all he could do was breathe and plead with his eyes. She took a step away from him.

"Billy!" Real fear took Katherine.

Fifty feet behind her, the ice exploded, and the Gargoyle shot up high into the air. Katherine turned and screamed; Billy had never heard her scream before, other than in his terrible dreams. He forced his useless right leg forwards. It moved an inch.

A thump echoed across the ice. It had landed. Behind Katherine, the half-headed Gargoyle trained its one remaining eye on her, then Billy, then back to her. Katherine stopped screaming.

Billy was desperate for her to run, but could do nothing to coax out his voice. He could already hear the offbeat canter as the beast scrambled towards them. He tried to scream a warning, but succeeded only in breathing out cold air and clenching his fists. He tried to pull the axe from under his arm, but it only swung through halfway. He heard stone scraping and skidding on ice. He forced fresh effort into his legs. They began to respond, but so slowly. Katherine glanced back at Billy, eyes wide and scared. In horror, he realised that without his touch she was falling back into the cold, and could not run if she chose to. Why hadn't he held the kiss longer and given her a chance? And now the Gargoyle was upon her with a triumphant scream. It threw her over its right shoulder, then looked for a moment at Billy.

"She is mine," it whispered through half a mouth. The Gargoyle stuck the stump of its left arm on the frozen river and with its hind legs it started to propel itself back towards the hole in the ice.

Billy found half his voice. "No!"

The scream found strength, and with it, he shook out the stagnation from his limbs. Ignoring the burning pain in his legs, he drove forward, reaching around for the axe. The Gargoyle was gaining speed. Katherine's eyes searched for Billy over the beast's shoulder, and he knew those eyes spoke of abject fear. How could it be this strong?

The Gargoyle spared him a second to turn and gloat, and Billy knew he'd lost the race. It lifted Katherine from its shoulder and held her high above its head.

"Mine!" it screamed, before falling back though the hole into the river.

Billy cried out, and caught a fleeting moment with Katherine's eyes as the stone arm dragged her down into the black water.

Her fingers scored the edge of the ice before following her into the water. Blind with rage, Billy arrived screaming at the hole, skidding forwards on his knees and following them both headlong into the dark water. He'd thought that the current would take him immediately, but the water below the ice was still; a dead river. He strained to see, but the ice took the moonlight, and there was nothing for his eyes to make out. The cold bit deeply. Adrenaline, running high, burned through the oxygen in his frozen lungs. Above him swam the hole, but it was confused and shifting. He looked again for Katherine, but there was nothing to see. With a final effort, he slung the axe upwards and hooked it hard into the lip of the hole. He pulled himself up the axe handle. A gasp of precious air. Air he couldn't give Katherine. Another pull, longer this time, and he was flat on his front on the ice.

Only a moment passed before fists and tears rained down on the ice. He'd kissed her, he'd finally kissed her, and it had killed her.

SOMEWHERE BETWEEN GASPS A QUIET thought found him. He fumbled in his pocket for his mobile phone. Somehow it had survived the soaking. It was a quarter past eleven. He had time. His mother was depressed, his father still lost, but no one was supposed to die over this. Not over this Christmas. He could still change his wish and save Katherine.

He picked himself up, steadying himself on the axe, and started to skate back up the river through the bridge and on to the church. The lock to the vestry was just below the ice line, but in any case, the door opened outwards and was blocked by ice. He chopped his way through the door without hesitating, pouring his fury through the wood with the axe. Once inside, he stripped off completely, knowing that if he attempted to get home whilst wet he would certainly fail; his last attempt had taught him that. The cassock he found was itchy, but at least warm. As he turned back towards the door to collect the axe and knuckleduster, he spied a huge bonus, his mother's bike, which he collected before heading for the door.

WITHOUT WARNING, THE VESTRY LIGHTS went out. Billy's eyes shot to the floor. The ice below his feet was starting to glow white, lighting the room from below.

"I think you'll find that garment is in my possession," said a familiar voice.

To Billy's horror, the cassock he was wearing squirmed tightly against his skin. His arms wrapped themselves across his body, causing the bike to clatter to the icy floor. The gown pulled itself tight before lifting him from the ground. Billy cried out in anger, twisting his head around as he tried to see which direction the voice had come from. He could make out nothing. The cassock flew backwards and upwards, lifting into the air and back until he was pinned hard against the wall near to the ceiling.

"Billy, Billy, Billy," came the voice again. "You are such a trusting young man."

The door to the main body of the church opened; still Billy couldn't see who was there.

"I thought you might have learned along this little journey, with all the opportunity you've had," said the voice, "that you, of all people, cannot afford to rely on anyone at all."

The floor revealed a little more light, and now Billy recognised the shape, before he even stepped into the room.

"You," he said, fighting the disappointment in his chest. "You?"

"Yes, me," said Mike Hayter, stepping fully onto the lit ice. "And very soon she will be mine."

"You're too late," Billy clenched his hands against the cassock. "It killed her," he said, still hoping he was wrong.

Mike threw back his head with a rich laugh. "Oh, she may soon wish that were true, but she is alive, there are plans for her." Mike strode towards Billy. "Though I'm willing to bet you still don't know who she is, or what this is all about, or why I took your father?"

Billy's rage spiked, pouring out in a pure scream. "What do you know?"

Mike paused and smiled, then came towards him, crossing the room with his arms outstretched, as the cassock pulled Billy towards its owner.

Mike started singing, softly at first, but quickly getting louder till his voice filled the room and made the air above him shake as he repeated the words. "Do you see what I see? Do you see what I see? Do you see what I see?" He grasped Billy by the shoulders, the cassock pulling him ever tighter and squeezing the air from his lungs. Billy just had time to notice three green sores on the vicar's face, one on his forehead and the others on his cheek, before Mike pulled back his head and whispered, "I am the Grey Knight."

Then he rammed his head forwards, pulling Billy's in fast and slamming their skulls not against, but actually into, one another. Billy felt a screaming pain in his mind and his world went black.

"BILLY?" A WHISPERING VOICE THAT was only recently familiar.

He tried to open his eyes.

"No, keep them shut for now," a small hand with bark for fingers took his own.

"Senga!"

"Shhh, you must stay calm, I can only hold this space for a few moments before the knight realises something is amiss."

"Where are we?"

"You are in his memory, but we are in Seven Corner Alley…"

"Beside the church?"

"It is a gateway to many places, as you are about to see through the connection with this poor fool's mind. Billy, he is going to show you some of his part in this, and then you are going to have to make a decision. You will be freed from the cassock, and you can walk home and your father will be returned to you tomorrow. I ask you, I beg of you, to consider another path. Your friend, Katherine, as you know her, is now lost to us. The consequences are unimaginably dire. She was here to be kept safe, and part of that meant her not knowing her origins."

Billy shook his head in confusion.

"Well, who is she?"

"We have no time, little one. The advantage you have is that the knight thinks you captive, and you are not. The knight thinks you are spent, and you are not. The knight believes you are powerless, and I know you to have a warrior's heart."

"But what can I do? Why can't we both go get her?"

"I may not go where you must and she may not see me. Not yet. It is not that time. Now, open your eyes."

Billy blinked, and gradually the brick and stone alley came into focus. Senga was there in human form, black eyes wide with fear, like a deer sensing a predator close enough to strike.

"See what he shows you, his arrogance may reveal more than he plans. That may let you learn his weaknesses." With that, Senga drew a small piece of moss from the wall, turned and walked towards a corner with the moss outstretched in front of her thumb. Where the moss met the wall, it rippled and allowed her to pass. As she disappeared from the alley, the moss flared briefly and was gone. Billy's vision went dark once more.

THE NEXT TIME BILLY COULD make anything out, he knew he wasn't looking through his own eyes, but those of the knight stumbling through the alley. He was locked into the images, sounds and thoughts of his enemy. The knight picked a couple of pieces of moss and pressed one with his thumb against a corner in the alley. At once he was at the kitchen door to the Christmas house. Anger flew through Billy; this man had been in his home!

Waving the locks open, the Grey Knight pushed open the kitchen door. He paused and tasted the air, raising his hands slightly to feel subtle vibrations and see who was home. His left hand twitched and his little finger extended out, pointing at the cupboard to his left. His eyes shifted upwards and the box on top of the cupboard started to rattle and shake, but just as it tipped to tumble over the edge, the Grey Knight caught it. The lid of the box opened as if by itself, and three crystal glasses slid out suspended in midair. The glasses turned, splitting the low lights from the ceiling into coloured shards across the walls. The knight tasted the wretched sentiment that surrounded the glasses and clenched his jaw against the nausea it caused him. Whilst remaining in control of the glasses with his left hand, he brought the thumb and forefinger of his right together. As though drawing a bow across a violin, the knight drew his hand across his chest and raised the vibration of the crystal glasses. Further fractures appeared in the colours cast on the wall as the glasses began to splinter before a cloud of shattered crystal formed in front of the knight.

The knight climbed the staircase, three stairs at a time, and followed the sound of the sleeping adult woman. The stench of the deerhound grew stronger here; clearly the filthy, broken woman had allowed the beast to sleep in her quarters. It amazed him that someone with such poor breeding had sired such a potent foe. He could hear the spiders scurry away as he waved the door open. They could sense his nature and knew it was time to be anywhere else. The carpet at the foot of the bed had been the dog's cot. Just as the stiff hairs from the hound started to rear up at the knight, white flame marked their passing. The heady smell of burnt hair mixed with a deeper tone from the woman. He could actually smell the grief seeping up through her pallid skin. He moved closer, tempted suddenly to taste the woman, to draw the exact note of her sorrow. She stirred, arching her back awkwardly, her eyelids fluttering.

"Tom..." said Penny Christmas to a ghost in her dream. "Tom?"

Not Tom, thought the knight, leaning over her, not even close, and turned back out of the bedroom. This was risky. If he was caught at this now, it would throw off his master's plans, and there were other tasks to attend to in Marlow tonight. From the doorway, he waved the thin duvet back over the woman and, as an afterthought, fluffed her pillows. Then he turned into the hallway and froze.

Someone was opening the kitchen door. The smell hit him at once; it was the boy himself. He heard boots crush crystal and smelt the boy's gasp; tasted his dismay. The woman was awake, throwing off his tucked duvet and stumbling to the door. He waved open the door to his left and entered the boy's room.

"Billy? Is that you?"

The knight listened to the woman descend the staircase but was no longer paying attention to her. Before him on the foot of the boy's bed lay a blanket he knew covered items of great power. He waved the blanket up into the air where it hung like a sun canopy, took three steps forward and looked on the bed with widening eyes. Here was the very knuckleduster…and the axe and key. He felt a compulsion to take them. Why, he could disrupt the prophecies by simply stealing them here and now. Surely the master had thought that the boy would keep them somewhere safe, perhaps hidden by the Tree in some obscure dream. Surely he should take the tools now, and the master would be free of the risk. Voices were being raised in the kitchen.

The knight drew on his courage and reached for the items.

—*WHAT ARE YOU STILL DOING IN THAT BUILDING!*

His voice slammed into the depths of his brain like a hammer.

—*GET OUT!*

And now there were footsteps heading up the stairs. The boy was coming. In a trice, the knight waved the blanket down over the items, leapt across the bed, waving open the window at the same time. He dived through it. As he did, he heard the door flung open; it had been that close. Plummeting towards the ground, he plucked a piece of moss from his breast pocket and pushed it out in front of his left thumb. The moss and thumb touched down and the ground swallowed the falling knight, leaving only the barest indentation, a few ashes and a thumbprint in the snow.

BILLY BLINKED AND MOANED AS the Grey Knight pulled his head away.

"You see, we all have our masters, Billy Christmas."

Being locked into someone else's thinking was bad enough, but to feel their loathing of people and things he found dear made him nauseous. "Yours doesn't seem to like you much," he managed to reply.

Mike Hayter hadn't finished with him yet. "One down, one to go. Do you want to know how our stone friend got the scent of your girlfriend, Billy?"

Billy hung limply in the cassock. The disorientation was extreme. He'd spoken to Senga, hadn't he? There was going to be an opportunity to get Katherine back, wasn't there? The knight approached, singing again, and Billy drew in breath as once more their heads entwined.

BACK IN THE ALLEY, THE knight looked about for more moss, and found a wall with a thick covering. One moment he was running at a brick wall, the next the ashes of a piece of moss clung to the cement between two bricks before succumbing to gravity and the pavement below.

It took two full steps for the knight to control the inertia that he had carried from the alley. He had landed perfectly in the girl's bedroom, which was a terrific advantage. He had left this so late, and with the cursed Teàrlag approaching, it would be hard to judge how much time he had to do this.

Unlike Billy's mother, this young woman possessed none of the magnetic sorrow that he craved. This one's skin reeked of everything you'd expect from her breeding: measured courage, judgement and—most unpleasant of all—a great capacity for love. He felt repulsed. Still, he had a job to do here, a seemingly innocuous but vital component to the master's plan. Best not to question the orders. He bent over the girl. It was strange that the bed had moved with her; perhaps it spoke of her potential? Without touching it, he lifted a lock of Katherine's dusty brown hair; holding it midair above his left hand, he drew back across with his right, severing. The lock hung a moment in the air before the knight waved it into a pocket in his sleeve, taking great care not to touch or contaminate it. He looked back at Katherine, and wide-eyed, she screamed.

"Billy!"

Shocked and completely off guard, the knight bounced back off the bed, cursing. He could tell that she was already sinking back into the dead sleep, but the damage had been done. With sudden certainty of the Tree's presence, the knight spun, rolling neatly underneath the bed.

The door opened slowly. Green light swept over the room, and he could see the fibres of the carpet lift, being drawn by static electricity. The knight readied himself for battle, staying silent, leaving it to Teàrlag to decide the moment he would launch out at the girl. He could feel the wisps of her energy tickle the edges of the bed, and forced himself to wait. This would be brief and bloody.

He heard a note of change in the girl's breathing, felt the energy pouring from the Tree, smelled the blood beating deeper within her heart; she was close to waking up.

"Katherine? That's it, dear, just sit up. No, not too fast…"

The steady voice of the Tree refreshed the bile in the knight. Such sanctimonious, odious intent.

"Are you Billy's Tree? He told me in my sleep…" her voice was weak, and she coughed after speaking.

"I am my own Tree, thank you. But yes, I am with Billy. Just sit there a moment, will you? Stop trying to stand. You've been sleeping too long for that."

The knight flattened himself against the floor as Katherine sat over him on the mattress.

"Take these," said Teàrlag.

"Tiny skates?"

"They are for Billy. You are to take him skating in the park."

"Have you really seen him? He has bigger feet than my dad…"

"He'll know what to do. Does this bag hold your skates?"

"Yes, but…"

"Put this duffel coat on. I'm not supposed to, but I think I'll spare us the walk down the hill."

From under the bed, the knight felt the large French door open out onto the veranda. At the same moment, the knight heard needles fall from the Tree onto Katherine.

"What are you doing?"

"It's to help you fly, little one, no don't get up. I shall lift you."

The indentation in the bed lifted and now the knight began to panic. He could see the stump of Teàrlag's trunk floating inches above the carpet. He rolled out of the other side of the bed and froze as the Tree floated out of the room, cradling the girl. The French doors shut, and an ugly grin spread over the face of the Grey Knight. The fool Tree had not spotted him.

Suddenly three needles fresh from the Tree sprang from the duvet and whipped deep into his face. Two on his left cheek and one high in his forehead. They each pumped green light into his face, and the knight struggled to contain a deep howl of pain. Grinding his teeth and breathing out spit onto the duvet, the knight pulled out the needles one by one. He watched them writhe against his fingers for a moment before consigning them to white flame.

It became clear he hadn't contained his cry well enough; from below, someone was already running up the stairs. He scowled and waved open the French doors and was out of them with the moss on his thumb well before the girl's family arrived. Below the veranda, a thumbprint and slight ashes were the only imperfections in the empty snow-covered gardens.

THE KNIGHT CRIED OUT AS he pulled his head away from Billy's, who was shocked to be using his own eyes once more. Mike Hayter rocked back onto his knees as if briefly in pain. Shaking it off, he got to his feet. "How ironic that the evening I lose the father, I gain the son. I suspect he'll think his escape somewhat less lucky now."

Billy snarled and fought against the cassock.

The Grey Knight reached down and drew a large circle, about eight feet across, in the ice with his finger. A bright light raced around the ring, and Mike quickly stepped outside the circle. Within the line the ice floor began to fizz, then bubble, then boil before finally going still. Steam now rose from the pool of water in the vestry. Billy realised as it settled that he could make out the inverted interior of some building below. He could clearly see the night sky through the upturned space, with moon-light against the stone walls.

"You know, if you had only pieced things together a little quicker you might have prevented what is about to happen to your friend." The Grey Knight shrugged off the overcoat he'd been wearing, revealing a grey waistcoat over a white shirt. "Such a shame."

"Just don't hurt her. Please!" Billy fought the cassock in vain.

"Well, we already have Billy, thanks to you. It is down to you that I was able to find her at all. You helped track and then trap her. Who do you think clipped her with the car? Who arranged for the actual impact to arrive later and send her to sleep? After months and months of searching, it was all possible thanks to you."

Again, Billy cried out, and the cassock hauled him closer.

"You should struggle less. The more you move, the tighter that will get, and it won't stop tightening just because you need to breathe." Mike's smile faltered. "It's not my choice, Billy."

He turned and faced the edge of the pool. Time appeared to slow, as he stepped forward a few inches above the water, then slowly sank under, turning around so his eyes met Billy's just before they rolled beneath the surface.

Billy bellowed in pure frustration and then stopped as he felt the cassock snake ever tighter about him. He calmed his breathing. Hadn't Senga said he would be freed?

A new sound found his ears. The ticking of the vestry clock. Slow, steady and unrelenting. Tick, tock, back and forth, the losses mounting, and time roaring past and him bound against this stupid wall, without the first clue what to do if he were free, and still time poured past him. In his mind's eye, the candle's flame flickered dangerously low, losing touch with his father. And now Katherine's fingers were losing their grip on the ice with the dead weight of the Gargoyle dragging her low. Despite the obvious danger, Billy howled out in despair, almost welcoming the constriction with which the cassock replied.

"Now then young 'un! Whatever sort of noise is that to be making?"

The unmistakable bark of Saul joined the voice, and Billy already knew it was Agnes standing at the tatters of the door. At once Saul bounded in, and started sniffing and growling at the pool's edge before looking up at Billy and barking. He ran up to the cassock and began biting the edge of the garment. Instantly it recoiled, almost hissing, forcing the air out of Billy's lungs.

"Saul, no! No you mustn't!" yelled Agnes. The dog sat back and gave a low howl.

Billy was in trouble. With each small breath, the cassock tightened against him, acting exactly as the Grey Knight had threatened it would. He already knew he couldn't speak, but flashed Agnes a look of fear that he hoped looked as authentic as it felt.

Agnes appeared to pause and take a breath. "Don't you worry, youngster. I can help you, I believe." She delved into some cloth compartment within her many layers and drew out the Christmas pie. Saul whined, wrinkling his huge nose. It was clear he could smell more than just the surface aroma.

Billy's breathing grew shallow, and the room greyed a little before his eyes. He wasn't sure what he would or could have said when he saw Agnes begin to break open the pie, but he knew from the tears forming in her eyes that she was parting with her precious gift. She shot Billy a small smile, began to rub the open chunk of pie into the cloth of the cassock. The reaction was instantaneous. Billy felt his ribs gathered and pressed together harder than ever. Agnes moved quickly, rubbing more pie into the cassock over his shoulders. A pungent smell hit his nose, like the foul ash from the attack on Teàrlag. The cassock began to feel thinner and weaker. Smoke slowly rose from the possessed cloth, and Agnes moved faster. Finally, the last of the pie was gone, and quite naked, Billy slumped forwards through the tattered threads into Agnes's strong arms. He drew in air just as weakly as they had when he breached the surface of the water in the tank some days before.

"Thank you," he whispered.

"You're most welcome."

SOME MINUTES LATER, BILLY WAS dressed in spare vestry clothes and they sat on the couch observing the world through the pool. Agnes was making no sound, but tears rolled down her cheeks and she made no attempt to hide them. Billy reached over with both hands and partly on instinct and partly for warmth lifted her heavy arm over his neck and placed his head against the folds of her clothes.

"That was your only way out, wasn't it?"

Agnes shrugged a little. "Nothing lasts forever, Billy. Not stars, not stone and certainly not people. Even well-preserved ones like me will pass in time. I just hadn't wanted to see any more of my own go before me."

"Thank you for saving me," said Billy, feeling warmth through the weaves. "I can't remember anyone doing that for me."

Agnes smiled. "It was a good swap, young 'un. An easy swap at that."

"I need to get going, don't I?"

The old woman drew in a deep breath. "You don't need to go anywhere, son. Your father is safe and you've done enough."

"But Senga said…"

"Everyone has an angle in this, including me. I have as many reasons as any for sending you in. But you have to decide for yourself. Your dad will be coming home now."

Billy already knew he wouldn't be able to look at him if bringing him home had losing Katherine as a price. "I won't leave her there."

"I didn't imagine you would. But Billy, the Gargoyle, the knight and anyone, anything, you meet there," she said, pointing down through the water to the inverted world, "they ain't playing at this, son. They have an ambition and you will threaten it. Make no mistake, they will kill you if they can. You need to understand that before you go. You want your father to come back and have you missing?"

Billy lifted his head from her shoulder and stood up. "I don't believe he would want me to leave anyone behind. It's not who we are."

Agnes blinked back more tears. "I'm sorry I can't go with you, Billy, but you won't be going alone." She picked herself up from the couch and held out her hand. In it was Saul's blue lead. The deerhound padded across the room and dropped his head, allowing Billy to fasten the tie to his collar. Agnes slipped two fingers into her mouth and gave a low whistle. A whispering sound approached from the door to the vestry. Leafy extremities wrapped themselves around the door frame to be followed by a single beady berry, looking inquisitively into the room. The mistletoe caught sight of Billy and scarpered across the floor, running up his leg, then back and finally settled, nestling against his neck, making him smile.

"And then there were three," said Agnes. "Billy, you're about to go somewhere so different, I can't begin to describe it. When you've worked it out, which you will, please try to remember who you're going there for. Don't be distracted by what is about to happen."

Quite mesmerised by her voice, Billy hadn't realised that he, Saul and the mistletoe on his shoulder had also been drifting out over the pool. He looked down at his feet before looking back at Agnes and noticing that her eyes were now quite black.

"She's my great-granddaughter, Billy."

For once, Billy felt calm and threw a smile back at Agnes. "I *will* bring her back."

At once he, Saul and the mistletoe fell through the water and left Marlow, Agnes and the vestry far behind.

THE INVERSION WAS SO SUBTLE Billy barely noticed the flip, but now they were rising rather than sinking. Aware of the gift he knew Agnes had given up for him, Billy tried to dismiss the small knot of fear growing around the fact that for the first time he would be going up against more than one foe. How many more was not clear, but also mattered little. He wasn't planning on hanging around for an extended fight. If possible, he wanted to grab Katherine and jump straight back through the water. No point in giving the opposition the home advantage on top of everything else. Saul paddled hard and breached the edge of the pool above him. He saw him turn and take the lead in his jaws, drawing Billy up through the water. However, as he did, time seemed to slow, and the lead appeared to extend, so that the closer he got to the surface the slower his approach became. In the end, he floated just below the surface of the water, the lead still drawing him through but only progressing millimetres at a time. Curiously, he didn't appear to need to breathe in this water. There was some quality about it that felt nourishing and enriching. He felt the cold vanish from his body for what felt like the first time in days. His heart pounded, not with urgency but with strength and confidence. He felt power in his arms and legs, and looked down at his body in wonder. On instinct, he gave a terrific kick against the water and exploded through the surface, high into the air, still feeling as though time were running slowly. He completed the arc of his trajectory and landed one knee down and another raised, and took his first deep breath of air in this new world. Stars filled his vision. Billy smiled and passed out, falling to one side. The last thing he heard was Saul barking in concern.

"BILLY, YOU HAVE TO GET up."

Billy had rarely wanted to be woken less. His body felt strong and happy and warm, and he felt at peace.

"Squire, you must rise."

He shrugged and tried to roll over. The thought tapped the inside of his head.

Squire? Billy forced his eyes open.

The courtyard swam before him as his eyes struggled to adjust to the new atmosphere. Blinking, he raised himself up to a sitting position. Moonlight poured down from above and it was all he could do to map the contours of the room. As far as he could tell, it was a circular courtyard perhaps two hundred yards across. The walls were high dark granite, speckled with flint that threw the moonlight back across the open space, lighting the damp air and making it dance. All across the courtyard, moisture seemed to be rising up into the air. He fancied he could see water trickling up the walls, and over at the pool the odd drip from the surface spiralled up to the sky. A figure he knew stepped forward and cast her shadow over him.

"No, Billy. Don't look at me. Shut your eyes."

He did as she told him. "Katherine."

At once, they were hugging tightly.

"I knew you'd come."

"I thought you had drowned."

"The damp air in this place, it's restoring me. Restoring us. No, don't open your eyes yet."

Billy released his grip on her and teetered back uneasily to a sitting position. Katherine moved back around behind him and drew him back to her, so eventually she was sitting propped up by the wall and he could rest his weight against her.

"We have a little time, Billy. Open your eyes, slowly."

"But we should escape now, before they're back, we must go."

Katherine pulled Billy closer to her. "They won't be back whilst the air is damp like this, they can't stand it, but they needed to make me strong again. They had to let the good air in."

Billy opened his eyes and blinked against the bright moonlight again. "Katherine, you can explain once we're back home. We must go back, now."

"Through the pool? It doesn't work both ways. See the water rising from it? It's a one-way trip whether you arrived through your pool or down with the river."

Katherine shivered, which made Billy jump. "I thought you'd drowned," he repeated, his mind returning to the ice and the pounding of his fists.

"I think I did for a while, but they need me, it seems." At this, Billy tried to lift and turn towards her, but Katherine locked her arms tightly over his shoulders. "No, please don't look at me."

"Katherine, I thought I'd been protecting you, keeping what I knew from you. But you seem to know much more than me. Can you please explain what the hell is going on?"

Katherine took a deep breath. "Over there, back home, I don't know anything about here. It's security. It's protection. It's deception. It's politics. I wasn't hiding anything from you. I was in fact hiding, in the open, from myself, for everyone here. I'm from this side, Billy."

Billy's heart pounded as he tried to make out what this meant. "Why won't you let me look at you, Katherine?"

"I don't want to scare you. I'm something different here, Billy."

He gave a small laugh. "I'm getting used to different. How bad can it be?"

Billy felt Katherine's grip release a little, then completely. As her arms fell away, he slowly turned around, rolling onto his knees until he was facing her. His shadow covered her, so he tilted his head to one side. As he did, he gave a small gasp. Katherine's hair had turned to a willow weave, her green eyes black and as her hands withdrew they became covered in the bark of a silver birch. She looked at him briefly and then at the floor, looking a little lost and embarrassed.

"Katherine," said Billy, "you're not the first I have seen like this…"

Katherine's eyes twitched back to his, then instantly past his. She put a silver finger up to her lips, silencing him. She rose slowly and tasted the air. Billy got to his feet and looked about him. Saul was just a few paces away with the mistletoe riding on his neck from where they both stood guard.

"The air is drying out," said Katherine. "They'll be back soon."

Billy pushed down the hundred or so questions he was dying to ask.

"You're sure we can't just swim down through the pool?"

"Very," said Katherine. She picked up a small smooth stone and skimmed it over to the water. The pebble rested comfortably on the surface without sinking before beginning to skip around until it bounced back onto the dry edge. "It did the same to me when I tried."

"Do you know another way out?"

"The only thing I know about this place is that I am not supposed to be anywhere near it."

Suddenly the courtyard dimmed.

"Oh no. No!" cried Billy. "Katherine, I left the weapons in the vestry. I can't fight the Gargoyle without them!"

Katherine smiled and then laughed.

He didn't join her, still stunned at his error.

"I'm laughing because I couldn't have been sent anyone better equipped but less prepared," said Katherine with her black eyes sparkling. "Billy, how have you felt since you entered this place?"

Billy tried to still his spiralling mind and answered. "Strong. I've felt really strong."

Katherine looked up at the sky with a wry smile. "Here you will not need weapons, Billy. You already brought an army." Her hand drifted out to indicate Saul and the mistletoe, who padded over and stood facing Katherine, almost to attention.

Billy shook his head. "You know yourself how strong this thing is, and it's not coming alone either."

"I know this place, Billy, and you must try and understand your very thoughts have an impact here. You notice how dark it just got? That was you."

Billy frowned. "How is that possible?"

"You're very powerful here, Billy, more than you can imagine, but that has to change," Katherine took his hand in hers. "That is going to change, now. Light up the moon, Billy."

Billy looked at her blankly.

Katherine took his chin and pointed it towards the sky. "Light it up. I know what a strong imagination you have. Your dark thoughts sent the light scuttling. Imagine how light you think it could be and then push it out there, then pull it out here, into existence."

Billy frowned, but this made sense to him, deep sense, like breathing air and eating food. He'd felt so at home in his skin since he'd burst through the pool, he began to wonder what might be possible here.

"Do it, Billy. Light up the courtyard."

He remembered how the flint flecks had picked up the light when he landed. He wanted to see that again. He took a deep breath, poured the light from his mind skywards and began to swell the bright glare up at the planet before pulling it back down.

Katherine smiled and somehow, in this place, Billy knew that her skin was tingling with anticipation. He looked up and gasped. To his astonishment, he could actually see the moonlight welling up and rolling into the courtyard. It burst over the walls so hard it made Katherine shield her black eyes.

She took his hand and squeezed it tightly. "Here, Billy, here you can make anything happen. You don't need weapons. You are every weapon you can dream."

A loud clapping broke the spell, and almost at once dimmed the moonlight again as Billy jumped, startled from his new senses back to his old fears.

"Bravo! Spectacular light show…did the witch convince you that you did it, too?"

Saul ran to his side and he could hear the mistletoe audibly hiss. Katherine moved a little closer, but her eyes were still raised to the sky. The courtyard was empty.

"They're not here yet, Billy."

"We'll be here in moments," answered the voice of the knight.

A deep and dark voice barrelled out of Katherine. "Be gone till then, false priest!"

Billy jumped and the courtyard went darker still.

"The air is drying, Billy, and I am out of time to tell you all the things I know are within you, which you struggle so hard to see. Do you trust me?"

He looked back at the bark-skinned girl in duffel coat, jeans and jumper, still thrown by the aggressive tone that had just sprung from her. Then he smiled. This was Katherine, exactly who Katherine always was, a powerful creature, not a shrinking violet. He'd always known she had backbone, that she had teeth. He always trusted her, as long as he could remember. She had never deceived him, never let him down.

"I trust you completely."

"Then know they will try to convince you that I have bewitched you. Created tricks to fool you. The only possible way they can beat you is to make you doubt yourself, doubt your power in this place. Because here, Billy, if you believed it enough, you could stop this world spinning and carry every living thing out into the ether."

"But I have nothing to fight them with," blurted out Billy.

"Billy, you have everything you ever needed, you always did," said Katherine, reaching forward and looking deep into his eyes. She placed a long, slow, full kiss on his mouth. The moonlight erupted again at once, and the courtyard disappeared in the bright glare.

Eventually, Katherine pulled slowly away. "Focus now, Billy. Breathe this place in, feed from it."

Across the courtyard, there came the sound of stone moving on stone, the uneven canter of the stone beast. To Billy's horror, the Gargoyle appeared to be at least three times the size he remembered. The open wounds he had inflicted looked more painful and angry than in his world. From the good side of the Gargoyle's mouth, flame began to pool. The beast screamed and poured fire out over the pool, where the rising moisture hissed and spat, sending up a cloud of steam. Through it, the Grey Knight marched directly for them. Despite Katherine's words, the moonlight dimmed once again. How could he possibly protect them all?

"You don't have to," said Katherine.

Billy shot her a look. "How did you…"

The knight marched on regardless.

"Sleep now," he said, motioning to Saul and the mistletoe. They fell down heavily on their side. Katherine cried out and started to run towards him, but the knight held up a hand, and she froze mid pace. "And you just stay put. I need a word with your young man."

Billy thought fast, trying to assimilate everything Katherine had shown him. He still couldn't really grasp how he was supposed to free them from here. And why could he seemingly have some impact or power here, and yet apparently Katherine could not?

"It is her, boy," said the knight, jumping through his thoughts. "In simple terms, she has some skill as a conjurer, and this world is more susceptible than our own. Things appear a little more real, but I shouldn't be fooled. Why don't you try the moonlight trick again?"

Billy looked at the knight uncertainly. Saul was breathing, Katherine was frozen though not facing him. With the Gargoyle merely pacing by the pool, there appeared to be no imminent threat. He looked up at the moon, tried to remember the connection he had felt and draw the light down once again. Nothing happened.

"Sorry, Billy. It is as well I intervened. You see, I'm not making it up when I call your friend here a witch."

Katherine flinched, pulling herself up and down to tear away from whatever influence the knight had over her. The Gargoyle reacted immediately and ran around the side of the pool, preventing her from moving towards the gateway. It needn't have bothered. She merely turned to look back at Billy.

"There is one thing I imagine she hasn't yet shared with you, apart from her skin condition," said the knight evenly. "Did she mention that she offered up your father on a plate for us?"

Despite the strength he felt, despite Katherine's kiss and the echo of her warning, Billy felt doubt slam against his ribs. His father?

Katherine opened her mouth to speak, then hesitated.

The knight turned to her with genuine surprise. "Why, didn't you think I would just tell him the truth? What else haven't you told him, I wonder?"

Katherine's shoulders sank, and the sky went darker still as Billy's heart plummeted fast. What else did she know? "Just tell me, Katherine."

She looked at Billy.

"How do I tell him?" she asked out loud.

"It is a problem," conceded the knight, unable to conceal his glee at the tension, which Billy still could not understand.

"Don't make me do this," said Katherine.

Clouds formed in the sky above. "Do what? Tell me what?" said Billy, with his fear rising. "Is my father dead? What is it you both know?"

"You know we're just the welcoming committee, don't you?" said the knight to the girl. "Do you honestly want *him* to be the one to tell Billy?"

Katherine snarled and took a step towards Mike. "You're feeding us both to him! So don't begin to pretend that…" She took another two steps towards him. "He should not have to find out this way!"

"What is it? What do you know!" a huge new voice sprang from Billy, shaking the very ground they stood on. Saul stirred from his sleep, shook his huge head and let out a baleful howl. Billy's heart beat harder than he could remember. He spread his feet to hold his balance, and his hands became fists. "Just tell me."

Katherine sighed and turned back to the knight with some venom. "Go keep your pet under control."

The knight threw a look at Billy and then walked to the far side of the courtyard and the pacing Gargoyle. Turning back to Billy, she put both her hands over his fists and gently unclenched them, looking deep into his eyes and trying to calm his breathing and his mind.

"Did you make my father leave? Did you do this?"

"No Billy. He, it's complicated…"

"Just tell me!"

"He offered to…"

"Offered, but you knew?"

"No, not when I was over there, but Billy, that isn't what the knight is saying. This is something else, something much bigger, and perhaps simpler, to explain."

Billy's mind was still failing to find anywhere familiar to grip, to hold onto. He was lost and beginning to wonder if he was ever going to find a way back to the simple things he knew and craved. Katherine led him slowly by the hand towards the pool. She motioned him to kneel beside her at the edge. To his right, he saw Saul and the mistletoe shake the last of the effects of the knight's words off. High above them, the clouds scurried over the night sky. Katherine placed a hand on his cheek and returned his focus to her.

"You had some tasks to accomplish, with the Tree. With Teàrlag?"

"You remember that?"

"I know that here. And during these tasks, did you notice things change? A bit like the way you changed the moonlight here?"

"No. I don't think so." Billy thought for a moment. "Well, the sheet music moved on the page."

"I remember that."

"And, well the knuckleduster changed its shape. But those were magical items. They were supposed to…"

"Didn't Teàrlag say…"

"There is less supposed to…"

Katherine smiled. "There is no supposed to. Did she say anything else about what you…"

"…bring to the tasks. But…"

"There is no but, either. I'm afraid." Katherine took another breath. "You brought it all."

Billy shook his head. "It's not possible. I didn't bring the Tree. Teàrlag brought the decorations. I'm just some kid…"

"Some kid," said Katherine. "Look, it isn't supposed to happen like this. It really isn't, and you're not going to like it because, well no one would. Do you still trust me, Billy?"

Billy thought before answering. "I always have."

"That'll have to do. We're running out of time. If this other person arrives, then we really are in trouble." Katherine looked over her shoulder at the knight, who was waiting patiently beside the stone beast. "So, I'm sorry about this, but try to remember; all the things you are, you still are. And you are still Billy Christmas."

Billy started to lean back and away from whatever truth he was being offered here, but Katherine grabbed him by the shoulder and slowly pulled him to the edge of the pool and over. She looked down into the reflection, then back up to him and motioned with her head for him to look too.

In the smooth water, the clouds were scurrying above them both. Slowly, he let his eyes adjust and find Katherine's reflection; she nodded him gently towards his own.

He recognised the shape of his face, though it looked larger than he remembered, his jaw broader. His shoulders were wider and fuller, too, and his skin had a strange silvery quality to it. He moved back and forth a little over the water, trying to catch the light. It was then he saw his eyes. A low moan poured out of his mouth, but the tongue was alien and his voice rasped. His eyes were pure black, and now as he shook his head in horror he saw his hair was weaves of willow.

Suddenly his feet itched more than he had ever known and he fell backwards quickly, tearing off his shoes. Through his woollen socks, he could see white roots spiking their way through the weave, trying to snake their way into the soil. At this he rolled onto his front, and tried to throw up, but there was nothing to give. His fists, now also covered in bark, hit the dirt floor in fear and frustration. Across the courtyard, he could hear snorts of laughter from the knight and the beast.

"Katherine!" he barked out. "What am I?"

She held him until he caught his breath, then rolled and turned him so that his feet were in the pool. Almost at once, he felt nourishment and strength being drawn up and through his legs and, despite the sheer oddness of this, felt his breath ease and his temper calm.

Billy opened his mouth to speak, but could not string together his thoughts to form any questions.

"This is you. You are from here too."

"I am? What am I?"

"We don't have words for it in the way you are used to. You are from here. You are part of here, part of this place."

"Part of what? Of where?"

"Time's up, Billy." The knight appeared at his shoulder, and his tone had changed completely. Saul started barking, but abruptly yelped. Billy spun around to see the Gargoyle pinning his dog and blowing gentle flame at the terrified mistletoe. Katherine leapt to her feet, and the knight knocked her into the pool as if she were weightless. Billy roared and glared up at the knight, but didn't want to risk standing on his crawling, rooted feet.

"Leave her alone!"

"Or what, Billy? You'll chase after me?" said the knight. "You know you ask really terrible questions. I'd have thought you wanted to know whether your father is like you, or whether you're adopted. Or perhaps your father is from here, but your mother not?"

Billy turned around and threw out a hand to Katherine. She was already pulling herself out of the pool, spitting water and snarling at the knight.

"He's like you, Billy. He's from here, that's why…"

"But not Mummy," said the knight in a sarcastic tone.

Billy looked back at her.

She shook her head. "No, she's human."

Suddenly the knight had Billy by the neck and was dragging him away from Katherine. "Which, Billy Christmas, makes you a bit of a filthy hybrid. A mammalian plant crossed with a bad dream," he pulled him close and ramped the sarcastic tone higher. "Or a mother's worst nightmare. Why do you think she could barely manage to look at you in the last year?"

Billy roared in anger, but this was lost as the knight dragged him closer to the Gargoyle.

"It's time to greet the master. I think we should make ourselves a nice little bonfire, right here and now. Nebulous, could you…"

The Gargoyle took a deep breath and blew a fierce blue flame that crackled, and now Billy actually heard the mistletoe scream, inside his head—*Billy help us, please!* He realised that though the voice had registered in his head, he had heard it through a single root that had snuck into the dirt floor from a toe. As the knight paused to motion the Gargoyle closer, working on instinct he let as many roots as he could enter the ground, and asked, *Who can hear me?*

We hear you, Billy—replied the mistletoe.

I hear you—replied Katherine.

Billy took a deep breath and spoke—*I want to go home and see my father. Who wants to come with me?*

We're with you.

All with you.

The Gargoyle moved over to Billy, leaving Saul in a heap. The mistletoe crept off from around the dog's neck and made for a crack in the wall. Katherine shivered by the edge of the pool, teeth bared, waiting. Billy looked back at Saul and nodded.

"You know Billy," said the knight, "there are few smells I enjoy more than wood smoke…"

The Gargoyle blew a long stream of flame. It reached out from its split face and danced over Billy, but he barely acknowledged it. He felt Saul watching, preparing.

The knight leaned in closer. "Come on, Nebulous, we don't want to serve up our guest cold."

The Gargoyle took a deeper breath, and from where he was, Billy could see the ignition flicker in the beast's throat.

"Now, Saul," said Billy.

A single bark, huge and deep, echoed high above the Gargoyle's head, surprising the beast so much it swallowed the igniting spark. Smoke poured from its split head. Spinning around, the Gargoyle backed up quickly into the Grey Knight, who only now was beginning to register what was amiss.

The deerhound, now standing at least twenty feet high at the shoulder, snarled, revealing canines two feet in length. Billy saw the stone beast actually shake in fear.

"No," said the knight, turning back to Billy. "No!"

"Now!" shouted Billy and the courtyard turned pitch black.

At once, the Gargoyle spat a stream of fire up at Saul, which only served to reveal the dog was already on the move. The Grey Knight clapped his hands together, each time creating a small white light which quickly fizzled out again.

"Burn them! Burn them all!" he screamed.

More fire erupted from the Gargoyle, but this time revealing only that the courtyard walls were rapidly being covered in mistletoe, which was streaming up the stone walls. It blew fire once more and there was a sudden stench of burning leaves, as the green limbs engulfed its snout and body, pulling the creature in hard against the wall and trapping it fast.

The knight finally managed to maintain a small orb of white light above his head, but there was now so much moisture rising from the pool that it could not penetrate far into the gloom.

"You're out of time, Billy," said the knight. "You're an amateur at this. First day on the job. My master is almost here, and he will burn your creations down in an instant."

Billy appeared at his shoulder. "Then we won't trouble you much longer."

The knight had been waiting for such a moment and dropped to his knee, reaching back as he did and pulling Billy clean over his shoulder.

"Foolish boy, do you think you can creep up on me? I've been visiting this place for years. Mastering its ways," the knight stood and pressed a foot hard on Billy's chest, making him gasp.

"Yes, but there is one large difference," said Billy, feet again plunged into the ground and communicating away. "You always came alone."

The knight looked down at him, therefore missing the huge punch that Katherine delivered to his jaw. He screamed in pain, and the light above him snapped out.

"Now, Billy," cried Katherine.

In an instant, Billy whisked open the clouds and poured moonlight over the courtyard again, lighting it brightly from end to end. He allowed himself a single moment to revel in the ease in which his abilities had come to him. To one side, the Gargoyle was pinned to the wall by the mistletoe every bit as tightly as the cassock had held him. In front of him, Katherine was nursing a bruised fist but looking up in wonder. Above her with legs dangling in space, was the Grey Knight, held aloft by one arm in the great jaws of Saul, who had now reached twenty-four feet at the shoulder, and was shaking the vicar every time he moved or made a sound.

"Good boy, Saul," said Billy. "Don't kill him. Just yet…"

Katherine looked at Billy in wonder, and drew in her breath. "I said you wouldn't need those weapons."

Billy shot her back a small smile, which quickly fell. He realised that the knight had started chuckling.

"You're too late. He's here, and you still don't know a way out."

Billy looked over his shoulder and could tell the air was once again beginning to thin and dry out. Katherine's eyes suddenly looked hunted, just as Senga's had in the alley.

"Drop him, Saul."

The deerhound gave one last stunning shake of the knight before throwing him high into the air. He landed heavily at Billy's feet, groaning at the impact. At once, Billy was upon the knight and searching through his pockets.

"Billy, what are you doing? We must try and escape," said Katherine, with rising panic in her voice.

"Do you trust me?" asked Billy.

Katherine paused and replied, "Well, I always have."

"Then that will have to do. We're out of time."

Billy handed her a small piece of moss.

"No, you can't. You don't know how…" whispered the knight.

"You can't begin to imagine how little not knowing stuff bothers me any more," said Billy, making sure he had gathered all the moss the knight possessed. "And I'm willing to bet this moss only returns you to one place, right? And you're going to find it a lot harder to get there without this."

The knight grimaced and then looked fearful. "Don't leave me here, Billy."

Billy spared him no more than a moment's glance. Behind him, Saul has halfway returned to normal size, and a sprig of mistletoe had separated from the wall and was climbing the hound to ride his collar.

Billy turned back to Katherine. "Time to go home."

Katherine looked around the courtyard. "Wherever that is. How does this work then, Billy?"

Saul, now normal size, arrived by their side, as the air grew thinner once more. Billy suspected he could hear a low growling from the mountains behind the courtyard. It reminded him of approaching thunder and galvanised him.

"We have to run, at this wall, right here, about as hard as we can."

The mistletoe covering the wall parted enough to reveal an archway of bare stone.

"That would seem to be a painful thing to do, Billy," said Katherine.

Billy handed her a thumb-sized piece of moss. "I'm hoping this will cushion the blow."

"Oh. Good."

"You know the alley down by the church in Marlow? Imagine we're already there, close your eyes and run!"

Above them the moonlight turned an eerie red and neither could now pretend that the growling was thunder or far away.

"Go now!" cried Billy.

Billy and Katherine ran with moss outstretched, closely followed by Saul and the mistletoe. The wall melted and they stumbled out of the other world and onto the ice in Seven Corner Alley. Behind them, they heard the air dry, the growl rise to fury and the growing cries of the Grey Knight.

Katherine slipped, and Billy piled straight over her. Saul and the mistletoe followed, and there was a sudden rush of heat and air from the gap in the wall. Billy glanced back, and the courtyard was suddenly awash with bright flame. A body, dark and heavy, landed, and for an instant he thought he could hear Mike calling out his name. Then the wall snapped back into existence and the coolness of the ice was all they felt.

KATHERINE HAD SHIFTED BACK INTO human guise. As they picked themselves up, Billy looked over himself and ran his hands through his hair.

"You're back to normal, too," said Katherine.

Billy looked at her for a moment. "Do you remember everything that just…"

"Yes Billy," Katherine paused for a moment. "I think they disassociate me somehow, but I'm not sure if I'll let them this time."

Billy wanted to ask who they were, but for now decided they had better move on, just in case he'd left some moss behind. Saul decided to lead the way, and lacking a plan, they decided to follow him. He led them out past the church and onto the bridge. It had become slightly foggy, but as they passed the first tower of the small suspension bridge, Billy thought he could make out two figures. He paused and put out a hand to Katherine. Saul was working on different senses though, and bounded forward with the mistletoe, tail wagging hard.

"Oh, hello, Saul. Where are they then? Did he find her?"

At once Billy and Katherine rushed forward through the fog. The round shape of Agnes and the tall triangular outline of Teàrlag gradually sharpened. Katherine was soon tightly wrapped into the folds of Agnes, whilst Billy slung an arm tightly around the Tree.

"How were your travels, Billy?" asked the Tree.

Billy looked towards Katherine, then at his own hands and the bark of the Tree. "I don't know where to begin," said Billy. "In fact I don't know if I know where I begin any more, Teàrlag."

"Quite a journey."

"How are we for time?" said Billy. "Because I have some questions I'm going to need to ask someone here. I don't much mind who answers them, but someone is going to have to try." The sentence started out jovially enough, but suddenly there was emotion behind the tone, and Katherine instantly shot out her hand to his.

"We have time now, Billy," said Katherine, looking from Agnes to the Tree. "Don't we? We're safe now."

"We are safe, and we do have time," said Agnes looking at the Tree, "but…"

"…We have someone who Billy has been looking forward to seeing for almost a year."

High above the fog in the church tower, the bell tolled midnight.

❧ Christmas Day ❧

ake that exactly a year," said Teàrlag, "and besides…"

"…*Your* father," continued Agnes to Katherine, "is barely able to contain himself, and at the moment you know full well that we don't want him to…"

"…No, we don't want that," said Katherine.

Despite the potential proximity of his own father, Billy was curious. "Why? What does the General become on the other side?"

"Pray you never find out, dear," said Agnes, "but I must get Katherine back to him, or Marlow will have a few more lumps knocked out of it, and I think it is high time that this business took a quiet turn. Agreed?"

No one disagreed. Katherine took Billy's hand and walked him off the bridge. Agnes, Teàrlag, Saul and the mistletoe followed behind at a discreet distance.

"I am going to find a way to thank you for coming after me," said Katherine. "There aren't words, Billy, but you saved my life tonight."

Billy's eyes were edging over towards Seven Corner Alley.

"Hey, are you listening to me?"

"Sorry, I was just thinking that we should have pulled him back."

"The vicar?"

He nodded. "We just left him to die…"

"Billy, we have a lot to talk about. This probably isn't over, and I don't think that guy is dead. Just having a very, very bad night."

Despite himself, Billy smiled, and Katherine returned it.

"Can you tell me how it happened? How Dad came to…"

Katherine suddenly looked impossibly sad. "I just…"

"I'm not angry or anything," said Billy, squeezing her hand. "I just need to know what…"

"Mike, the Grey Knight, had been sent to find me. I'd been hidden here, and I will try to explain that, and your dad, well, he intervened. He didn't know he would be taken. He just tried to give me a chance to be somewhere else at a particular moment, but then they took him. He'd been held in that courtyard, in an enforced night, for a whole year."

"But why didn't he just use his imagination to blow the place apart? In fact, why didn't you?"

Katherine smiled, shaking her head a little. "Billy, you're a wonder. Not everyone can do what you can. They don't have your exotic breeding!"

Billy smiled uncertainly and began to wonder where his father might be now. "There is something you can do, Katherine."

"Name it."

"Tomorrow, can we meet up, before anyone tries to…reassociate you, and talk about everything?"

"I promise. We can." Katherine smiled and looked over her shoulder before giving Billy a kiss on his cheek that lingered a good moment longer than it needed. Billy looked back, unsure of his new ground in their old arena. Katherine shot him a mysterious smile, and peeled off to join Agnes for the walk home, with Saul and the mistletoe following them.

Teàrlag joined Billy and motioned towards Higginson Park.

"He's in here?"

The Tree bowed. "Merry Christmas, Billy."

They walked into the park in silence. Here the fog was clearing, and Billy could see further ahead through the snow, and still he didn't rush ahead. Rushing had never helped him find his dad, and even now he wasn't completely convinced he was going to see him again. Something would happen, and even if it didn't, there was still the matter of what his father was, and of course what he himself was too. He wished Katherine were still beside him; he felt alien and alone.

"You are who you always were, and so is he," said Teàrlag.

"Can you read my thoughts even when my feet, my roots, are not…"

"I don't need any such connection to know your mind, Billy," said the Tree. "I never did. It is so sad that your discovery was forced upon you in this way."

"I still don't know what it means, and I know you won't tell me," said Billy, smiling.

Teàrlag stopped her low bounce across the snow and turned to him at once. "I know it means you will never go home to the life you craved and that will always hurt some part of you. But I also know you're finding out you're part of something much bigger and have much more to do. If anyone is to have such an interesting life, Billy, with the chance to turn it into something magical, I know of no person better suited to take that on."

Billy smiled and allowed the second rare compliment from the Tree to land on him as they walked deeper into the park. After a while, they arrived at the statue of Sir Steve, and here Teàrlag turned to him.

"I must leave you now, Billy, for I only have hours left, and I'd like to see some more of this world in case it is my last trip here."

Billy looked around for his father. "But where will you go?"

Teàrlag branched a broad smile. "Why, I will chase the end of this night around the world. See my giant cousins from across the oceans, drink it all in, in case...new adventures are calling."

The Tree began to hover and turn slowly. With this, doubt and panic flew up in Billy. "The candle, what about the candle?"

"The candle?" Teàrlag looked at him curiously. "The candle is safe and the tasks were met. What is it, Billy? What is it really?"

Tears suddenly stabbed at Billy's eyes. "Please, just don't leave me alone, OK?"

The Tree threw him a small sad smile. "Why, Billy Christmas, you don't get to be alone ever again."

With that, Teàrlag exploded into the sky with astonishing speed and was gone, leaving a cloud of snow-dust covering Billy and making him cough. He spun around and around but could see no one. He turned again, panicking, tears still pricking his eyes.

He shouted after her. "That's not funny! You shouldn't say that if you don't mean it..."

"She's right, Billy."

His voice. Unmistakably his father's voice. Again he whirled around, trying to clear the snow from his eyes. Something reminded him of meeting Teàrlag for the first time, not knowing where the Tree's voice came from. He stopped spinning and just waited.

Slowly from behind the statue, a tall figure emerged. Trench coat and hat, gold-rimmed glasses, taller still than Billy, though the gap between them had reduced some over the year. He instantly recognised the shape of his parent.

"Dad!"

"Come here, my boy."

At once, he closed the final distance and Billy fell hard into the arms of the man for all he was worth. Tears fell on both sides, curtailing words. "I'm so sorry, son. I never knew I would be gone this long."

Billy pulled back just a touch to look up at his father's face. "You look human."

"I can pass as both. I think you know now what I am?"

"Part of there?"

"Yes, I am part of there."

"We are?"

Tom Christmas looked down at Billy. "*You* can be part of wherever you want to be, my boy. We'll explain everything now."

"We will?"

"I still haven't seen your mother. I waited here until you came back. In case I had to come find you."

Billy suddenly looked sad again. "The knight told me that she hated the fact that I'm…different?"

Tom Christmas's brow furrowed. "After I was taken, the people charged with protecting Katherine hid your mother's memories of the other place and our kind. It was done to protect you, son. I can assure you she is very comfortable with my—with *our*—kind. It's a long story, but we didn't meet each other in this world. We met back there. You should never, ever doubt her love, son."

Billy gave a half smile, wondering what else he was going to learn about his family.

"But tell me, Billy, how she is doing?" said Tom.

The boy paused for a while before replying. "She's going to be really pleased to see you."

They walked slowly away from the statue. Billy let go of his hand for a moment and ran back. He slapped the knight across the backside once more. "Thanks, Sir Steve," whispered Billy, before returning to his father.

"SO YOU KNOW WE'RE A little different then?" said Tom Christmas to Billy.

"Yeah, roots, bad hair, the works..." said Billy.

Tom Christmas smiled. "Did Katherine not show you how fast we can move when we have to?"

Billy smiled, "No, Dad. There wasn't much time to go over the details."

Looking up he noticed his father's hair thickening and shoulders broadening. "Fancy a race?"

He looked down at his legs and could tell the change could now come at will. He slipped off his shoes and felt the roots offer purchase against the snow. His hair rippled into willow and skin flashed silver. Looking back at his father with jet black eyes, he smiled and said, "Why not?" In a moment, where two tall beings had once been, all that was left was snow dust sparkling in the night sky.

Through the snow his footprints linked the ancient trees of Higginson Park.

ACKNOWLEDGEMENTS

Here are a few of my dues:

I am beyond lucky with my parents; please accept this small token to brag about me in exchange for thirty-eight years of dubious progress, hurried loans and keeping the worst headlines out of the newspapers.

My siblings: Christopher, Matthew and Kezia and their partners for much love, enthusiasm and a steadfast acceptance of primogeniture.

And in the order they fall out of my brain today:

Danielle Cronin, who suggested a competition and cooked supper while I wrote. Larry Andries, for raising the bar and passing it on. Daniel the Spaniel from Green Curve. James Clark and Gaby Hinsliff, who laugh *at* me; the mark of true friendship. All the King Alfred College troops, but of course: Barry, Mark G, Niall, DC, Polly, Joanna, Jo and Zoe; may you carry your secrets silently to Valhalla... The spoils of Oxford—the Studio Theatre Club, Matt Kirk, Stephen Briggs, Dan Booth; I will buy drinks to forgo listing all names here. X-175, Xenon—John (Skipper), Richard and Mark, who remind me I live too far from the sea. Owen and Claire Jenkins, the rain dance kids. Robert Gilbert, fellow Scillonian, chief scientific advisor and the best dinner date in Oxford. A few old friends who always understood—Mark, Rob, David, James, Julian, Dominic, Carlo and their ever-growing families; please own comfortable couches always.

Sarah Viner, the first editor, which taught whom that too.

Steve and Jane Homewood, my fellow honeymooners and dear missing parts of my brain. In these pages, constant velocity joints have pink spots and sound like plucked harp strings, though not on Tuesdays.

Katherine Grainger, MBE, who once beat me in a race over Westminster Bridge; she has gifted the book immense love and me a stronger spine.

And again in order:

Randy Stanard and Jack Brougham, who saw things I could not and shared their gifts.

Nita Congress, unparalleled copy-editing genius bar none.

Rose Solari and James J. Patterson, the bookbinders who dance where others fear to tread. You prove the rule about trusting the word of good Americans. Thank you for rolling the dice, holding the line and believing in the book.

To my daughter—well, now you know what Daddy does! Te quiero infinite hija, x.